I0535577

Imminent Domain

Finding Goldilocks

Neal JB Verne

Copyright: *APP #: 1-3044517111*

ISBN 13: *978-0-9972280-1-4*

ISBN 10: *0997228016*

Disclaimer and Legal:

Acknowledgements:

AVC Proofreading- Proofing: Alicia Carmical

AVC Proofreading- Editing: Alicia Carmical- Thanks for the sleepless nights and dedication to excellence and being so much support!

Barren Acres Editing: Karen Hrdlicka- Thanks for the extra time and dedication to the work.

Dawn Sullivan- Thanks for helping with graphics, formatting and being such a great encouragement!

The Blue Focus: Kim Miller, Johnny Miller- Thanks for the help with the graphics!

Chrystinia Joy Carmical- Thanks for the feedback, help with proofing and encouragement!

Holly Mae Carmical- Thanks for helping out early on and the encouragement!

JS Scott- Thanks for the inspiration.

Sri Bonthu- Thanks for the advice and answering so many dumb newbie questions!

Glossary of terms:

- **Buckingham Dolly: Powered dual wheel device with a hydraulic lift for moving large heavy objects.**
- **FEMA: Federal Emergency Management Agency.**
- **FMEA: Failure Mode Effects Analysis- A study during a design of a device to determine possible reasons for failure and ways to circumvent.**
- **FTL: Faster Than Light.**
- **Goldilocks: A habitable environment.**
- **Holograph: Three dimensional image producing device.**
- **Ionosphere: Area of the highest layer of the atmosphere between a planet and space.**
- **MELS: Microwave Exceeding Light Speed- Communications device for long distance transmission.**
- **Red Giant: The change of state of a star nearing the end of its life cycle.**
- **Replicator: Three dimensional printing device used to reproduce an item. This device can print many different substances.**
- **WRC: World Relocation Coalition.**

Contents

Chapter 1 1

Finding Goldilocks 1

Chapter 2 10

Message In A Bottle 10

Chapter 3 18

Goldilocks Speaks 18

Chapter 4 27

The Parche I Phones Home 27

Chapter 5 35

Loyalty, Betrayal, and Secrets 35

Chapter 6 45

First Impressions 45

Chapter 7 53

First Contact 53

Chapter 8 61

The Prototype Transport 61

Chapter 9 70

Eavesdropping on Goldilocks 70

Chapter 10 77

Foreign Relations Commander Jacob Style 77

Chapter 11 85

Imminent Domain 85

Chapter 12 93

Charles Phillip's Arc 93

Chapter 13 100

Malpeada in a Giving Spirit 100

Chapter 14 110

Determining a Heading 110

Chapter 15 117

Welcome to the Jungle 117

Chapter 16 124

Welcome Wagon 124

Chapter 17 130

The Production Race Is On! 130

Chapter 18 138

It's So On Now 138

Chapter 19 144

Packing To Move 144

Chapter 20 151

Goldilocks Came Upon a Cabin in the Woods 151

Chapter 21 160

Exit Strategy 160

Chapter 22 172

The New Frontier 172

Chapter 23 184

The Departure 184

Chapter 24 194

The Explorers 194

Chapter 25 209

Mass Exodus 209

Chapter 26 221

Breaking New Ground 221

Chapter 27 233

Next Stop Goldilocks 233

Chapter 28 246

Go South Young Man 246

Chapter 29 254

Grand Union Station 254

Chapter 30 266

Well Oiled Machine 266

Chapter 1 272

Charmed Life 272

Chapter 1
Finding Goldilocks

The year is 2116, and a spacecraft named the WRC Parche I orbits a planet. It is a blue planet in the light of its sun and lacks light on the dark side. It appears to have a glow from large campfires in some areas that can be seen from miles above, but not the big city lights that one would expect of a modern society. The current task for the crew is scanning for communications and signs of inhabitants. This mission is a reconnaissance and fact gathering endeavor from a distant planet that received intriguing data from a probe that was sent. This society has an assumed technologically superior society than the world they are investigating. The Parche I passes over the dark side. Light gleams and glitters across her shiny blue and white swept wings, cockpit, and large triangular propulsion system affixed to each wing as it passes into the brilliantly lit sunny side of the planet. The craft is a magnificent state of the art piece of engineering. Only two of its kind is built to date. They are the WRC Parche I and the WRC Parche II. It is a reconnaissance ship and uses atomic propulsion that creates a type of FTL (Faster Than Light) drive that can propel the craft at twenty times plus the speed of light.

The replicators are preparing to run nonstop back home, in every colony, to incorporate the successful new FTL technology into many vessels of this style in order to create a mass exit from their planet to a suitable one. Thus saving as much of the inhabitants as possible. An estimated half a million spacecrafts and approximately two years will be required to evacuate much of the population, about two and a half billion souls of the chosen from modern societies, of the world. Every available resource is being consumed in this endeavor. It is an unprecedented effort that has every civilized and modern society on the planet sharing technology and resources to this end. This craft's home base realized the world's impending doom in their year 2085.

Their sun is dying and all the leaders of the world created the WRC (World Relocation Coalition). They are desperately searching for a Goldilocks planet and some means to relocate as many people as they can before the end of time. A Goldilocks planet is one that is considered inhabitable in that it is not too hot and not too cold, it is just right. It must also have enough natural resources to sustain life. It is a very commonly known term on this world, as it is their only hope to survive. They are unable to precisely predict when the sun will begin the first stage of morphing into a red giant. The scientist of this world all accept the data that is at hand and approximates it will occur within fifty years of the discovery in 2085.

When this occurs, the sun will become less intense and will radiate much less heat, causing an ice age and in time, kill all life on the world. It will eventually be released from its current orbit to be an asteroid that floats around the solar system. It had long been believed that the sun would become excessively hot when this phenomenon occurred. In 2021, a star was observed actually morphing into a red giant. This was studied using a telescope that was launched in the 1990s, and the findings were significantly different than this long time belief. It was observed that although it became larger, it actually put out much less heat because of the depletion of fuel. Other efforts are being sought, such as building enormous shelters. Another ship, the WRC Parche II, is exploring a probe in another region of space, in the opposite direction.

The commander of the ship is Jacob (Jake) Conley. He is a highly decorated, twenty-eight-year-old official with the WRC. He is a fit and athletic man in appearance and fairly tall at near six-foot-two, clean shaven, with dark brown hair, and he sits among his crew of five. The five all wear official blue jumpsuits with a white stripe down each side and made of a material similar to leather. He sits in the middle seat that is slightly raised from the floor, in a darkened cockpit that has dark gray automobile style leather, high-back swivel seats. There are lights from the controls lighting his face and room, lighting that is of a blue hue and lit with the intensity similar to a black light. The others all sit at control stations, with colored lights dancing over their faces from the panels that each of them administer.

The others sit two to each side. To the left of him and slightly behind is Heather Lawson, a beautiful, highly decorated, dark haired female, twenty-eight years old, that serves as his navigator. She monitors a station that is against the side of the cockpit but has a console that protrudes from the side in a manner to allow her to face forward. It is much like a dashboard that has rounded edges. It has flat color displays embedded into the light gray sloped top.

Next to her and further forward is the pilot, Ted Snyder. He sits behind control panels of multi-colored gauges and indicators that extend out from the front of the cabin. His console is sloped for good ergonomics and is below a three-dimensional hologram that is projected like a movie theater within a recess, in lieu of traditional glass windows. It is currently showing the front and sides of the outside of the craft. Ted is thirty-five years old, with black hair slightly graying in areas, and has been in aviation and space exploration his entire life. In appearance, he is a typical fighter pilot.

To Ted's right and at a very similar console is the copilot, Greg Compton. Greg is a younger, brownish blond haired guy. He is always very clear and concise when corresponding with his superiors. He is somewhat shorter than Ted but very muscular. He has strong ambitions and has great respect for his fellow crew members. Opposite of Heather, at a rather larger station that protrudes nearly twice the distance of Heather's and has four different monitors, is the Parche I's engineer, Dean Stinson. He is a forty-four-year-old man, with dark brown hair and gray highlights. He is a witty fellow with a bit of sarcastic overtones at times but speaks with a great deal of authority in his voice. He has been a member of the Coalition since it was formed in 2090. Dean performed much of the design work on the crafts and their newly designed engines.

The crew members are some of the most skilled at their respective positions that their home world has to offer. It has been six months since they left on this mission traveling at FTL speed from their doomed home planet. Everyone was relieved to find signs of confirmation of data retrieved from the deep distant galaxy probe. It returned data that indicated the planet was inhabitable and this is

3

becoming reality. They pinged the planet for satellite communications activity and monitored it for any type of modern broadcasts. They monitored it for UHF or VHF from its surface and within its orbit, only to find no indication of life, or, at least, nothing that indicated technology of any sort.

The group had to perform multiple roles to accommodate each other throughout the endeavor. Heather and Greg shared grooming duties such as haircuts and medical care, along with some other obligations that intertwined. Each person would rotate to assist in filling each other's primary obligations while they slept, but while en route, the schedule—although official—was somewhat lax, as they tended to not have great obligations other than interpretation of additional scans from the probe in the area that continually returned data. They also performed functions like replacing filters or performing routine maintenance within the spacecraft. Ted would fill in for Jake while he slept. During the time that Ted and Greg slept, Jake would fill in at the controls for a while. Dean had no one who could perform his specific duties. He was thrown out of bed on occasion when alarms and warnings were annunciated from the spacecraft's controls that were not understood by the crew. Dean could fill anyone's role if necessary.

The spacecraft's sensors are currently performing scans to determine if it is possible to sustain life on the planet. Dean and Heather are both administering equipment that performs these scans and taking real time images on the surface. Heather monitors her station and she sees images in the water, on the beach, and walking around on dirt roads. What appears to be an old style of wood shingled roofs also shows up.

She speaks up and says, "Jake, there are inhabitants on this planet." Dean confirms this by a resounding, "YES!! I see movement, and it looks like these individuals were not always without technology. I have discovered facilities that appear to be comparable to our own and what appear to be runways for aircraft. They all seem absent of any activity, though." Jake considers what this means to the efforts of finding a planet. *We can't add three billion souls to a planet's population*, he thinks to himself. Jake tells

4

Dean and Heather to continue gathering data and they will present a full report to headquarters when appropriate.

"I can break through the atmosphere, and we could land the ship in an unpopulated area if you would like," Ted explains.

Dean responds, "Ted, you're a little rambunctious, it's a bad idea. We are unsure at this time if we would be landing in someone's backyard." They are passing over the darkened area of the planet.

"All of the movements we are seeing through the scans are beings, Dean?" Heather asks, with a surprised sounding voice.

Dean replies, "All of that movement is something, it can't all be beings, but we must clearly find a non-obvious location if we decide to set this little bird down on the surface without being discovered."

Jake questions, "What is it that you two are speaking of?"

"We are seeing movement all across the dark side of the planet," Dean replies.

"Movement, as in water? Or as in biological, animals, plants, robots? What is the movement?"

Dean explains, "That is just it, Commander. We don't know what it is precisely. Much of the movement is on the dark side of the planet and does not appear to be anchored in a way that it could be plants or anything growing from the surface. Much of it is obviously water, as the probe indicated, but the other movement is unclear. It is as if there are billions of beings that are moving around, with less than a meter of space between them in some of the most condensed areas. It is likely marine life. The water will have to be of unprecedented purity, as my scans do not indicate that this life is within the water that we have detected. "

"Please continue the scans and give me some assurances of what this is and some idea of the best approach to investigate the surface," Jake responds.

"Aye aye, Commander," says Dean.

Ted speaks under his breath and says, "Smart ass," and Heather chuckles. Ted feels that he is just as capable and competent, perhaps more so than Dean in piloting the craft and resents some of the wisecracks he hears from that corner of the cabin, at times. Ted knows that Dean has a superior knowledge of the systems and respects that, but is never appreciative of his sense of humor at his expense.

Dean later determines that much of the unrecognizable activity is heavy fog and some wildlife. He reports this to the commander, and Heather determines that the planet's population is much more conservative than initially thought.

They continue the scans and Heather says, "I have spotted what appears to be a radio tower, and I am detecting a weak local signal."

Jake asks, "What format is it transmitting? Can we intercept and perhaps interpret the broadcasts?"

"It is coming across, but it is a language that I have not heard before," she says as she listens to the communication through her headphones.

"I want to hear it," says Jake.

She then begins to play a sound that is foreign to everyone in the room, through a wave-type of a sound producing device. It consists of two large rectangular impressions near the console, one on each side of the holograph.

"What type of communication system or frequency is this?" asks Dean.

Heather answers, "I picked it up on an Amplitude Modulated frequency 'AM'." She turns the sound back down.

Dean responds, "AM is an amplitude carrier based format that is very rudimentary and takes very little to produce. I think it is possible to use stones and fishing line to produce this technology."

"I am, with your permission, sir, going to send a feedback to base for a possible interpretation "plug-in" so that we may find the meaning of these transmissions," she explains.

"How long will it take before we can get this to base, interpret it, and have it returned?" asks Jake.

She looks somewhat perplexed as she struggles for a reply, as she has no idea how long it takes to build such a complex program, and simply says, "I am unsure, Commander."

Dean says, "It will take weeks, perhaps months. The transmission to base will take two, possibly three, days before they get enough data from a file this large for a full character set to perform an analysis. Why don't you let me see if I can put together some type of program for interpretation?"

Jake asks, "Can you create a program to make sense of this?"

Dean replies, "I don't know. I have never done this, but I have created systems to interpret other languages that were coded, surely this one has some similarities."

"So be it," says Jake. "Please do what you can and send out the transmission to base as a second method."

Greg has a yellow light illuminate on his display, and he reports to the others that the long range avoidance detection system is detecting something other than debris in orbit. Ted begins to work with a screen on his console.

Ted looks at Jake and says, "There is a satellite with a decaying orbit at 5,000 Kilometers ahead of us."

"A SATELLITE? Are you certain?" asks Jake. "I thought this planet had limited to no technology, and now not only do they have a population here, but they have a satellite in orbit?"

Ted and Greg both look back at Jake and Dean. Ted says, "Yes, this is a satellite." Jake considers that perhaps these beings are victims of their own vices.

"I am now detecting what appear to be power generating facilities on the surface," says Heather as she continues looking at her monitor.

Jake wonders if it is the wind or some natural resources and asks Heather, "Of what method?"

She replies, "This facility is no longer in operation. It is emitting a slight amount of radioactive traces and would appear to be of a nuclear reactor."

"Is it strong enough to pollute the atmosphere?" Jake asks.

Heather replies, "No, it is only trace amounts, and it appears it was shut down in a professional manner." She wonders if the fuel rods are present and how stable the system could be. She has superior knowledge of power generation, as she studied this in school.

Following the discovery that a satellite was in orbit, Dean started a secondary scan of the orbit of this planet and found over three hundred satellites in orbit. All appeared to be decommissioned and have a decaying orbit.

"Jake, if one satellite made you uneasy, then you should have a seat because there are satellites in 'LPO' (Low Planet Orbit), 'MPO' (Medium Planet Orbit), and 'HPO' (High Planet Orbit), all decommissioned and have been for several years, or so it appears. Did these beings all turn into non-technological morons or something? It is as if they just turned off the technologically advanced portion of their existence," Dean explains.

"Let's not judge so hastily. Our society would be blissfully content if we were unaware of our own planet's certain future," Jake replies.

Heather begins detecting a signal from one of the objects and it is in the AEHF (Advanced Extremely High Frequency) range. She speaks up and explains, "Commander, there is a transmission that has just started from one of the objects in orbit. It is in the AEHF range."

"That is the most advanced communications frequency that we can transmit back in our own world, short of our MELS (Microwave Exceeding Light Speed) systems," Jake replies, and considers that they typically use this in conjunction with weapon systems. The MELS system would be commonly used, but it requires so much energy that it is only generated for long distance communications for space travel. "Is there any chance this is a weapons' system or a defensive measure of some type?" He then prepares to enable defensive operational procedures.

Heather replies, "It does not appear to have any conventional style of weapons' systems."

"Can this transmission be interpreted?" he asks.

She states, "No, it is not a vocal type of transmission, only data. It can be downloaded and potentially interpreted on a common platform. This data will help Dean in his efforts, as it must be a communication from the civilization below. It could be a time capsule or some type of warning in data format."

Dean downloads the data and says in a southern drawl, "I hope like hell some computer virus didn't cripple this world's technology because if it did, then I'm not sure it wouldn't shut down our little flying saucer." He pauses. "I began the download when I saw what she had uncovered, and the initial files are a map to their language, with similar traits for programming to our own. I will have it converted in a compatible file format within minutes. I should be able to translate their language within an hour using this data. It is as if this society is some parallel civilization to our own."

Ted sits studying the horizon, being certain to plot their course to avoid the abandoned satellites and space debris as Greg looks on, checking long-range scans. Heather continues to find abandoned technological facilities and begins creating a map of the world, and Jake sits quietly, wondering why a modernized civilization would abandon all of their technology in this way. They all await the data that Dean is working to reveal.

Chapter 2

Message In A Bottle

Dean continues to work with the data he downloaded from the device in orbit. He finds files that contain text documents, graphical images, and quickly learns to adapt all of the software to a format that can be used on the computers within the spacecraft. He starts to review the data himself, prior to releasing what he is finding.

Heather continues to scan the surface and finds a facility that appears to have missile silos and she feels compelled to point this out to Jake. "Commander, I have now revealed another facility of particular interest."

Jake says, "It was our directive to understand what the data packet revealed prior to getting distracted with facilities that are on the surface, Heather."

She replies, "Yes, sir, but I thought you would want to be apprised of a weapons' facility."

"WHAT? A weapons' facility, Heather? My apologies," he exclaims. "If there is something down there that poses a threat to our vessel or mission, then it shall take precedence over any fact-finding efforts."

She explains that she has revealed what appears to be a missile silo, and although it is not active, it appears to be capable of being activated by emergency power. Jake then considers if he must treat this as a threat, or if he is dealing with a meek group of individuals that are incapable of defending themselves. He then explains to Heather that she should parameterize the scan with characteristics of this device, mark this location on the map, and focus her probe on locating any other facilities that appear to have weapons. The room grew very quiet and everyone is wondering if the world is meek and peaceful, then why is it that the commander is so particularly interested in their weapons' capability?

Dean, who had been engulfed in his program interpretation, rotates his chair to Heather and Jake and glances up through his glasses and asks, "Jake, if they are meek and peaceful, why would their weapons and defense capabilities be of such interest to us?"

Jake looks back at Dean, with an obvious outrage over his face, and says, "This is not of your concern. If I feel a need to defend this ship, or if I determine it is necessary to eradicate the inhabitants of this world, then it is my choice as the commander."

Dean shrugs. "Okay, I got ya. You are undoubtedly the boss. I am not questioning your position or authority, but if you determine this world must be attacked, then I believe we must discuss this, as we all are subjected to the laws of our world. We are a civilized group, and I have morality issues with bringing harm to a peaceful world. I don't want to sit on trial, explaining why we let you destroy a group of non-hostile individuals who we may cohabitate with."

Jake just looks away and thinks to himself, if *an attack is necessary, then Dean may be a liability* as he scowls and looks away at the holographic projection at the front of the cockpit. He then looks at Dean's displays and realizes he has pictures that he is looking over. He gets up and walks to Dean's workstation and looks at his monitor, and says, "Images? Is this what was transmitted from the object?"

Dean quickly minimizes the images that he is decoding and looks directly into Jake's eyes and says, "This is what I am working with currently. It is not a complete data set and the images that were on the monitor may have colors inverted or the round surfaces may be square. This software must be decoded perfectly prior to releasing any information that I believe to be true. I do not, will not, and have never allowed anyone to examine what I am preparing through my work prior to completion, or at least a confident rough draft to present. When this data set is prepared, it will be presented to you and our group in a way that I am confident in what you are seeing is factual. I am not and will not hold back any data, but I shall not present any false or unconfirmed data for review. If you will kindly give me time to complete my task, then I will be glad to review it with you. If you can't do this, then I shall give you the data and you can extract and decode it yourself!"

Jake responds, "Duly noted. I apologize for interrupting you. Please continue and I shall not interfere again."

Heather finds hundreds of these missile sites and she continues to build her map. Greg thinks Dean was a little hard on the commander for simply asking a question, but stays out of it. Ted is ready to set the Parche I down somewhere and considers the potential of the world below. He wonders if Jake decides to attack them if they are as meek as they seem. Is their technology defunct or just turned off? A few hours pass and none of the crew has slept in at least thirty-six hours.

Jake yawns, and asks, "Who is tired?"

The crew is silent. No one wants to stop now, as they have traveled so far in anticipation of this moment of learning about this new and unusual place. After about a half hour of cold silence and only the sound of the crew's fingers tapping on the control stations and an occasional yoke movement from Ted for speed or course corrections, Dean says in a loud, distinctive voice, "I AM!"

Jake replies, "What? You are what?"

Dean answers, "I am tired. I'm an old man, I could use some sleep!"

Jake thinks to himself, *is the old bastard serious?* He said a freaking hour and now we are on at least hour three with the data decode. "Do you need to sleep, Dean?"

Dean replies, "I could damn sure use it, but I do have a decoding method. I can confidently interpret the majority of this information." He considers rather it is prudent to go on without sleep. Is Jake going to piss him off again asking stupid shit?

Jake is just dying to hear what the packet has to say. He is a mature, strong leader and considers if he should just tell the old man to go take his freaking nap so that he will make sense when he explains the data. He speaks, "Dean, look, I have had you working

12

for many hours, and I know all of you must be tired. I know everyone would like some sleep, including me, and no one is at their best. Dean, you, Greg, and I are going to hit the rack."

He looks at Heather and says, "You wake Greg in four hours. You hit the rack then. Greg, you take the helm and let Ted and Heather get some sleep. Greg, you get us all up after Dean and I get eight hours, or if something unforeseen happens."

They take off to get some desperately needed sleep. Ted thinks, *damn, I'm holding down the fort with Heather, well, at least I got someone to keep me awake and she is freaking HOT!*

Heather sits quietly, building her map of the world's liquid and solid masses and pinpointing the defense facilities as instructed. She looks at Ted, thinking he is really kind of overrated. She speaks up and asks, "Is it difficult piloting the craft?"

Ted answers, "Much easier than putting together a three-dimensional topographical map of the world below, I would say." He wonders what the population is looking like and if there is enough room for the people of his world to live in conjunction with these beings. He asks Heather, "So, do you know what they look like?"

"Yeah, just like us."

"Wow, I guess I thought they would be little green men." He chuckles.

She giggles. "Some with green hair, but no little green men that I have seen." She smiles confidently and an image appears on the holograph of a person just like the people of their world.

"Why have you not presented this to the others?" he asks.

"They had been gone fifteen minutes before I was able to get a clear, unobstructed image of one of them."

He thinks that will make it easy to coexist with them. The panel on Jacob's station then illuminates and a high-pitched beeping sounds, indicating a message was received. Heather pushes a button on her console and a voice comes alive. *"WRC Commander-in-Chief Charles Phillips to the Parche I - trials for the first prototype*

13

transport ship have been postponed. We hope to have the ability to transport individuals to the planet within six weeks, depending upon the test being performed on these vessels. We have received your two-day updates and are very excited here about the new world the Parche I mission discovered. Please pay reverence to your sister ship, the Parche II, as it was destroyed, losing all souls on board. Details to your commander to follow: end of transmission, WRC Commander-in-Chief, Charles Phillips, over."

Ted wonders what happened to the Parche II. He had friends all the way back to his academy days on that ship. With slightly glassy eyes, he says, "Heather, isn't it about time to wake Greg?"

She responds, "No, you wake him. The last time I woke him, he had parts of his manhood hanging out."

Ted chuckles, thinking that she broke up the monotony and sadness of the moment, and says, "Very well." He transfers the helm to Heather and takes off through the back of the cabin. Greg then appears after a short time and jokingly asks Heather, in a rather sleepy voice, "You got it?"

She just looks at him and says in an obviously annoyed voice, "Transferring helm control."

"To the pilot's seat?"

She speaks loudly, "COPILOT."

Greg laughs. "Ah okay."

Heather gets up, and says, "Stay awake, asshole!"

"I thought a beautiful woman would wake me. Jake even said!"

"Yeah, I want to pass on seeing the ole ball sac hanging out there again, Greg."

Greg laughs. "Your loss. Sleep well, beautiful lady." He looks at the back of her tight jumpsuit, and jokingly says, "I will wake you, darling."

She stops and turns, explaining, "You know my alarm gets me up!"

An hour passes and the long range detection system shows a vague image that appears to be a space station. He thinks, *Wow, I wonder if Dean picked that up*. He then takes a screen shot of it from his display and saves the coordinates.

Time passes slowly for Greg as he mans the helm and after a couple of hours, he hears the automatic door open and Dean walks in. He greets Greg and sits down at his station. He appears freshly bathed but still has a little sleep in his eyes as he sits a plate of replicated bacon and a cup of coffee, "black", on his workstation.

Greg says, "I picked up what looks like a space station, perhaps."

Dean replies, "Hmm, where?"

"I will send you the coordinates."

"Similar to ours?" Dean asks.

Greg states, "Not exactly, and I can't be sure that's what it is."

"Well, I'm not sure what comes next, but maybe we will have time to investigate." Dean gets back to work on his imagery and documents.

Greg says, "Heather had images of the people down there on the holograph when I came in earlier. They look just like us."

Dean exclaims, "Really! Well, she could have sent me the images. I can decode their data, but a picture of a being would give me a reference to validate my code by." He decides that's enough guess work, and if she has images, then he can compare them for validation. He then starts looking at her logs in the file server and discovers people, pets, and billboard sign images. He begins using these items for reference.

A few minutes later, Jake comes walking through the auto-cabin door and looks surprised to see Dean working away. He sits at his console with a replicated glass of orange juice and opens a yogurt. "Dean," he says, "dare I ask how close you are?"

"Sure," Dean replies. "I'm there." Dean gets up and walks out of the room.

Jake wonders if he got any sleep, is he pissed now? Dean makes his way down the corridor to the crew's quarters and slowly walks into Heather's pitch black, dark room. He goes to her bedside when suddenly the automated door to her bathing area rapidly slides fully open, revealing a twenty-eight-year-old, dark haired, green eyed beauty with an olive complexion, without a stitch of clothing. Dean stands in awe of this goddess that has just stepped into his sight, and he tries but cannot look away. She does nothing to prevent him from looking and kind of smiles and says, "Uh, may I help you, Mr. Stinson?" An old rock-n-roll song is playing, Are You Going To Come My Way by Lenny Kravitz, in the background.

As he turns away blushing, he stutters, "The stuff, uh data, my mm, uh presentation, I'm ready."

She replies confidently, "Are you ready to present the data from the object?"

He stutters, "Yeah, I-I thought you might, you know," as he looks back at her, "like to join us."

She nods. "Please tell them I will be right there, and Dean, you are the only crew member that I don't mind seeing me this way." Surprised beyond belief, he smiles and leaves her quarters to go and wake Ted.

Ted is walking out of his room and headed to the break area to get something to eat from the food replicator as he sees Dean coming out of Heather's quarters. He peers down the corridor at Dean and shakes his head, thinking, *What? Are those two camping together now?*

Meanwhile in the cockpit, Jake speaks to Greg about Heather. Jake looks at Greg and smiles. "You and Heather argue like brother and sister."

Greg chuckles. "I know, she doesn't get how damn sexy I am, I don't believe."

Jake just chuckles and starts to check on the message from command. He privately listens in his ear-buds, unaware that Ted and

Heather heard it hours earlier. Dean and Ted walk in and Jake says, "Okay, guys, are we ready to review this package yet?"

Dean nods, and says, "As soon as Heather gets here." Ted peers over at Dean, thinking, *you dirty old man.*

Jake starts to speak, "Well, is she–" interrupted by the automatic door abruptly sliding open and all eyes go to her. Jake then continues, "Just like a woman… fashionably late."

Dean speaks up, "Actually, she still has about fifteen minutes before her downtime is over, and besides, you and I got eight hours, *she* only got four." Jake looks at Dean and thinks, *you're awfully damn accommodating for her.* He clears his throat and says, "Gentlemen and Ms. Heather, can we begin the review of our findings, please?"

Chapter 3

Goldilocks Speaks

Dean begins, "I haven't actually gone through a great deal of this information, only enough to feel like it has been interpreted adequately. There is about 50Gig of information, including over a thousand pictures, so we will begin by randomly going through some of the images. Many have captions and I have the text decoded. I have also created a "plug in" so that we may interpret the transmissions from the AM stations from the surface."

Dean then brings up a hologram on the screen. The caption reads HUNGER and has a picture of a child with a blue hue to his complexion. The little one's skin is sunken in around his poor little bone structure, his hair matted up, and sores on his little forehead, arms, and legs. His lips chapped and swollen to the point he can't close his mouth and his teeth are dark yellow, almost brown. He sits in front of a rundown old shack on a dirt, almost desert-like, ground. Another image appears that is similar to this one, but the caption reads WE NEED HELP WITH FAMINE IN AREAS OF OUR WORLD. The image changes and a muscle-bound bodybuilder is on the screen in tights, with long hair, flexing his biceps, and the caption reads: BODYBUILDING. Another shows a picture of men and women in a large park with a lake in the background and the caption reads WE ARE DIVERSE WITH A WIDE RANGE OF INTERESTS.

The image changes and scenes from a war are shown, with a person's leg blown off in an alley with smoke from what appears to be bombs in the background. The caption reads WAR OF TWO NATIONS. They continue through the images and a band that appears to be playing music, with big long hair, the singer wearing leather pants, and young, beautiful, half-dressed females are shown, however, the instruments are very unlike their own and a caption reads MUSIC CATEGORY 1. Another image with people wearing large beige and black brim hats appear, along with horses and a dirt arena in the background, the caption reads MUSIC CATEGORY 2. An image of a flying saucer looking device is shown. It is silver, with sleek smooth edges, darkened in windows, and below it is an isometric drawing of the details, showing dimensions and materials required with a caption that reads TECHNOLOGY/SPACE. The next image shows a picture of a missile resting in a silo, only the nose cone peaks out of it with the word Daringranka that reads OFFENSIVE SYSTEMS.

Jake says, "You think that should be defensiv?"

Dean replies, "No, not really. The road map they gave me to follow was pretty clear. Offense is offense and defense is defense."

The next is a picture of a man holding a machine gun, wearing a white shirt that isn't buttoned, with what appears to be a tattoo that says DARINGRANKA'S RESISTANCE, and a crowd of others standing behind him, with a wooded area just beyond that and the caption reads STRONG MILITIA.

Again, Jake comes back with, "Military?"

Dean replies, "Not to be rude, but it's pointless to continue explaining the same thing over and over about that."

Ted speaks up, "Do we believe that there are a bunch of vigilantes running around down there?"

"Stranger things have happened," Heather says.

The image changes and a large blue and silver commercial airliner is shown, with the name Longenthros Air, with a caption of TRANSPORTATION. Another image displays water that is so clear it appears that large, expensive yachts in the image are floating on air, and the caption reads H2O AND RECREATION.

Jake comments, "This is all very similar to our home world. Is there a way to search the images or documents for keywords?"

"Yes!" Dean exclaims.

"Search militia," Jake adds.

Dean has fifty hits. The first image is an article in a newspaper, showing a bearded man, who has a dark complexion, with an ammunition belt and machine gun, shooting into what looks like a government building. The article says, "Today in Daringranka, a mob of 200,000 militia overthrew the Daringranka government. They promise peace once they rid their country of the corrupt government."

Another image is shown with ten militia members standing in a parlor area, with flags behind them and the article reads, "Today in Daringranka, the militia members begin to set up a new government in that region. The members of parliament are imprisoned for committing crimes against their own people. The new interim leader made a statement. Interim President Gryntha Haulk explains, "We are not ruthless, cruel, or even unruly people, but we shall have peace and equality in our nation. The nation has a population of about one billion people."

Jake, with a perplexed look on his face, asks, "The people overthrew the government in a nation of one billion people? That is near a quarter of our home country."

Dean nods. "Okay, fine. But why no technology? Overthrow, take a new approach, but why eliminate your technological advances?"

A new image appears and another article with a picture of a vacant hydroelectric generating facility. The article says, "Today, the new president in Daringranka was elected. His first decision as president was to rule that any job solely based on money to make money and does not create anything tangible, either directly or indirectly, be ruled illegal and punishable by death. The major industries of the nation closed their doors due to the accountants, CEOs, and leaders requiring clarity of the law. They feared being dealt with in what they considered an extreme fashion if they continued in their current professions.

Jake shakes his head. "Wow, not a big fan of bankers, I suppose."

Dean says, "Our world has had similar laws. Look it up in history books."

Heather thinks about it for a minute and realizes the history books in their world had some of the same laws. She looks with admiration at Dean as the next picture is presented. The hologram shows a two-dimensional video of a town meeting, in a room lit with torches, and entitled: "Dark Ages To Fall On Daringranka." The residents of Daringranka met in their capital city today and looked for answers from their leaders. President Haulk spoke saying that all of the businesses that produce electricity and large producers of goods all refuse to try to operate without accountants. He asks the crowd of over a thousand people if they want the corrupt royal leaders to have everyone else's 90% that each hardworking individual deserves. The crowd cheers, and yells, "NO".

He continues his speech and asks if each one is in a bad situation? The crowd yells, "NO". He says, "We will face some difficult times and we may determine that our society requires large corporations, but don't you want an opportunity? An opportunity, if only for a short time, to be free? To determine if we want to provide for each of our communities for one another? If our nation wants a power generating plant, then we can vote. Vote for this need that we have, but it shall not be the government's plant. It will not be Goliath Power and Light, with the CEO bringing in more money than all of the people of this group combined. We will not be a communist society, and we shall not be a slave to the corporate giants any longer. We will all share in our triumphs. We will all suffer from some choices, but we shall be free!"

Ted speaks, "Seriously? A total nation has come together as one and has determined that they will rewrite the book?"

Dean again says, "Not rewriting the book, merely lightning striking twice. This happened on our world, then lawyers and bankers convinced everyone to forget these values."

The image changes and Dean skips to the end, and a video begins. The video shows a news reporter hunkered down beside a building, explaining that Daringranka was attacked by Longenthros.

She is obviously in fear for her life as she trembles, terrified while she shares this very disturbing story in the development of the world below. She speaks as she kneels down while bombs and machine guns light up the night and make it difficult to clearly hear her and explains, "The war has come down to the war of two world powers. Many of the bankers and businessmen fled from Daringranka to here in Longenthros just two years ago when the new president took office and came to Longenthros, causing some very bitter international relations between the two nations. Longenthros' government decided to try to take back what many felt belonged to them, but Daringranka is now on the offensive. The ship is about to leave to deposit this time capsule into orbit and I must end my coverage. Let's all hope that Daringranka and our own rebels save us from this evil empire that has become Longenthros. The rich torture the poor for entertainment and servants starve to death while serving wine and fine meals to the rich so that they may over indulge and grow bigger each day."

The room falls silent. "Well," Dean says, "judging by the lights being out, I'd say Daringranka won." He continues, "I think I'll take a break."

Jake responds, "Very well." *If ever I needed to speak with Charles Phillips one on one, now would be that time*, he thinks to himself.

Dean goes into his quarters, pulls his jumpsuit off, and puts on some gym clothes. A white pair of athletic shorts, an "A" style shirt, thinking, *Heather, huh, with all those young studs in there, she seems to like me* as he chuckles to himself. He grabs a ball and racquet and whistles as he makes his way to the recreational facility. He gets near and hears what sounds like someone in the miniaturized racquetball facility that is fashioned near the break area. He slowly opens the door, with his racquet and ball in hand, to find Heather. She says with a smile, "Would you like to play?" Dean gladly obliges her.

Back on the bridge, Jake says, "Enough of our home movies and history lessons. I want to know current events. I need to get on the surface. Ted, look for a suitable landing area."

Ted explains, "I will need Dean and Heather to provide the map."

Jake says, "Well, then let's get some rest, I suppose 'when in Rome'. Wake me in four hours, Ted." Jake tells Greg he is also relieved for the next four hours as well. Ted thinks to himself, *that is not how I seen that going there!* He then chuckles to himself and sits alone at the helm, piloting the ship for the next three hours while everyone is resting, staring out into the stars. Four hours seem to be dragging by when Greg enters the bridge.

Greg asks Ted, "I wonder if Jake would mind if I sat in his chair?"

Ted replies, "I wouldn't...*respect*!"

"Yeah, you're right. You ready..." interrupted by Ted climbing out of the pilot's seat, Ted says, "Yes! I am beat!" He turns to walk away and says, "The controls are transferred to the copilot's seat so you don't get confused about seats again!" He chuckles as the door opens and he exits. He makes his way down the corridor past Heather's quarters and hears the faintest sound of talking as he passes by the metallic gray sealed door. He goes to the replicator and says, "*Woman*!" The replicator responds with *Request not found.* Ted says, "I figured as much. Well, then give me something to make me not think about it. Bourbon and make it a double on the rocks." A clear brownish beverage appears, with a few cubes of ice and a little stirring straw within it. He goes and lies down in his quarters, still fully dressed as it has been over twenty-four hrs since he has seen his bed.

Greg sits at the controls and a red light illuminates. A red banner on the display says, Filter #1 High Pressure. Greg presses the compressed air #1 button on the screen and the light goes yellow and the alarm banner turns to yellow and says, Filter Compressor #1 Inoperable. He goes to another screen and two buttons are displayed. They say, Purge Air Filter #1 and Air Filter #2. He pushes Purge #1, a few seconds pass and the light goes green.

About an hour passes and Dean and Heather walk in smiling, laughing, and teasing each other. Greg thinks to himself, *Yeah, we know who is getting freaking lucky on board this pile of bolts*. He speaks up, "Did y'all sleep…" and pauses as if to imply that he may say together, but then he says, "well?"

Dean answers with a loud thundering reply, "I feel like a new man!"

Heather says politely in a humble voice, "Very well, thanks."

Greg just peers at her as if to say you have done wrong. They sit down and Dean asks if they want to try some of the AM broadcast for interpretation. Then the door slides open and Jake walks in with a muffin and what appears to be a Coca-Cola and says, "Y'all ain't getting started without me, are you?" with a muffled sound of a fellow with muffin in his mouth.

Dean says, "Wouldn't dream of it."

Jake continues, "If you can interpret the broadcasts from the radio tower, then let's hear it."

Dean speaks up, "There will be a delay."

Jake considers his answer. "How long?"

Dean answers, "I have been processing the signal for hours and enough should be interpreted that we can get something tangible from it." Heather presses a couple of buttons and looks over at Dean, he gives her a little wink and nod. Sounds begin to be produced from the system and a bunch of static is heard. Then it says, Today we will have fresh produce and purified water at Jinkas' market at 5th and Main. Jack Shaw will be raising a barn on the east side of Miltyburg on the Shaw farm and is soliciting help from his neighbors. The general store is low on fresh eggs and is looking to barter ammunition or other items of value. As always, platinum is always welcomed if you don't have eggs or other tangible items to barter. Our store has good stock on shovels, axes, and mining tools.

Jake says, "Okay." Heather turns the broadcast down. He continues, "We have a society that is as advanced as our own. They barter, have no electricity to speak of, and are more concerned with a barn raising than building a new sleek automobile, plane, or train?"

24

Dean shrugs. "Yeah, it looks that way. Perhaps Daringranka won the war."

Jake comes back and asks, "Could it only be this community?"

Heather says, "This is an advanced community. They have a radio station and some way to power it."

"Where geographically is this?" Jake asks.

"120 degrees latitude and 255 degrees longitude." She is sure of this because she has scanned over half of the planet now and found 1,200 radio stations of this type.

Jake wants more, he wants answers. "What else have you found?"

"Well, what do you want to know? I have 40% of the world's statistics and have plotted every military sight…2,800 so far, and a fairly comprehensive population count plotted."

"Give me the details as best as you can," he replies.

"Okay, the scans have produced the following data: at 40% of the total completed: the population so far is one point four billion people, it is 30% landmass at 149 million sq km and 70% water or 349 million sq kms, making the total at 40% on 498 million sq kms. Overall area has been calculated at slightly over 1.245 billion sq kms of total surface area and if the 30/70% continues to hold true, then the total landmass will be 374 million sq kms and populated with three point five billion beings, or a little over ten beings per sq km." Everyone is silent trying to ascertain her findings. She then says, "Roughly triple the landmass of our world and two-thirds of the population."

Jake asks, "So, there is plenty of room for us?"

Dean chuckles. "Room at the inn if they will have us. We may have to leave our bankers and lawyers at home."

Heather speaks up and explains, "This is only 40% done. It could change dramatically the more we scan." Jake considers what this means. He feels sure that he will know what home base will think about these numbers. "I want to speak with the inhabitants," Jake says.

Greg speaks up, "Me, too. Fine little farm girls down there surely." He chuckles.

Dean speaks up, "I guess that is what happens when you remove a vibrant, male adult from society for six months."

Heather says, "Uh, yeah."

Jake replies, "Well, enough of the facts and figures are here. Now I must send WRC the news and ask permission to make first contact."

Chapter 4

The Parche I Phones Home

Jake leaves the bridge and goes to his quarters. He has very lavish accommodations compared to the rest of the crew. He enters his door and to the left is a 60" flat screen television, with a living room that would rival any of the mansions back home. It is done in earth tone beige colors, with skylights that open into the star filled sky. It has a fine leather sofa, matching loveseat, and recliner. He walks past the living quarters to what looks more like a study than his office. This room is also much like home, with dimmed lights and a fine large oak desk with three large screen computer monitors and a bookshelf full of all of the great authors behind the desk. He sits down in his leather high-back chair and opens a communications program on his computer to call back to Earth.

He starts the communication with: "Commander Jacob Conley WRC Parche I to Charles Phillips. Greetings, sir, and we here pray that things are going well back home. Today we found that the people of this planet have been ruthless. They appear to be a war-torn group that will likely never be civilized. They seem to have a militia that has taken over the country below and will likely never accommodate peace for our own existence. It appears they despise technology also. It is my perception that we must study this group for a period of time, or eradicate them prior to trying to coexist…or plan to be at war with this civilization. We have gathered intelligence and exhausted all efforts from afar. It is my belief that we must go down to the surface and meet with the leaders of Alfa Kantabury I— Goldilocks—to ascertain our path forward. Sir, please do not think that I wish to cause unnecessary harm or destruction to them, but my primary directive is to save our Earth at all cost. I have a copy of the data obtained from a time capsule that we found in orbit. I will send it, following this correspondence. There should also be an application to serve as an interpreting device. Commander Jacob Conley, of the Earth Vessel WRC Parche 1, out." He plays the message back twice to review it, to ensure it presents factual information, and presses send to get the communication off and on its way to headquarters. It will take eight hours to transmit a small message such as this and likely six hours to receive a reply. The spaceship's communications system is not as powerful as the ones at home base due to power conservation.

Jake then makes his way back to the bridge to find everyone still working at their stations and says, "WRC Commander-in-Chief Charles Phillips sent a message yesterday that will affect Dean and Ted more than the rest of us. They both worked closely with two of the men on that mission." He goes on to explain that the Parche II was lost to a solar storm. The shielding in the front of the vessel was adequate to protect the ship against solar flares and cosmic debris, but the designers apparently didn't consider the potential of two opposing storms from two different stars in close proximity of one another.

Dean speaks up, "This was considered, but the directive from WRC's committee determined that the possibility was low and the time to protect against all possible scenarios was too time-consuming. I imagine Keith Heavener wishes they had taken the time now. He was their engineer and an advocate for being able to safely outrun these flares and debris. RIP Parche II."

Jake goes on and says, "I have two transmissions. The first of which I will forward in its entirety and the second one will be relayed on a need to know basis."

Understandably shaken, Dean says, "Permission to leave the bridge, sir?"

Jake shakes his head. "Granted."

He walks out and Heather looks at Jake, and Jake says, "Yeah, you, too."

In a quick walk, Heather catches up with Dean but walks behind him, with a look of concern just as he reaches his quarters and they go inside. Dean's room is much more humble than Jake's. It has holographs projected above gray carbon fiber tables of every portion of the ship. It shows a miniaturized image of the engines and the bridge, along with faceless beings and their current positions. It also shows every other section of the ship, including one of the entire ship that is transparent in blue and smoky gray.

Heather quietly says, "Dean," as he looks up from his seat near his dining area. The dining area consists of a modest and simple bar and a small booth, with a nice, small chandelier above each, and a floor that is similar to a ceramic tile texture. "Are you okay?"

"When a choice is made concerning safety in building these crafts for exploring space, you have to consider every eventuality as fact. It seems like you sat in on some of the FMEA—FAILURE MODE EFFECTS ANALYSIS—meetings. We considered flares, debris, meteors, and I brought up the direction of these items. The group determined that in the interest of time, forward shielding was adequate. They simply didn't think these objects could catch us in flight. I agreed, but I did bring up the potential of sitting in orbit when debris collided with the ship from behind. They determined these items could and would be detected and the spacecraft would be pointed toward this threat so that the forward shields would deflect it. In the interest of feeling as if I was beating a dead horse, I let it go, but I did wonder *what if*. What if two threats existed in close proximity, what if the sensors were damaged and didn't detect them? My *what ifs* seemed trivial then. The crew of our sister ship would still be alive if I had beat the dead horse! I just feel awful. I am physically ill over this, as I had the authority to change this condition and I didn't. Where is that time machine we were promised by now?"

"You haven't built that time machine yet. Look, Dean, don't beat yourself up over it. It just as well could have been us."

"Yeah, that, too."

She doesn't know if she can say anything to console him but decides to try. "I was in some of the meetings. John accepted the risks. Would you want them beating themselves up over this if it had been us?"

He thinks she is just too freaking smart, beautiful, and correct to argue with. He gets up and grabs his racquet, looks over at his

29

beautiful, young girlfriend and says, "Play some ball?" And off they go.

Meanwhile, back on the bridge, Ted states, "Dean did raise several questions concerning this. I sat in on the meetings."

Jake shrugs. "And we may still be waiting. Our sun could be freezing our Earth as we speak. We had to take some chances and move on. Let's take this a little further. Greg, what about Shelly?" Greg looks back, and asks, "Shelly? My sister?" Jake continues, "Yeah, and Ted, how about your daughter, Alicia? Don't you gentlemen think it is worth risking our lives to outrun the power of the sun that will undoubtedly destroy our planet? We have to get them out now!"

Ted agrees, "You make a very valid point, Commander."

Greg thinks about Shelly and daydreams of his and her younger years, growing up in the same house as his beauty queen sister. How she had the entire football team chasing her and what a truly wholesome and proper young lady she turned out to be. She is two years younger than him. He always had more friends than he needed because guys wanted to be friends with him to try to get close to his sister.

Ted stares at the multicolored monitor, thinking of little Alicia who is all grown up and away at college as he left. He pictures her in her baby blue "Rockers" uniform and how her softball team must have set records for being the worst ever. But he was proud of her and attended every game, with a big goofy smile on his face and pride in his heart as they left the ball field, even though it was usually a loss. Ted also thinks about that beautiful wife that he had to turn free and wondered how Katrina was doing now with her newfound love back in her home state of Minnesota.

Jake gives none of the past much thought, as he is too busy analyzing his next move and next challenge. What if they order him to wage war? What if these people welcome him and he has to kill them all for the good of his own planet? He has some awful thoughts going through his mind about *what ifs*.

Hours pass by and Jake speaks up, "What of our two lovebirds? It shouldn't be long before we hear from base. I requested a trip to the surface and to make first contact with the inhabitants." He asks Ted and Greg if they are ok.

Ted answers, "Now that I've had a little shuteye, I am fine."

Greg sheepishly replies, "I don't mind getting some rest, maybe I can pilot the ship to the surface if you're too tired?"

"Yeah, I don't see that, but maybe."

As Greg walks toward the back of the bridge, he looks behind him at Ted. "I will be back up in about four hours."

Commander Jake decides to retire to his quarters for a while in anticipation of an end to their holding pattern."Yeah, me, too. Maybe Charles will have a communication for me by then. I know they have received ours by now." They both leave the bridge.

Greg walks by the recreational center and hears some laughing and the sound of the rubber on their shoes screeching around on the gym floor, also loud pops of a ball being struck by a racquet and hit against the walls. He stops to peek in on Dean and Heather through a small transparent window in the door, and he sees they are both drenched in sweat, giving it their all as they bat the ball against the wall. Greg pulls the heavy metal hatch open as the ball hits the back wall and bounces across fairly energetically. The large, brightly lit, white room becomes silent as they stop playing to acknowledge Greg's presence.

With a smile on her face, Heather asks, "What's up?"

"How long y'all been playing?"

Dean, with a sarcastic smile, looks at Greg and says, "Oh, you mean we haven't told you?" Heather chuckles. Greg scowls. "No, not really." He kind of scratches his head as it becomes clear that Dean just told him it was none of his business in an unconventional way. "You two might want to get some rest. It sounded to me as if we are headed to the surface in about four hours."

31

Heather agrees, "Yeah, we need to get some rest. The ole man has got to be getting tired 'cause I have worn him out." Greg says, "Whatever," as he closes the hatch.

Dean asks Heather, "Are you tired? 'Cause the old man still has enough in him to spank your little ass again."

"Nah, you have worn me out, but Greg doesn't need to know that."

Greg is still standing by the hatch, hearing everything they say as they gather their towels, wiping sweat from their red faces. They grab their gym bags and open the hatch to see Greg standing outside the door. He just looks at both of them, shakes his head, and takes off to the break area.

Dean and Heather go to Dean's quarters and both get in the shower together. Dean says, "I think ole Greg thinks he should be your choice of fellas," while the water from the shower muffles his voice.

"Sure, and he would have been a few years back. Guys like Greg think of themselves too much. Most do not understand what a female really desires."

"You could be giving me way too much credit, little one. I don't understand women in the slightest."

She laughs. "You know enough to know that I am a person. I have my opinions. I don't have to have you treat me like a queen and agree with everything I say to get into bed with me, then act like you don't know me the next day."

"Nah, not really, but then you aren't like a lot of the ladies that I have known."

She has a perplexed look on her face. "Okay, what's that supposed to mean?"

Dean defends himself. "Well, just your attitude. You act as if you want to be my friend and you know things don't all have to be your way. Like right now. You could demand we be at your place, you could have had me playing cards or computer games because you like that better."

"I guess I could, but honestly, I don't like those things better. I enjoy racquetball and talking about things that interest both of us."

"Exactly! I can play cards, we can play computer games if you like those things, but if you want everything your way, then you can get it. But there is the possibility that I could get tired of it all being your way. I like how it is. We do things that we both like and the things we have in common." They climb in bed together for a peaceful night's sleep, without a stretch of clothes on.

Ted sits alone on the bridge, once again piloting the vessel and watching more footage from the archives they have decoded. He watches the footage of the reporter they all seen earlier, and he wonders if she is still alive. Was this package sent last month, last year, or a hundred, perhaps a thousand years ago? He passes by the dark space station that Greg tagged and wonders if it is inhabitable. Could they power it up and have an out station for the large vessels that will be en route soon? He hears a familiar beep at Jake's communication's panel, signaling an incoming communication from base. He wonders if that is the one they are all waiting on. Should he wake Jake up? He looks at the time displayed on his console and decides it is impossible for this to be a reply from Jake's message. He props up his feet and checks a couple of status screens and decides he will let them all rest peacefully, and sit there for his boring journey in endless circles around this planet.

Greg sits in his quarters, watching a transmission that he gets each day from base. A bunch of college-aged kids is on the beach, in what looks like Ft. Lauderdale, having a big party. A live popular band is playing, and dark tanned, half-naked ladies and men are in a big crowd, listening to the show. He nods off to sleep to the sound of the MC calling out the winners of games they are playing there on the beach.

The group gets daily communications, events, the news, and each member got to select some type of media they enjoy from their home world. It is about six hours later than when it was broadcasted back home, but it is as current as they can have. And they feel fortunate to have that.

Chapter 5

Loyalty, Betrayal, and Secrets

In a conference room atop a great skyscraper in Nevada, with windows for walls, a group of leaders sit at a large hardwood table. The room is warmly lit and darkness plumes outside the windows, where lights from the wild city below and stars from the sky can be seen. The leaders of the WRC are having a meeting. They each have dark colored leather, high-back, roll around chairs and a plaque with their respective titles and a triangular wooden trinket. The first seat is Charles Phillips at the head of the table. He is a large athletic man in appearance, with brown hair. He wears jeans and a dress shirt without a tie. He is the leader of the group and the top official of the WRC. Around the table are representatives from every nation in the world that have chosen to participate in the relocation efforts. The view out of the windows of the room reveals no buildings that are comparable to the size and height of this one.

Charles starts the meeting by addressing old business. "Gentlemen, we are on a very tight deadline to start our journey to our new world. It is of utmost importance that our deadline and testing of the new transport ships begin as soon as possible. We have passed the original deadline of our agreement and this is detrimental to the success of our timeline. I have threatened our builder with a change of leadership if he can't get the project timeline back in order. The Parche I has located a Goldilocks planet, and they are currently investigating feasibility for our inhabitance.

The ship has returned a communication to us that includes a partial copy of a dataset, in the form of a time capsule, from the orbit of the planet. The coalition's software and graphic engineers are reviewing the means for interpretation that Dean Stinson provided for us to ensure the message is accurate, clear, and properly interpreted in each language that is necessary for review." The leaders all begin talking amongst themselves - many in foreign tongues. Charles determines that it is prudent to give the leaders some time to digest the fact that a world was found that was already inhabited and the information from this will be transferred to each leader. He exclaims, "Order please, ORDER!" The room goes silent as this large powerful six-foot-eight-inch man stands up and reveals displeasure in being ignored by the group. He speaks in a very stern voice, "Gentlemen, I realize that you all have different perspectives on this discovery, but please realize the individuals that are interpreting its contents were appointed by this group and are from each of our countries. We must allow them to do their job prior to us passing judgment on the contents or speculating on anyone's motives. It is simple; we can't go on misinformation, and the only way I know to reveal the contents of this package is to:

1. Ensure the contents and understand it clearly.

2. Present the information to our group for discussion of our path forward based on the interpretation by interpretation and it being sent to each leader and their respective advisor.

Please do not second guess my decision as your leader as this…is…the most logical path that I see."

The group once again begins discussions among themselves. Charles stands up and hits the table with his gavel and says, "LET US RECESS for an hour. We shall reconvene and discuss the remainder of the matters that are of interest to our efforts at 7:35 pm."

The group then leaves the area. Each of the members has an office in the building and on the same floor as the boardroom, with the exception of Charles Phillips. Charles has the entire floor above this one…the penthouse. He gets in the elevator and goes to the top floor. He goes into his lavish office that is more like a condominium and sits down. In walks the President and the Vice President of the USA, accompanied by their respective secret service members. The Republican President, Robert Lynch, and the Vice President, John Garland, sit and want to discuss the reaction of the committee.

"Mr. President, I have not deceived anyone, and this transmission was received only hours… not days ago."

President Lynch replies, "I have no issue with what you are doing here. We have made you our leader for this endeavor because we need an intelligent, non-emotional, and non-biased action to the challenges that must be taken. I believe that this is the direction necessary for all things within this endeavor and for this information gathering as well."

John Garland, the VP, sits quietly and considers what is in the package and if there is a potential for misinformation coming from the group that is interpreting the information. VP Garland speaks up and asks, "Can we trust them?"

Charles says, "Trust who?"

"The engineers that are interpreting the communication."

"I don't know. Can you trust me? Can I trust you? Does the President of the US have reasons that he may mislead the group? Who can and can't be trusted at a time like this? I can tell you the way the engineering team was assembled. It is several different individuals from several different countries. I do not believe that one would allow the others to be misleading. We are all trying to save our own countries. This is a joint effort and certainly should be viewed as such. I do have the original file, and I have saved it separately from the information I released to the engineering team. Our ole buddy, Dean Stinson, has already translated all of the information. It is simply this team's obligation to confirm his findings and interpret it into their respective languages."

"I didn't mean to sound judgmental or that I am not in agreement with your choices, but I would like for you to have a little preface of the questions that will come from the other committee members. They are fearful that the others wish them to perish and to take the new world for their own."

President Lynch speaks up, "Dean Stinson? The same man who designed the FTL drive technology for our new fleet of transport ships?"

Charles replies, "Yes, Mr. President, I don't think he would be willing to accept full credit for the design, but he led the group. This man is not only a leader, he is also a craftsman and the finest engineer that I have ever worked with. The fathers of modern day technology would be quite impressed with the work Dean has done, as he has practically confirmed the cosmic speed limit and developed a method of manipulating it in a way that allows our spaceships to effectively exceed this. I do not believe that anyone within our little young engineering group will find anything that is incorrect with his work. He would not have released it if he didn't think it was accurate, and he is rarely incorrect. I felt it prudent that the other countries' engineers have an opportunity to review the data to be certain there are no misconceptions or fears of the perception of deception, or of anyone withholding data."

The President says, "That is why you are sitting where you are, Charles. It didn't take a committee to decide to take this action, did it?" He chuckles at Charles' wisdom.

"Nope, I knew that these guys would be fearful of deception, and I am doing my best to avoid any fear of dishonesty. Honestly, from what I gather from Commander Jacob Conley's transmission, it is likely we will have to wage a war with the inhabitants on the planet. I am not at liberty to discuss it in depth without the group, as I can't be swayed by any one leader, but it is a strong possibility."

"I see. This may turn into a morality issue."

"I have said more than I feel comfortable with at this time. Please understand that if President Vasquez from Mexico, or President Skuratov (Скуратов) from Russia sat in front of me at this time, I would feel the same way. I am not any more for or any more against any of our nations within our coalition. This includes the USA. This is a world event. It is bigger than any one nation."

"Agreed. We are all just desperate for survival."

"Well, it seems that many of us are fearful of a power play," Charles replies.

The group all enters the room and everyone has a seat, as the time for the break has passed. President Skuratov from Russia turns a triangular wooden trinket, lying on the table in front of him, with the point up—indicating he has a question.

Charles starts the meeting back up. "I hope everyone enjoyed their break and are positive about discussing the new information that has been revealed. I would like to call on President Skuratov from Russia. Please speak your mind at this time, Mr. President."

The salt and peppered hair Russian stands and asks, "What Russian interpreters do you have with the group that is interpreting the information?"

Charles replies, "I will have to review to see all of the names that are assigned to this group. This committee has appointed all of these individuals to the taskforce, and if there is not a Russian engineer involved, it is because the group didn't assign one to them."

The President's advisor, who is sitting beside him, places his triangular piece with the point up on top of his nameplate in front of him.

Charles says, "Advisor Drygin, do you have something to add?"

The advisor to President Skuratov stands and replies, "Sir Vladimir Lachkov—Владимир Лачков—is our engineer on this task force."

President Skuratov nods. "Acceptable. I must feel as though there is total transparency to our mother country."

Charles responds with, "Gentlemen, let me assure you that all precautions are being made to accommodate an open and honest interchange of information. There will be times that some representatives from some nations will not be involved, but there is a large enough consortium across the board that it will balance out. We all must trust that we are all supporting the directive of relocating all of our societies to a new world. I must admit that time is of the essence. We have a great amount of information to cover, and a decision needs to be made in reference to what the next step is for our reconnaissance spacecraft the Parche I.

"Okay, to continue with the direction that the meeting was started with, I have our committee confirming the findings of the mission engineer. Does anyone object to this direction?" He pauses and a few rumblings are heard throughout the group, but no triangles go up. "The next order of business is that the decision was made that no one over the age of sixty years old is to go, with the exception of government defined special cases. Does this stand?"

He looks over the group and looks at the stenographer and says, "Please let the record show that it is agreed that the individuals that will be included in the first transports will be less than sixty years of age and in good health unless WRC officials identify a reason for the other." Charles continues, "We have uncivilized and underdeveloped poor nations that do not have the resources to contribute that may be afforded an opportunity to join us." Triangles point up all around the table. "I solicit the group for thoughts concerning this. I am not interested in an open discussion, as it typically doesn't end with a clear agreement of what we plan to do. But I would like for you all to remit your consideration, along with justification of why you are for or against it, in an email to me and my administrative assistant, Brenda Smith." The triangles all go back flat on the table, except for one.

Charles asks, "President Vasquez, you have thoughts?"

He stands and says, "Much of my country is considered uncivilized. It is acceptable to me to only include the people of good standing in our community if it pleases the group. We have drug dealers, warlords, and undesirables that do not need to pollute our new world."

Charles looks on as this man has just condemned a portion of his society to death and responds, "President Vasquez, please recall that in February we had discussions concerning criminals on our world and if they shall or shall not be included with our voyage. It was determined that each country would decide the community members that would be allowed to be included, with the exception of age and health. The coalition will not determine the selection of criminals or upstanding citizens from each country. Each leader must be prepared to support whatever choice they make as their new country will be their own to facilitate. I would not want to start a country with a prison that is full, but this is each individual leader's choice."

Vasquez nods as he understands that it is to be his choice.

"Currently, our reconnaissance ship, the Parche I, is requesting permission to make contact with the inhabitants on the surface of the planet. I would like to grant them permission to gather additional intelligence through this means."

Triangles from the US President, Russian President, and the Egyptian President are turned upward. It appears that the Egyptian President was first to turn up his triangle, so Charles calls on him.

President Mohammad asks, "Do the inhabitants appear civilized?"

"Somewhat. I have limited information concerning the people of the planet. I was told by Commander Jacob Conley that they have gathered all of the information from orbit as is possible. As I mentioned earlier, we are in possession of the findings they currently have gathered and will make it available as soon as our interpreters complete this package." President Mohammad takes his seat.

He then calls on President Lynch of the United States. President Lynch stands and asks, "Are we in such a hurry that we can't take a few days to study the data they have gathered and make a clear decision of what the next logical move is?"

"Well, sir, I have to explain that we didn't haphazardly appoint Commander Conley as leader of this mission. I trust his judgment, and he feels this is necessary to do. Quite frankly, he is so far from home that he could choose whatever direction he deems necessary, but he has solicited our input. I believe if this is what he suggests for our next step, we should grant him permission."

President Lynch replies, "Well, if there is no additional information that can be obtained short of them going to the surface, then I agree with you." He sits down and the Russian President flips his triangle flat on the table.

41

Charles says, "President Skuratov, did you have some thoughts concerning this topic?" He looks at Charles and replies, "Would it matter? It sounds as if your mind is made up to grant permission and you lead this coalition. If I tell you no, I don't want them going, would it stop you from granting them permission? Have you already?"

Charles smiles and thinks to himself, *if I let you guys in on every step of the process, it would take two weeks.* He says, "Yes, sir, you are correct. I am in the position to determine what happens next. You all have chosen me for these types of decisions and to not let you stop yourselves from moving forward with our detrimental objective of relocating and saving as many people of our Earth as possible. You and every other member of this group have explained to me that it is unacceptable to allow you all to stop yourselves. This by no means indicates that your opinion does not matter. NO SIR! I have not granted permission for the group to go to the surface. If you tell me that this is unacceptable, then I will tell them that it is not possible at this time, however, I would expect a very good explanation and your particular insight of why we should tell them no. We are prepared to wage war against these individuals if necessary to save our planet. We must invoke Eminent Domain regardless of the world's response. We don't want to endanger our reconnaissance ship, but this is a dangerous mission regardless."

President Skuratov says, "I understand and I agree. Please grant them permission. We have too many varying and diverse personalities in this room for us all to agree each time, and you are our decision maker in the end. Young man, I hope you realize the responsibility that you have."

"Indeed, I do, sir, and please believe that I don't mean to make choices that are not agreed with, but when this coalition started the search for a new world, I was appointed to govern it. Each of you have told me and have sent affidavits for my consent to have full control and the authority to do what is necessary and to not allow politics to stop the process. If this occurs, we will all surely freeze to death, with half-constructed transportation ships, and each feeling content that they made their point but died because they stopped our overall progress. I shall not let any one man or group stop the progress. I also have the power to release a country from the group. I don't wish to flex my muscles, but this is the agreement from the entire coalition…and was each of yours and your country's choice. I will do what is necessary. I promised this then and I am happy to reconfirm now. This meeting is now adjourned. I look forward to reading your inputs and suggestions in the emails."

The meeting has been adjourned and all of the members exit the room. Charles heads back upstairs to his office. The walls are windows, much like the large conference room where everyone met. He stands at the window, considering what the leaders of their doomed world have conveyed. He just thinks that it is preposterous that they would be holding on to their political positions when all of this will change within the near future.

He gets a musical tone from his work station, and he goes and checks his email to find that the engineers have completed their confirmation. Their analysis finds that the app, which Dean sent, along with the package, was accurate and nothing other than an interpretation into various languages was necessary. He begins to review the data and reads the analysis that Heather put together for the statistics of the planet. Silently, he considers the population of the landmass being three and a half billion inhabitants for a landmass of 425 million sq kms. He looks up some statistics for planet Earth, to find current population data as being seven billion people on 149 million sq kms. Forty million are sixty plus years old and 100 million have life debilitating illnesses. The Asian governments have determined that 80% of their population will want to stay due to religious beliefs and will not be leaving their homeland. This reduces the total number of people eligible to transport by 3.4 billion. Considering most areas of Africa have not contributed and only have one representative on the coalition's steering committee, they will not have the rights to more than 200 million people. This gives the total of all inhabitants that will make the trip to be approximately 1.2 billion from Asia, 500 million from Europe, 300 million from Russia, 300 million from North America, 100 million from South America, 120 million from Australia, and an odd number from Antarctica, along with a possible correction factor of +/-5%, results in a new world population of approximately 2.65 billion people. If the current inhabitants remain on Goldilocks, which is three and a half billion individuals currently in place, this will make the statistics of the new world about six billion individuals on a landmass of 425 million sq kms. Depending upon resources, it sounds as though the new world will have three times the landmass of Earth and about two-thirds of the population.

This sounds like some excellent numbers to report to the members. This calculates to the Earth's population as fifty-four people per sq km as compared to the new world being ten people per sq km. He feels confident that it is possible to coexist with the current inhabitants.

He begins his reply to the Parche I. "WRC Commander-in-Chief Charles Phillips to Reconnaissance vessel WRC Parche I. We hope that all things are well in orbit of the planet Alfa Kantabury I—Goldilocks. We have begun reviewing the information you have sent. We have determined that it is acceptable for you to make contact with the government officials of this world. Please perform due diligence in determining who and where you need to be and who you must speak with prior to breaking the atmosphere if this is possible. If not, please–as always–use your best judgment, as I am sure that your crew has and will. Commander-in-Chief of the WRC over."

Charles then forwards each respective package to each member of the coalition, with the properly interpreted information. He puts a standard personal note in each one that explains the statistics of the world compared to planet Earth. He reminds them that the information contained in the packet is sensitive and shall not be shared with anyone other than a trusted official of each representative.

Chapter 6

First Impressions

Ted looks at the holograph in front of him and sees the abandoned space station. He focuses one of the exterior cameras in the direction of the unit and sees a dim light on it, then turns on an exterior spotlight. He sees nothing but a shadow and the faint light appears to be the size of an ant when the spotlight is not focused on it. He quickly begins to focus and it passes before he can get a look at anything. He thinks this is unusual as no electrical impulses were detected coming from the unit, but something had to be powering the light. He thinks out loud to himself, "I don't know…I am pretty tired, maybe that was a reflection." Dean walks in and sees the fixed image of the space station that Ted had been looking at.

Ted looks back at Dean and says, "Odd; it looked like there was a light on it."

Dean shrugs. "Well, not really that odd, as they could have some type of exterior lighting that uses less power than what our scanners can pick up. It is impossible to know what frequency, or type of power, to check for. It will not be 60Hz – 110Vac or 12, 24, or 48Vdc as we would expect on our world, I wouldn't think. They may not even use the same type of electricity as we use. We may learn something new from them."

"Where is Heather?"

"She wasn't ready to get up. I told her to sleep in, and I would let her know when we are ready to progress in going to the surface, or what our direction is from WRC." Dean sits down at his workstation and says, "It looks like we have time to check out the space station if Jake is cool with it."

"Hey, think you can take the wheel for a bit? I may crash for a few minutes."

"Yeah, I think I can handle her for a bit. I was at the wheel the first time she went into FTL drive."

"Great, I am transferring controls now." Ted leaves the bridge and goes off to his quarters. He goes into his humble room with navigation holograms on the wall that looks like pictures of the ship but are three-dimensional. He has a cloth-covered couch and recliner. He also has a small kitchenette with a bar and mini fridge. He goes to the fridge, gets a freshly replicated beer out, sits at his easy chair, and looks on a coffee table at his little girl, *Alicia,* and wonders what she is doing as he looks at his clock on the wall. It is 2:30 am back home. He says out loud, "Well, she better be in bed sleeping on this Friday night." Then he looks at a picture of his ex-wife, Katrina, and thinks of times they spent on the lake in his little cabin and thinks to himself, "What am I doing? I am six months away from home at 20X light speed. It is possible that to them I am dead. It is like I am near Heaven. What if this is Heaven below us? What could we be in for? I am a Christian and have a strong belief in my Lord." He clicks on the TV in his room and dials up some old videos of his ex-wife and little girl and kicks back in his chair and watches an Easter clip, then dials up preschool graduation, Christmas, then high school graduation. He is feeling a little homesick but knows what he is doing needs to be done for his little girl and everyone else's little girls back on planet Earth, to ensure the survival of the human race.

Jake walks onto the bridge and says, "Well, good morning, Dean. Where is Heather?" With a big smile.

Dean says, "Everyone asks me where Heather is. Don't y'all like to see me?"

"Yeah, ole buddy, everyone has to give you a little grief. I got to tell you she is an awesome catch. You are a lucky guy, even if this is just for the time that we are away on this mission."

"Well, I find her awesome, and we have a great deal of the same interests. This could really be something for us. She is somewhat younger, and I am a little worried about turning on the TV or playing some music. I like documentaries, action shows, old time

Rock-n-Roll, and old Country. I fear she is going to want to watch MTV and listen to some kind of Hippity Hoppity BS."

Jake laughs."Anything going on up here? Where is Ted? I thought he was good since he had a little rest."

"That was hours ago."

Jake looks at the time. "Jeez, I have been down for a while, huh? It seems like I just laid down."

Jake sits down at his panel and sees the indicator for a new message received. He opens it and it is a file sent from WRC headquarters, showing the anticipated evacuation headcount from Earth.

Commander Conley,

Attached, please find approximate numbers for the population that is calculated to come to the new world. We have corrections for Asia, taking into consideration the number of people that would prefer to stick it out here, and a limitation on age and health of individuals. I am uncertain of people that are incarcerated, as they will be selected by each country's government, but in short, the entire count is expected to be between 2.5 and 3 billion people. This will require thousands of transport ships. We anticipate a constant circle of a one year trip for a mission, with a fleet of about 400,000 ships making approximately two trips each, with 4,000 ships a week that are capable of carrying 5,000 people per ship beginning as soon as it is possible to accommodate people on the planet and the ships are ready. We expect to begin time trials with the first transports as early as next week. We are behind schedule currently on completion of the prototype. Once completed, the units will be replicated at a very fast pace. We shall be sending about 16,000 transport ships each month until all are deployed. It will be possible for our citizens to live on resources from military supply ships for up to three years if necessary, but it will only allow us to evacuate about half of the people if they have nowhere to go. We will have to dispose of the existing population if necessary. Please do not divulge any information concerning what lengths we shall go to, to anyone on the planet if you decide that you must go to the surface.

Sincerely,

Charles Phillips, Commander-in-Chief WRC

Jake knows Charles hasn't gotten his transmission yet when WRC sent this and thinks, *Hell,*

didn't know it was my choice.

Dean looks over at Jake. "You want the helm?"

Jakes shakes his head. "Not particularly. I will go get Greg up if you are tired of watching it."

"Nah, let him sleep. We have had him going for hours on end, and I suspect when we get approval to go to the surface, we will all be needing a little beauty sleep."

"You're right. Transfer the helm if you are tired of it."

"I'm not tired of it. Thought you might want to drive for a bit. I know you like to pilot it occasionally, but it isn't bothering me."

Jake nods."Thanks, but I do have plenty to do over here. I got a communication from WRC headquarters giving status on transports I need to study. I also want to review some more data from the time capsule prior to trying to meet them."

"Suit yourself. I am good. Is the transport prototype complete yet?"

Jake scowls. "No, it is behind schedule."

Dean, with a perplexed look, says, "We kind of need to find a spot for them before they start sending people. What is the capacity, did they mention? The one I helped design would hold 5,000."

"They must be going with that one. Can you imagine losing one, though? That would be pretty tragic."

Dean agrees, "True, but the idea is to not lose any."

The door slides open and in walks Heather. Both Dean and Jake look back and Dean remarks, "Damn, you get sexier every time I see you!"

Jake cuts his eyes at Dean as if to say, "Very unprofessional of you." Dean realizes his error and replies, "Oops, sorry, Jake."

Jake just nods. "Good morning, young lady. Are you ready to tackle the new world?"

"Of course! Do we need to set a course? Have you got the okay? Should Dean go wake Greg, Commander?"

"Not yet, but let's get prepared. We need to determine where their headquarters are located."

"Is that what you need to know?"

"Yes, please, and since we have two on deck, I think I will go work in my office for a while." He starts down the hallway to his quarters and comes upon Greg. Greg says, "Good morning, sir."

"G'morning, how are you?"

"Well rested. Have you heard anything about our trip down there yet?"

"Not yet, but I anticipate something soon."

"Great!" exclaims Greg.

Jake gets to his quarters and goes to his office, sits into his chair and brings up his PC to read the data from WRC again. He thinks to himself, "I wonder why only a small portion of the Asian people are coming. Hell, that is a small portion of their population. I wonder if they will be content in their crowded homeland after the others have gone. Who will be left in the US? Radicals? Will China decide to move in on the ones that are left?" Then suddenly a new transmission comes across from Charles Phillips' assistant, Brenda Smith.

Dear Jake,

I miss you as always. I really worried about you when I heard we lost your sister ship. Charles asked that I contact you and let you know that we have received your communication and data package. He wants you to know a meeting is scheduled for the coalition this afternoon and shortly following that he will be responding to your requests. He also realized there were a few gaps in the last correspondence that was sent and you might like a little deeper explanation about them. The Chinese are deep in tradition and many don't want to leave their homeland. They have decided not to accept anyone over sixty years of age unless they have a permit and anyone seriously ill due to not having established medical facilities. The African and Middle East nations are poverty stricken and can't afford to contribute to the coalition and are not included at this time, but he anticipates the coalition providing a number of them with a free pass.

Jake, I want you to know that I care deeply for you and I want you to take care.

Love,

Brenda Smith

Administrative Assistant to WRC CNC, Charles Phillips

Jake says, "Hell yeah!" *I guess things didn't pan out with ole Dale, her long time love interest, following their short marriage together. I sure look forward to seeing her again.*

Meanwhile, on the bridge, Greg is back at the helm. Heather and Dean are working to find a landing site and monitoring to determine a capital city. Dean says, "I have it." Heather asks, "What do you have?"

"Shortwave from a capital city in Daringranka."

"No way, Dean! I have tried all of the channels."

"Conventional channels. They're transmitting on an inverse carrier frequency. It is a negative going signal."

Greg speaks up. "Bizarro world."

Dean agrees, "Yeah perhaps, but we may have done the same thing in our world, but our foundation is positive. We may need to reconsider all of our scans." Heather cuts her eyes over at Dean. He explains, "We shall calibrate to monitor for negative DC voltages, and at all frequencies. It is just impossible to believe that all of these installations are dormant!"

Heather is astonished. "I already have a hit. I changed the possible scan to negative DC and frequencies from zero to the microwave range. I show DC voltages at a negative potential all over. I also see square waves at ultra high frequencies carrying electricity everywhere."

Dean nods. "I see it as well. Heather, do you see any power transmission lines on the surface?"

"No, and I did not earlier, but I assumed when the power went off perhaps they removed the poles or they were buried."

Dean exclaims, "It is lit up like the Fourth of July down there!"

Excitement seems to fill the room as Jake and Ted walk in. Jake asks, "What is going on?" as he sees smiles all around the room and everyone seems to be excited.

Dean says, "Look at the holograph." They all look up at the scan of the surface and city lights light up the night.

Jake questions, "How can this be? I thought we determined no light, no power."

Dean says, "Heather, would you like to explain?" Heather says, "Certainly, Mr. Dean. It was you who discovered it, though. We discovered there was a light on the space station and no trace voltage was found. The exterior camera on the ship was set up for ultraviolet light earlier. Dean determined the voltage was likely negatively rectified DC. This is an unusual way to create a DC voltage as you clip the negative going portion of the sign wave. On Earth, this would only raise zero to some value. For this planet, they create negative voltages. It's a pretty neat trick! We decided to recalibrate our scan parameters to include this as well as sawtooth, triangular, and square waves from zero to microwave. We discovered hits all over the world at a very high-frequency square wave. I can't understand why this is this way or how it works, but I can explain the lights."

Dean asks, "Okay, Ms. Smarty Pants, why couldn't we see the light?"

She says, "Dean re-parameterized the cameras to interpret ultraviolet light. There it is. We can see down there, but we will require glasses at nighttime. I still can't understand the value of the high-frequency square wave for the electricity, though."

Dean speaks up, "These folks aren't without technology. They distribute electricity better and more efficiently than we do back home. They don't use any copper conductors to transmit electricity. They use a superconductor and perhaps a cryogenic gold substance. It would then be fed into coils, and they use air as their medium to transport power from what I can tell. Nikola Tesla had performed this on our world but did not share the technology prior to his passing."

Jake says, "Awesome, perhaps they can be reasoned with. I just got the transmission from home base and we have five tickets to the surface. I do want to do as much research as is possible to determine where we need to go and who we are looking for prior to breaking into the atmosphere. Perhaps we could make contact with them via wireless communications prior to arriving unannounced."

Heather says, "I have the capital city transmissions but can't understand a damn thing."

Jake says, "You been hanging with the wrong crowd, girl, you potty mouth," as he gives her a mischievous smirk.

Chapter 7

First Contact

Heather and Dean both have headsets on and it is apparent they are *tuning in* to a plethora of broadcasts from Goldilocks. Dean and Heather devised an application that allows real-time interpretations of both languages in both directions. Dean pulls down his headset and says, "Commander," abruptly interrupting him.

Jake looks up from the latest correspondences from Earth and looks his way and says, "Dean? You called me Commander, that is nice and pretty respectful to the leadership of this vessel. I just got the promotion before we left headquarters, and it is music to my ears to hear that. We do have to live with one another for a very long time, though, and I do not mind being called Jake."

Dean has called him Jake this entire voyage. Dean continues, "Sir, we are receiving a televised newscast."

"On the screen please," states Jake.

Three broadcasters are sitting at a desk that is not unlike a news broadcast desk on our own world, but the desk is decorated with what appears to be a healthy layer of gold.

The anchorman starts by saying, "Good evening from our capital city of Novaraca. I am Kelvik Carrolt, along with my co-anchor, Mrs. Stellita Mickgowia, and Juthamba Zelicwi with the weather.

"We begin our story tonight with news from our governing body. The leaders of Longenthros met in our capital city to discuss the future of subsidies for failed farmers. They explained that if a farmer is not skilled in raising food, he should find a different line of work. The farmers complained that their failed crops are due to the weather. The official of Agriculture rebutted their claims due to the other farmers that were successful. In the end, the group determined the subsidies from the government would continue throughout the end of this year, but if unsuccessful during the following year, unless there is a catastrophic weather event, they would not profit from our other citizens who are ultimately finding a way to be successful in their chosen crafts.

"In other news, the carnival is in town to correspond with our yearly crafts festival in the south end of Novaraca. Our reporter Kanancy Kalitina is reporting from there." The picture changes to reveal a young, red-haired female that has some food that no one on the bridge recognizes but appears to be a corn dog that is black with some type of coating of gray. She starts reporting, "Loads of fun to be had here at the carnival. There are prizes to win, rides to ride, and a lottery to give away a baby goat, oh, and the food is delicious and very unhealthy for you, as always. For Novaraca city news, I am Kanancy Kalitina."

The picture then reveals the news crew and Stellita begins speaking, "In other news today, the leaders of the carnival based from Carsanalia city – Johnohka Barrent was indicted on charges of not contributing, neither directly nor indirectly, with the day to day operation of his carnival. The government has reported that there will be a very deep probe into his daily interaction with his business, but if found guilty, he faces the penalty of death due to the constitution put in place four years ago following the civil war."

Kelvik Carrolt takes over again and says, "A probe to investigate the murder of a businessman that was murdered last year revealed today that the perpetrator had taken illegal drugs prior to murdering the man. The nation was shocked by the outrageous act of harming another citizen, and although they spared the man's family, after putting him to death by hanging in the town square of Novaraca, they are placing them under close surveillance to ensure there isn't some family gene defect that would dictate this type of socially outrageous act. They have been performing mental analysis on the family since the tragedy and are now ready to move to the next phase. They are sparing their lives, unlike with the last heinous crime of this type. This was the only murder within our world over the past two years, as many will recall the other murder back two and a half years ago resulted in the man being hanged in the street. His mother, father, and descendants were disposed of humanely by lethal injection to stop the bloodline. They had immediately found traits that could have led to further actions such as this from his other family members."

Stellita Mickgowia begins again, "Okay, let's get on to the good news of the day. Juthamba Zelicwi, how is our weather looking?"

On the bridge, Jake says, "Okay, let's record the rest and each of us can study it a little and give this some thought. They are killing one's family because of their actions? Wow!"

Dean shakes his head. "Our best Christians may not live up to these standards."

"We will have to learn to coexist it looks like, if that is even possible. I fear what perspective they have toward *spacemen*. If they do not like the way we look, does that mean they will hang us? Heather, you and Dean please find a way to identify the government officials, find a way to contact them via a wireless communications link, and let me know when we can do this. I am going to my quarters. Patch that link into my system so that I may watch their TV stations. I suggest that Ted and Greg do the same with this station or others. It may be prudent to try to find a religious station."

Jake gets back to his quarters and starts a new communication via email.

Charles,

I have some deep fear of this society and their methods and tactics. Their way of life would seem barbaric to our bleeding hearts on Earth. They have very little tolerance for any un-adherence to their laws. They have only had two murders on the entire planet within three years and the suspect was hanged in the street in both cases. The most disturbing thing is that in one of the two cases, they also killed the man's parents and descendants, humanely, but they were killed by the government, according to the news report I just watched.

Honestly, sir, I fear with such a hard line that we should postpone travel to the surface until we feel we know the laws that we must abide by. We should have the ability to communicate directly with their leaders within twenty-four hours. I would very much like to be able to sit down and have a discussion with you to determine our best path forward. I must trust my training and gather data and we can discuss through correspondence. This email should only take four hours to reach you and two hours for your reply to reach me, without any attachments. If there is some information that you can give me that may help my predicament or advice that may lead me in the right direction, please let me know ASAP, as I will be speaking with the inhabitants at my earliest opportunity.

Sincerely,

Commander Jacob Conley WRC Parche I

He hits send and a little musical note plays on the screen and an email from WRC Engineer Jeff Briscoe has arrived.

Jake,

Charles asked that I inform you that the time trials begin today on the prototype transport ships. It will be performed by me, Dalton Coleman, and Bill Hogan, with a minimum complement of crew, approximately four people. We will be back in touch to inform you of our results.

Sincerely,

Jeff Briscoe WRC SR Design Engineer

Jake thinks this is great news. He closes the computer screen and turns on the television set and sits down on his easy chair to see what can be learned about the world below.

Back on the bridge, Heather has a headset and mouthpiece, like a telemarketer, plugged into her workstation and she is speaking with someone on the surface.

She says, "I am trying to get in touch with Senator Marliklez." Dean then hears her say, "Hello, Mr. Marliklez? This may sound very unusual, but my name is Heather and I am in orbit above your planet." The response on the other end is, "Who?" She replies, "Sir, I know this is very difficult to believe, or understand for you, but I am in great need of getting in touch with your top leader." The Senator comes back, "Why? Why do you have a need to speak to our government leaders?"

"Sir, I have the commander of my ship that would very much like to discuss a relationship between our world and yours. Is there some frequency or number that President Haulk can be reached? Is it possible that I can give you a way to connect back to me?" Senator Marliklez pauses for a bit. "Yes. Give me your contact information." Heather, with a smile on her face, replies, "Okay, I have a link at 765-555-5678-1-1 on your communication device. I await your leader's response and, Senator, thank you greatly for your cooperation."

She gets off the phone with the senator and Dean says, "You looked pretty nervous there, Heather." Ted and Greg both are deep into their TV shows, with their headsets on.

Heather makes a humphing noise. "Wouldn't you be?"

"First contact and trying to get them to let you talk to their President, or to ask they get in touch with you…uh yeah, guess it would maybe make me a little apprehensive."

She pushes a button on her panel. Jake, in his quarters watching his television program, hears a beep, then Heather's voice comes over the panel. "Jake, I have made contact with a Senator Marliklez on the surface and he will have President Haulk call a number that I have linked to my comm center."

Jake's voice comes over the comm link. "Heather, can you come to my quarters? I believe it prudent for us to discuss something."

Heather gets up and Dean asks, "What's up?"

Heather shrugs and replies, "Jake asked that I come to his office. He wants to discuss my correspondence with the senator I suppose."

"Ah, I see."

Heather arrives at Jake's quarters, and he says, "Have a seat." She sits down and wonders what is on his mind. "Heather, I really have to admit that prior to the last few days I was uncertain how good of a choice you were to be on this mission with us. I thought that you are a pretty lady that will ultimately distract my crew."

She tries to speak up. "Sir, that is un…" and she is interrupted by Jake to hear him say, "I know that sounds harsh and unfair toward you, but it is more than just stereotyping for me. I have worked with a lot of women and have found that some of the attractive ones want special treatment. I want to promote you and increase your compensation, for what that is worth, due to the strengths that you have shown. The relationship with Dean is a bit of a nuisance to me at times, but I don't believe that it is harmful to our mission or I would forbid it. It has actually seemed like a benefit to your work and his. You are now promoted to Sr. Research Navigator for the WRC, with a 15% increase in salary."

Heather is shocked. "Sir, I don't know what to say. It is disheartening to know that you have a stereotyping tendency toward me, but I am very happy you have acknowledged greater value in me and that you are discovering more of my talents as a member of our crew."

"Now, what was the senator like? Did he believe you? What did he say?" Jake asks.

"I honestly don't know. At first, he didn't believe me but promised he had a direct link to the president and he would put him in touch with me."

"Do not put him in direct touch with me when he calls. I would very much enjoy putting him in a waiting game for me to return his call. It is more likely that he will have an aide call. If an aide calls or the president calls, you set up a meeting time. It doesn't matter if it is within an hour of the call or at midnight. When he is available, I will be ready for the communication. Immediately contact me once they make contact and record the conversation."

"I recorded the senator if you care to hear. There is not a great deal of content."

"Yes, please send me a link to the communication or send me the recording, please. And that will be all."

"Of course, and Commander, I have a great deal of gratitude for what you have said and done here today."

"You deserve it, keep up the good work and GET BACK AT IT!" He laughs.

She takes off back to the bridge. She walks in and Dean asks, "Well, did you get your ass chewed?"

"No, on the contrary, I am now a Sr. Research Navigator, and he told me what a great job I am doing."

"Really? I had the idea that he didn't like you much."

"Me, too. He was afraid that I was going to mesmerize all of you with my amazing beauty." She laughs.

Dean looks at her and says, "That is not so farfetched, my little beauty. It has happened before. Commanders and Captains have had mutiny in history due to a beautiful woman causing dissension among a crew of men on long, lonely voyages."

"I just want to perform my duties. I enjoy my job. I am astonished at a promotion. It feels very fulfilling to be Sr. Research Navigator Heather Lawson! It also came with a large increase in compensation!"

Dean says, "I don't think there is anyone on the ship more deserving," as he looks toward the pilots that are still watching their episodes of what looks like Friends ~ Alpha Kantabury I style.

"You sincerely mean that, Dean?"

"Yes, you have contributed a great deal to this journey, much more than to give us something other than a cold hard display to look at, especially for me!" as he chuckles.

"Yeah, well, you have given me a little eye candy, too, big boy."

Ted looks back, shaking his head, and says, "Y'all get a room, damn."

Dean laughs. "Got one! Don't you need to get back to your episode of *The Love Boat* there, ole buddy."

"Say what you want, but their TV is better than ours. They have beautiful women, violence or action more than gore, it seems, and sex, but nothing goes over the top. It is G-rated or maybe PG13. No one kills anyone else and an underlying theme is that there are no outsiders. They all help one another and work together. There doesn't seem to be different classes of people. They have social differences, but I have seen nothing within these TV shows that appears to be royalty."

Dean nods. "That makes sense, from what we have learned about them so far."

"It is terrible to think what our society will bring to this world."

Dean says, "We could learn from them if our leaders will allow us. We do stand a chance to follow with Charles Phillips at the wheel."

Chapter 8

The Prototype Transport

The sun beams across the top of a field that starts where the tarmac ends. It must be miles of flat land until you can seemingly see the curvature of the Earth. It's almost like being on the ocean, but the grass makes the morning sunlight glitter, shimmer, and sparkle as it breaks the dawn of a new day in America's largest test facility. The first transport prototype, the Arc 0, sits on the runway. It takes up more room than a music hall. She is much different in appearance than the shiny Parche vessels. It is a dull, flat black ship and reminds the officers of the WRC of the stealth bomber that was first launched in the United States back in the early 1980s. Charles Phillips stands at the front of the first one built, wondering how on earth this mammoth ship will ever take flight. This ship is not terribly different from the Parche I and II, with her swept wing design and engines that you could park three locomotives in side-by-side. In front of the ship are Charles Phillips–CNC WRC, Dalton Coleman–test pilot, Jeff Briscoe and Bill Hogan–leading design engineers and pilots on the project.

Charles starts explaining how he expects things to go. "Gentlemen, this test shall take five days. After day one, I expect a communication to inform us of how the ship feels once she hits FTL speeds."

Jeff responds, "Sir, it shall take in excess of thirty-six hours to get the engines wound up to FTL speed."

"I thought the human body G-force dictated the acceleration time of twenty-two hours, Jeff."

"Yes, sir, but with a prototype craft, we give it a fourteen-hour leeway to ensure the accelerometers are properly calibrated and the vessel does not take itself apart. This is her maiden voyage. Once complete, we have a battery of tests that include faster acceleration rates."

Charles says, "When you get it at top speed, call me," in a fairly stern annoyed military voice.

Jeff goes to attention and says, "Sir, yes sir, Commander!"

Jeff, Bill, and Dalton climb the flights of stairs to enter this colossal ship. Charles climbs into a white Ford Super Duty, WRC truck and heads to the control tower. Dalton sits at the front of the bridge, much like the bridge of the Parche I, and Jeff sits at the commander's seat, with Bill at the navigator's station. They all click feverishly through their preflight checklists on their consoles.

Charles arrives at the control tower after about a ten-minute ride and him and his assistant, Woody, climb out of the big truck. They walk into the air conditioned control tower lobby, with armed guards holding AK style weapons on each side of the door. Each one salutes Charles, as does he when he enters the room.

Brenda Smith meets him in the lobby. "Sir, the committee is all in the tower, awaiting your arrival."

"All of them, Brenda? It is steaming hot out there."

Brenda says, "All of the regulars."

He says, "Very well," as they step into an elevator.

They arrive at the top, with a room full of committee members. A large hologram of the ship levitates in the middle of the room. The group all look out at the enormous ship as the engine exhausts go solid blue.

President Lynch remarks, "That is a color blue that I've never seen."

Steve, the traffic controller, speaks up, "Yes sir, it is the glow from the fuel. If it is the same as the Parche engines, it will glow to a dark purple, almost black, then go to a lime green and the craft will take off."

The President of the United States says, "Interesting."

The glow from the gigantic engines then begin growing darker until it is purple, almost black. A few minutes pass and the ship springs into the air like an arrow launched from a bow. A strong loud noise is heard within the tower, then a shockwave rocks the tower as if an earthquake has hit the area. The committee members look at Charles as if the ship has just blown up.

The Russian President speaks up and asks, "What happened?"

Charles says, "The ship launched."

The traffic controller explains, "It is so powerful that you have to look closely or it is gone before you can see it go down the runway."

President Lynch speaks up, "I don't see how the human body can handle that much force."

Charles nods and explains, "The ship is equipped with anti 'G' compensating dampeners, but even with the force that the ship takes off at, it will take it thirty-six hours to get to the speed of light at constant acceleration. The force on the crew is well within limits." The committee looks on in disbelief. Charles continues, "In practicality, most people think that we push a button and instantly go to FTL drive. If this actually occurred, it would rip the motors from the vessel and leave our crew flat as a pancake. The speed they took off at will set them back in their seat, but nothing like the engines are capable of. We run the ship faster and faster until it eventually obtains the speed of twenty times the speed of light."

President Lynch speaks up, "I don't mean to trouble you smart fellas with dumb questions, but once they are in space, is it like other spacecraft that we have seen where everyone is weightless?"

Charles says, "No sir, and that is a really good question for the group because we haven't discussed that. Could you imagine 5,000 people on a ship without gravity? Oh my. Could you imagine what all would be floating around the cabin? The ship is equipped with a gel around the outside of the hull. This gel is agitated by the motion of the ship and is circulated at an extremely high rate of speed, creating something like a gyroscope due to the direction and path the gel takes. This action causes a phenomenon that is not that much different from the rotation effects of our Earth. It is like magnetism for all items within the spacecraft to be pulled toward the bottom of the vessel. In the early stages, this was troublesome for a space pilot to become accustomed to. The fact that the craft being level doesn't matter as it has artificial gravity and gravity is wherever the bottom of the spaceship is located. It can cause confusion as it pertains to the horizon while it is still within our atmosphere and due to the pilot can't 'feel' the craft's descent like he can in a conventional aircraft."

President Lynch says, "This is all very fascinating stuff. It is the best gee whiz stuff I have seen since I have been in office. How long before the spaceship is out of our atmosphere?"

"It is now and has traveled about 1,000 miles into space, if that gives you some perspective."

The President scratches his head. "Man, that thing is fast, especially for how large it is! Will it be able to land on the runway when it gets back home?"

Charles is beginning to become somewhat tired of the inquisitiveness. "Yes sir, but it will take it twenty-four hours to slow back to a safe speed in order to reenter the atmosphere, and if he misses it, he will have to travel several thousand miles and make a strong tight turn to make another attempt. Once it enters the atmosphere, he will circle the Earth once to slow his speed and line up on the approach. The runway is about 10X the length of a normal jetliner's.

"Gentlemen, please forgive me, but I must get back to the office to check in on the mission and take care of things."

President Lynch says, "By all means. Thank you for being so free with your time and information on the craft and please know that not all of us are up on the basics of the thing," as he smiles.

"No problem." He nods, "Gentlemen. Brenda, Woody, let's head back to headquarters."

He gets back to his office and settles into his office chair. He has the automatic updates that were emailed from the craft. He pulls up the first one and it says hull temperature: actual, anticipated, and ideal then a percentage from ideal that is green. One field is listed as

Hull Integrity, then an inside temperature, engine core temperature etc. all with green indicators all the way down the screen. He brings up another email and the same information is being sent every fifteen minutes. Another email shows the vital statistics of the crew and any notations taken from the crew members.

He opens an email from Bill Hogan, who has not been on an FTL drive system, that says, HOLY SHIT! THIS OLE BIG GAL CAN MOVE! Charles chuckles as he considers that Bill is unaware that his comments are being transcribed and aren't personal and half of command can see them.

Brenda comes in and says, "Commander, who designed the gravity system for the craft?"

Charles says, "That smart-ass, Dean Stinson did, why?"

"Well, it just sounds ingenious and I could admire a man that has the ability to create something that will mean so much to space travel."

Charles says, "You should, all the rest of us that are in the know admire that old fella. So is that why you came in? To inquire about the gravity generator in the spacecraft?"

She responds, "Oh, heavens no, and if I was out of line I apologize."

"Not at all, but it is an odd inquiry coming from you, Brenda."

"I know, but I find that one interesting. I came to explain that a scientist in Russia devised a laser that can penetrate the sun and monitor its progression into the stages of burning out."

"Fantastic, if they are correct. Who has tested it? Can they confirm their findings? What basis do they have to compare it to?"

"I didn't make this thing, Charles. I was simply asked to tell you about it."

"American in conjunction with German scientists have determined the fate of the sun within about a year, but if there is a method of predicting precisely when through some real-time

65

measurement, it would be of great benefit. Who asked you to tell me about it?"

She says, "President Skuratov's assistant, Russian advisor Drygin said that the president wanted me to tell you. He said a Russian scientist created it and it is being evaluated by Andrei Yolkin and you could contact them for details."

"Thank you, Brenda, and I didn't mean to give you the third degree. You must know what this means if we can gauge the time that we have left prior to doomsday."

"You have a lot of pressure on you, and I completely understand. I won't get upset unless I think that you're disappointed in something I have done."

"Understood and no problem with you, young lady." She leaves his office.

Charles then has a musical tone and he sees that he has received electronic mail. He opens the program and clicks on a new line that is bold and says Jacob.Conley@WRC.com. He reads the correspondence from Jake.

Charles,

I have some deep fear of this society and their methods and tactics. Their way of life would seem barbaric to our bleeding hearts on Earth. They have very little tolerance for any un-adherence to their laws. They have only had two murders on the entire planet within three years and the suspect was hanged in the street in both cases. The most disturbing thing is that in one of the two cases they also killed the man's parents and descendants, humanely, but they were killed by the government, according to the news report I just watched.

Honestly, sir, I fear with such a hard line that we should postpone travel to the surface until we feel we know the laws that we must abide by. We should have the ability to communicate directly with their leaders within twenty-four hours. I would very much like to be able to sit down and have a discussion with you to determine our best path forward. I must trust my training and

66

gather data and we can discuss through correspondence. This email should only take two hours to reach you and two hours for your reply to reach me, without any attachments. If there is some information that you can give me that may help my predicament or advice that may lead me in the right direction, please let me know ASAP, as I will be speaking with the inhabitants at my earliest opportunity.

Sincerely,

Commander Jacob Conley WRC Parche I

He sits alone, with the lights slightly dimmed, considering just how much control he has of things at this point. He has a lot of thoughts going through his head. When the world leaders get to the new world, it will be up to them what happens next as their armies and respective groups will follow them. *Why should it be this way?* he thinks. They are all abandoning their country, and by all rights should be at the mercy of the leaders of the new world, respect and abide by their rules and wishes. I know that some of the leaders would want to conquer the land if they are subject to such laws, as each can't charge a fee for lending currency or employ tax collectors and bankers. If I table this for discussion, what will become of the talks? I see no choice but to discuss this concern. The survival of our world is all that is critical to the people of our world.

He clicks a button and says, "Brenda, do you have stats of the first transports that are planned?" A voice from Brenda comes back over the intercom and says, "Yes, Commander, would you like for me to send them or print them?" He says, "Print and bring them in, please."

He speaks out loud, "Well, Brenda isn't exactly my advisor but she is levelheaded, and could at least be a sounding board to see if my thoughts are reasonable."

Brenda walks in and hands Charles the papers. He says, "You look nice today, Brenda."

She very rarely gets praise for her appearance from her boss and says, "Thanks, Commander. Is that all you need?"

Charles replies, "No," as he looks at the list. "Who put this plan together?"

"General Brett Silvers did, sir. He is a special advisor from the US Military and specializes in mobilizing large groups for the US military."

"The first fleet of ships to leave will have 1,000 military vessels. They will be hauling supplies, temporary command posts, shelter, and armament," Charles says.

Brenda looks at him and says, "You do have a military man planning support for our venture and I seen that, but wouldn't you have to in order to secure a place for the people to go?"

"Of course, but I haven't actually seen 'the plan' like this. I know that I have received it but haven't opened and reviewed it. Perhaps it was disbelief in the fact that we would actually figure out a way to leave Earth. The people of this world have their own army. Perhaps they will see this as an act of hostility."

"Is what we are doing not an act of hostility, sir? What would we do if aliens came and was going to move in on us?"

Charles says, "It would be war. I have to put together my recommendations to the board. I have to do more than that actually. These leaders are essentially just tokens from their nations, who do not actually get anything accomplished. They only angle to make themselves look like they did the right thing. I actually have to make a choice and ask for their review and make this happen. If no one will agree, then I will have to decide what we do, Brenda. I like the plan. I can't think of a way for anyone to survive unless food, water, and semi-permanent shelters are in place. He suggests enough provisions for the first group for six months before another arrives. He even has provisions for animals, plants, and sustainable fundamentals. I believe the world has many of these resources. Our people will have to adapt. Aye, yie yie. This is horrific to think of businessmen having to build a shelter with potentially primitive tools. I have no more to add." He says to himself in a low voice, "Please let Jake reply with good news about their leader and an understanding of our predicament. Brenda, pray for us, and thank you for lending me your ear."

Brenda says, "I pray every day for all of us, and Commander, I am here for you for anything that you require and I am happy to be in this position for you."

"Let's not get too accommodating. You do have a fella named Dale out there somewhere that I have met a time or two."

She looks at him without the desire to leave an inappropriate tone to their conversation, and just says, "I am tired, it's late, and I think I should go home."

"Very well. Get some rest. It has been a long, eventful day for us all. This is a big day and a bigger one to come soon!" She walks out of the room with him looking at her tight jumpsuit, thinking she really is a very attractive lady.

Brenda closes the door and says, "Well, the other fella's name is not Dale, he is my ex, it is Jake."

Charles brings up the latest correspondence from the Ark 0 and all green lights, with the exception of Bill and his vitals are a bit excited but only in the yellow zone. He drafts a response to Jake and explains that it is important to try to befriend the leaders on Alpha Kantabury I and he regrets that he can't be there to assist with the difficult situation that he is in. He explains the only thing that needs to be impressed upon their President is that we are coming. We have our own society rules of conduct that shall be adhered to by our people, and it is as much of a fact as there are stars in the sky that three billion earthlings and a complement of nearly one billion various animals will be arriving within the next two years, like it or not.

Chapter 9

Eavesdropping on Goldilocks

Twelve hours have passed on the Parche I, and the communications link has remained silent. Heather and Dean have continued to research the structure, names of the governmental officials, and the topology of the land. They now have all of the names for the key players, country name, state names, and layout of providences. They discovered that time is different than on Earth and are prepared to report on their findings.

Following the deafening silence, Ted steps in well rested. "Maybe if we are going to the planet's surface, you all ought to get some rest."

Dean replies, "I have just started putting together a way of keeping time so that we can be in sync with the planet. I have examples of their system, and I have to put together a program so that we may be able to determine what time it is there."

Heather messages Dean on his workstation. "I'm not tired either."

Ted nudges Greg as he still has his headphones on, watching television and Greg pulls down his earpieces. "Yes, sir?"

"Do you want to go get some sleep?"

"Not right now, Ted. This show is about over, then I will be ready. It is a strange time allotted for the episodes. It is less than an hour."

Dean says, "This planet has shorter days than us, and a longer year."

Greg speaks up, "So time isn't the same here?"

The bridge door opens and Jake walks in. Dean looks back and sees the commander. Jake says, "Go on."

Dean replies, "Greg inquired about time keeping here on the planet." He continues, "Time is an absolute, there is no change to the fact of one second then we progress into another second that is constant, and can't be changed. Our entire time system of tracking this phenomenon can be considered relative. It is based on our Earth's rotation for units that are used to represent one day, and for days, weeks and months, we use the orbit around the sun. This planet's time is unique and different from ours. The planet rotates at a faster rate than Earth, and this makes their day shorter, and it has a wider orbit around its sun and this causes the year to be longer."

Greg says, "It is strange that I have never considered that our timekeeping on Earth wasn't universal, and in fact, it isn't a constant in the universe."

Dean replies, "It is for us, or has been, but will not be feasible on this world."

Jake then says, "Are you all ready to give me an update on your research?"

Heather says, "Sir, we have found they have a networked system that is similar to our computers and mobile phones. It is something like our Internet, but it doesn't appear to be as sophisticated as our systems back home. I will refer to it as the A.K.1 Internet (Alpha Kantabury 1 Internet)." She continues, "We have been able to retrieve data from it, and we have discovered the framework and layout of the society through information from it. I have discovered that the country of Daringranka won the war between it and Longenthros. Following the war, they created a new country, Malpeada, from the two very large landmasses and changed them to states that are separated by water. The states' names are Daringranka and Longenthros. Each of the states has hundreds of providences that are further broken down into cities, then, of course, individual communities. The representatives that make up the government all come from the individual providences, with the exception of the executive branch and cabinet that is located in Daringranka's capital city of Novaraca, with a satellite location in Tridonca, the capital city of Longenthros. They elected a president,

Gryntha Haulk, and he appointed a vice president, Seltico Haulk, his wife. The two states have governors. The providences each have senators that serve as their representatives and some of the larger cities have mayors. It is a democratic society. The population is so small and the landmass is so great that most of the towns are very small, and most families are self-supporting and miles from their neighbors in most cases."

Jake says, "When our world relocates here, that will change. It sounds like they have a reasonable and somewhat simple structure to their government. We have not had any reply from President Haulk, Heather?"

"No, sir."

"This is important information, but I think we have enough to have an understanding of their structure. Please focus all efforts on finding a direct link to the president. I fear that Senator Marliklez may have thought that we were juveniles crank calling him. It would be a difficult thing to believe when someone calls telling you that they are calling from a spacecraft in outer space."

"Understood, sir."

Jake looks over at Greg. "Greg, please give me a report on your research. What have you learned by watching these sit-coms?"

"They have a healthy sense of humor, they are allowed freedom of speech, they mock officials as we do on Earth, however, they do very little that is overly offensive or harmful toward one another. They don't seem to do this from fear. It seems that they do this out of respect for fellow beings. They seem very content and happy with their situation, for the most part. This, of course, is a judgment based on TV shows."

"This may seem like a strange research tool, but you can learn much from television. When I was younger, I traveled to Europe. I had a translation app and I watched TV quite regularly. It was a convenient way to understand the mindset of the people in Italy, and later in Belgium. You are excused, Greg, if you are ready for a break, please don't put a great deal of hope around going to the surface. We can't do this until we can determine if they are going to be welcoming to us or hostile."

"I understand and thank you. I am happy to stay for the remainder of the briefing."

"Very well." Jake then looks at Dean. "What have you found?"

Dean says, "Their time tracking methods are different from ours."

Jake nods. "I expected this from your earlier comments. The planet is much larger, but I expected it to rotate slower than Earth."

"I am impressed that you had some insight, Commander, as this was my first impression as well after Heather gave us the statistics of the size and diameter of the world, however, on the contrary, it actually rotates faster than Earth. Their day consists of 17.4 of our Earth hours, and I am still working on a program that can be used to reference the way they track time."

Jake chuckles. "Send someone down to buy a watch." He continues, "I was joking, of course. Have you also been able to interface with their Internet?"

"I have been able to intercept files and upload some that are on the system."

"Great, I would like to see the hard drive of the president's computer, a copy of his most recent emails, phone calls, something to have an insight into who he is and what are his capabilities. You didn't obtain any of this type of information I assume."

"No, just common items. I don't guess you want a menu from a restaurant. Getting into the president's computer could be a little tricky, Commander."

"I didn't bring the most intelligent man in the WRC along to be able to tell me what time it is or to order a meal, Dean."

"I understand, sir."

Jake finishes up his questions and decides to head back to his office to get some sleep while waiting on the call from the surface.

He makes sure that Heather is going to get some rest, but that she also has a back-up set up for if the call comes in while she is sleeping.

"Heather, one more thing."

"What is that, Commander?"

"If we don't hear anything from the surface, and we do not have a valid line directly to the president within twelve hrs, then I want Senator Marliklez back on the phone, and this time, I shall speak with him. He will be clear that we aren't a crank call after I speak to him." Jake leaves the bridge and Greg leaves shortly after him.

Ted asks Dean if he is ready for some shut eye. Dean says, "I'm not real sure that I can sleep after that. I have the time tracking program working now, and I need to allow it to run for some period of time to ensure that it is working properly. It sounds like I need to start hacking into some systems down there, though, from what Jake was saying. What are you going to do, Heather?"

Heather shrugs. "Well, if Ted is okay alone, then I would like for us to get something to eat and I want a shower."

Dean agrees. "A thick steak with all the trimmings does sound good."

Ted says, "I am fine. Should I try to capture a scan or images from the space station when we pass it later, Dean?"

"Yes, if you know the coordinates, I would suggest that you scan it and video the lights. When we get there, for all we know at this point, it could be occupied."

Ted nods. "Good, because the TV shows are about to wear me thin, and it didn't sound like Jake was very interested in that."

Dean and Heather leave the bridge and walk down to the cafeteria. Dean gets a steak, baked potato, and some bread. Heather gets a salad and a pasta dish. Dean tells Heather that he would like to go to a different spot to eat. Heather follows Dean down a small hallway outside of the cafeteria, and they make their way to a hatch that opens to reveal a ladder that is dimly lit and has a small passageway. They go up to the very top of the ship. It is a conservative sized room, but the floor is covered with a light brown plush carpet type material, the ceiling is not as tall as the others, and the walls are all a light gray metallic color. A large hatch with a big metal hand wheel extends from the ceiling in the middle of the room.

Dean hands Heather his supper and opens a door to a little utility closet that contains a small blue ladder. He pulls the ladder out and climbs up to the hatch. He turns the wheel counter clockwise and it opens and swings downward at a slow pace, then the hinge rotates all the way back up to the ceiling and locks in place to reveal a glass dome that is on the top of the exterior of the ship. Dean walks over to a series of switches that control the lights within the room and turns two of them off. The light in the room lowers to a relaxing level. He takes the ladder back to the closet and pulls out two beige colored, padded, cloth folding chairs and positions them beneath the dome.

He looks at Heather, "Romantic?" And chuckles.

She smiles. "More so than you may think actually."

They sit down and start eating. Heather asks, "How secure is this place? Can we speak openly?"

Dean nods. "As openly as you want." And he winks at her.

Heather and Dean have a candid conversation about Jake not exactly pointing them in the right direction on what he was wanting and needing.

Dean looks at Heather. "How about we stop talking shop and just enjoy the view, our supper, and each other's company?"

"You're right, Dean. Enough about work."

She looks up at the stars and the glow of Goldilocks. They both see lights that look like fires as she eats her pasta and drinks a replicated Pepsi. Dean reaches in his pocket and pulls out a pair of glasses. "Here, give these a try." She is impressed that he would take the time to replicate these for her and puts the glasses on.

She looks out of the hatch to see groups of lights. She says, "Longenthros and Daringranka at night. They are so beautiful with the glasses." Dean puts on a pair that he created for him and a large dark planet below has clusters of lights: white, blue, red, and green, some flashing. Some of the blue and purple lights have the same hue as the exhaust from the engines on the Parche. He wonders what the reason is that the people below must use ultraviolet light in lieu of the light frequencies that human beings can see.

He takes the last bite of his steak and sits the container on the floor beside of him and looks at this beautiful lady sitting across from him, thinking what a lucky man he is. She props her ankles on his lap and leans back in her chair, revealing a silky smooth, dark complexioned ankle beneath her blue jumpsuit, with the small white top of her little sock peeking out of her small brown leather boot. She finishes her pasta and sets her container on the floor near Dean's. He can tell how relaxed she is and can see how much she is enjoying a break from the complexities and stress of the bridge while Jake was quizzing them. He puts his hand on her ankle beneath the cuff of her pants and massages on her calf.

"The glow is almost like having a campfire here, Dean."

"More like the glow of a new world."

She smiles at him, thinking he is always the witty one, as they unwind for a few minutes.

Chapter 10

Foreign Relations Commander Jacob Style

Heather and Dean sit in the observation deck and Dean opens his eyes and says, "Heather! Wake up! We must have fallen asleep." Then over the intercom they hear, "Ted Snyder to Heather Lawson. Please contact the bridge."

Heather jumps up from Dean's embrace and says, "Oh my! We are late!" She wonders if the president called. They pick up their trash, throw the chairs back into the closet, close up the hatch, and rush down the ladder. They both rush through the entrance to the bridge, with Jake, Greg, and Ted looking at them. Heather's hair is not brushed, as she always keeps it, her jumpsuit looks wrinkled, and Dean's boots are untied. His chin has an after five o'clock shadow.

Jake tries to hide his chuckle. "This isn't an emergency, you could have called. I need you both to report to your stations in one hour."

Heather responds, "Did the senator or the president call, Commander?"

"No, but we are calling him."

"Okay."

Dean leans over from behind her and smiles and says in a mischievous tone, "We'll be back!"

The guys all chuckle as soon as the bridge door is closed back securely. Greg says, "I wonder where they were."

Jake says, "They were up on the observation deck. They fell asleep."

Ted says, "I didn't detect anyone in that area, but I did note that the inside hatch open indicator came up earlier."

Jake responds, "I know, but did you detect them anywhere else, Ted?"

"That is just it, they disappeared."

"They disappeared from your monitor, not Dean's holograph. Dean built this ship, he knows how to disappear, but not from his own monitoring system. If they weren't on it, then I would have been a little worried." Jake continues, "Not only could I locate them on Dean's system, but I could tell you what position they were in."

Greg looks back and smiles. "Really?"

A few moments pass and Dean and Heather come walking onto the bridge. Dean sits down at his workstation and sits a cup of coffee down, eating a cup of freshly replicated yogurt. Heather brings up her monitor and looks at Jake, then at Ted. "Still no call?"

Ted shakes his head. "Nope, but I got a great scan of the space station."

Jake looks at Heather. "Heather, please call the senator." Heather begins to press buttons on her panel as Jake puts on his headset.

Heather says, "Senator Marliklez? Hello, I have Commander Jacob Conley of the Earth Vessel WRC Parche I on the line to speak to you."

The senator, with an obviously shaken voice, says, "Okay, ma'am."

Heather changes the audio for all to hear and Jake pulls his earpiece back down and says, "Senator Marliklez, Senator Stevex Marliklez?"

The voice on the other end of the line says, "Yes, uh…yes, sir, this is Senator Marliklez," with a slight delay through the interpreter program that Dean programmed into the communications channel.

Jake responds, "Senator, my Sr. Navigator here on the vessel contacted you and said that you agreed to have the president contact us."

The senator comes back, "Yes, sir. I told her that I would, but–as his voice gets shaky–you must realize that in my position I get strange phone calls all the time. My phone number is public information. She said that you all are in orbit of our planet. Is this true?"

"Yes, do you need me to prove this to you?"

"No, but what is it that you are in need of?"

"I thought that my Navigator was quite clear of our needs. We require a discussion with President Haulk, Senator."

"Sir, we can't just give out a method of contacting our top officials directly. Did you contact his office staff?"

"Senator, we did not waste our time with this. We called you. You said you would contact him. Do we need to come to the surface to contact this man?"

The senator clearly unsure of what to do. "If I give you a way to contact him, is it possible to leave my name out of it?"

"Certainly, I will now give you back to Heather and she will take the information. Thank you, Senator."

Heather comes on and the voice goes away. Everyone can hear Heather taking down the number and ending the call.

She looks at Jake and says, "Are you ready?"

Jake shakes his head. "No, but I am well-rested and in a good mood. Go ahead." Heather puts the audio on so that everyone can hear.

Soon a voice is heard. "Hello, President Haulk here."

Heather takes a big breath and speaks, "President Haulk, I am Heather Lawson of the Earth vessel WRC Parche I. We are in orbit above your planet and I have Commander Jacob Conley here. He would like to have some discussions with you."

The president comes back and says, "Ma'am, put this man on the line."

Jake speaks up, "Mr. President, I hope that we have not startled you."

"No, no I'm not startled. I am in need of knowing what it is that you want."

"Well, sir, we have much to discuss. Do you have the time to spend now on what it is that is necessary for us to talk about?"

"I can make the time, however, I do not have the resources necessary to discuss many things without having my advisors with me."

"Well, could we arrange a time and a method for this?"

"Yes, we can do this fairly quickly. I would very much like to sit down face-to-face with you for these talks, though. That is generally the way we do things here on Malpeada."

Dean speaks up and asks, "Mr. President, is the current time 1156 Daringranka time?"

"No, it is currently 0856 East Daringranka time. Who is speaking, please?"

Dean says, "Sir, this is Dean Stinson. I am the vessel's resident Sr. Design Engineer."

Jake asks, "Sir, could you give me a few minutes to discuss with my crew members?"

"Certainly."

Heather then mutes the communications link and Jake then says, "Ted, how long would it take to take flight from the ground if we were in an emergency situation down there?"

"If we shut down the engines, it shall take fifteen minutes Earth time to prepare for lift off, sir. If the engines are left at idle, then she will take flight almost immediately, no more than thirty seconds."

Jake then looks in Dean's direction. "How much can our shields withstand as it pertains to conventional weapons that they may have, and what is required for them to have full power?"

Dean replies, "Well, sir, on the surface, there is nothing in front or behind the ship that they can throw at the ship with full shielding that will scuff the paint, sir. In order to have the shields up, the engines must be at 30% power, though."

Heather speaks up, "Sir, the president is waiting." Jake cuts his eyes at Heather. "You don't think I know that I have this mission critical important man on hold, young lady?" Heather says, "Sorry, sir."

He then looks back at Dean. "Does the time synchronization app work properly at this time, Dean?"

"I thought you wanted to buy a watch."

He snaps back at Dean and scoffs, "I have no time for a smart-ass answer, Dean!"

Dean realizing that the commander is very stressed replies, "Yes, sir, my apologies. The time program will keep within one microsecond over 60,000 hours from what I can tell. This will be well within the window that is required for a meeting time. It was merely necessary to synchronize with a specific part of the planet."

"Okay, Heather, let me have the president once more." Jake continues, "Mr. President, I'm sorry for my delay. Sir, our primary directive for this trip is to make contact and discuss some key items with you. I can be anywhere that you can assure my vessel's safe passage both to and from and that has room to land my vessel."

The president responds, "You shall have safe passage as long as you and your crew have no intentions of bringing harm upon our people here. I need to get you in touch with General Davrex Zelicwi. He is my general that is in charge of Daringranka's air defense base located in the capital city of Novaraca. He will be able to give you the meeting place and accommodate any size vessel that you need to land. His mobile device can be reached at 765-555-7224-1-1. I will call him and tell him to expect a call from you and the nature of what you will require. What is the approximate size, shape, and requirements for landing your vessel?"

Ted answers, "Sir, our vessel can land in a vertical descent and ascent in an area of 100 square meters."

The president asks, "Who is speaking now, please?"

"I am Ted Snyder and I am the pilot of our vessel, the Parche I."

The president then inquires about the number of crew members. Jake speaks once again, "Sir, our ship has a complement of five. Our crew consists of Heather Lawson our Sr. Research Navigator, Dean Stinson our Sr. Design Engineer, Ted Snyder our Pilot, and Greg Compton our CoPilot. I am the Commander, Jake Conley." Each says hi as he called their name.

The president speaks again, "It is nice to make your acquaintances. I would very much like to plan for a meeting in eight of our Malpeada hours, 1700 East Daringranka time. The general will give you the coordinates. Is this possible?"

Ted speaks, "Yes, we can land anywhere on the planet within six hours."

"Sir, this is Commander Jake Conley, we will contact the general and we very much appreciate your time and look forward to meeting with you."

The president says, "Goodbye." A collective sound of several of the crew speaking at once and at slightly different times comes back with, "Goodbye, sir."

About fifteen minutes pass and Heather looks at Jake and inquires if he is ready for the call to the general.

"By all means, let's get this setup."

Heather comes back and speaks, "Hello, General Davrex Zelicwi?"

"Yes, this is General Zelicwi."

"Sir, President Haulk asked that we contact you and set up a place to land our vessel."

The general comes back with somewhat of a surprised voice and exclaims, "You are real? I thought our president had eaten some Zolitof Stew or something. I am concerned with your intentions."

Jake comes back and replies, "Sir, don't be alarmed. We look nearly exactly like the people of your world, and we only require information and safe passage by you and obviously a place to land our vessel. We are on a peaceful mission."

"You're not little green men?" The whole crew starts laughing.

"No, sir, perhaps we had the same creator. I would like to have Ted Stinson, our pilot, speak with you and obtain the coordinates and any additional information required for our meeting."

"Sir, this is Ted Snyder. I am ready for the location."

After getting the measurements of the spacecraft and speaking with Ted about locations, they finally come up with a space big enough to land the spacecraft safely. The general proceeds to give Ted the coordinates at which he is to land at. He also told the Parche I that they are going to shut down the airspace around the runways during the arrival time to make sure they have safe passage and no obstacles. Ted was told to contact the air tower within an hour of landing so he could be given a few flight plan options. He was given the code EARTH—Zelicwi—CODE EX to use when he answers any tower that may question him.

"General, I believe that you have covered everything required, sir."

"When you speak with other aircraft and control towers, they will believe that you are an experimental vessel from our base. I look forward to meeting your group. Goodbye for now."

"Goodbye, sir, and we too look forward to meeting you and your representatives."

Heather says, "Earth vessel WRC Parche I out."

Jake says, "I am going to go draft a correspondence to Charles Phillips to let them know what happened in the event that we do not return." Jake then leaves the bridge and enters his quarters. He sits at

83

his desk and sees an electronic mail, Charles.Phillips@WRC .com with the Subject: First Contact. Jake reads the email and continues focusing on the final lines of the correspondence.

He explains the only thing that needs to be impressed upon their president is that we are coming. We have our own society rules of conduct that shall be adhered to by our people, and it is as much of a fact as there are stars in the sky that three billion earthlings and a complement of nearly one billion various animals will be arriving within the next two years, like it or not.

Jake sits for quite some time thinking about how he can tell the inhabitants that this is their intention.

Chapter 11

Imminent Domain

Ted comes over the intercom in Jakes office, "Sir, we are now prepared to begin our trip to the surface. Permission to travel to the coordinates required."

"Affirmative, let's go."

Ted then throttles up the engines and begins to break away from the holding pattern that they have been in for weeks. The ship moves into the area of the world that is lighted and the bright sunlight beams off of the shiny vessel. They begin a descent into the outer atmosphere. The cameras located on the outside of the ship are displayed on the large holographic displays at the very front of the bridge. It shows brilliant blue lights, almost like the strobe of an arc welder, as the ship travels through this area. Everyone feels a little uneasy, as they know if something goes wrong, the ship could be damaged during this time. Suddenly, the flickering of bright lights cease, and the bright light of Goldilocks' sun is constant.

Ted comes back on the intercom in Jake's quarters, "Commander, we are now in Alpha Kantabury 1's atmosphere."

"Entry is never a boring thing, Ted. Do you know our ETA?"

"No sir, reentry is never boring on any planet and a little nerve-racking. Sir, our arrival time should be six hours from now, Earth time."

"Ted, has Dean shared Goldilocks' time program with you?"

"Yes, sir, it indicates that we will arrive at 1550 East Daringranka time."

"An hour and a half early. Ted, can you adjust the vessel's speed so that we arrive twenty minutes prior to our planned time, please?"

"Certainly, sir, this is not a problem, or we could change our path for some sightseeing."

"We do not need to go joyriding, as they may view this as an unauthorized passage or it may appear that we are not good navigators if we do not stick with our flight plan."

"Understood, sir. Our new ETA shall be 1640 East Daringranka time."

"Thank you, Ted."

They spend the next few minutes staring at the holograph that has cameras focused on the world beneath the ship. Heather speaks up, "Ted, I have an air traffic controller requesting that we identify ourselves."

"Put them on the comms, please."

They hear a voice that says, "Unidentified Heavy, please identify yourself."

Ted replies, "This is the unidentified heavy and first I would like to convey a code, EARTH – Zelicwi – CODE EX."

The controller responds, "One moment please."

A few minutes later, a second voice comes on, "This is the manager of the Longenthros, Sarinca air defense base tower. Please identify your exploratory vessel."

Ted speaks up, "We are the vessel WRC Parche I."

The tower comes back on, "You are cleared to pass through our air space and please maintain your altitude and advise us of any heading changes." He then continues, "Impressive craft, what the hell kind of exploratory crafts are they building over there in Daringranka these days? I am detecting high heat from your propulsion system exhaust."

Jake comes onto the intercom, "We are not at liberty to discuss the details of our mission with anyone other than General Zelicwi."

The tower comes back on. "Understood, Sarinca tower out."

An hour passes and they begin to see the ocean on the holographic monitor. It is a beautiful, seemingly never ending inverted blue sky beneath them, with a large ship out on the water occasionally.

They hear another transmission that says, "Sarinca tower passing control to Daringranka." Then another voice says, "Daringranka tower, Lovarica air base to unidentified vessel, please identify yourself."

Ted speaks up, "Don't you pass data from one tower to the next?"

The tower comes back, "Affirmative, but you must give us positive confirmation in an exploratory vessel."

Ted, with an agitated voice, says, "Very well, EARTH – Zelicwi – CODE EX. We are the vessel WRC Parche I."

The voice replies, "Lovarica tower grants permission to continue at your current altitude to your predetermined coordinates, we are apprised of your mission. We shall track you for fifty-seven minutes and release you to Novaraca tower for your descent and final coordinates. Please inform us if you require course corrections or to change your heading or altitude."

"Thank you, Lovarica tower, will do."

The voice comes back on, "Parche I, are you of our world?"

Jake comes on the intercom once more, "We must ask that you inquire of General Zelicwi or President Haulk for questions such as these."

"Lovarica tower out," the voice says.

"How much longer, Ted?" inquires Jake on the comm.

"We are on time, Commander."

Another hour passes and the voice returns and says, "Lovarica Tower now passing control and correspondence of your vessel to Novaraca Tower." Then the voice changes and says, "Parche I, this is the capital city of Daringranka's control tower, located on the military installation of Novaraca. Please give me your clearance code."

Ted speaks up, "<u>EARTH – Zelicwi – CODE EX</u>."

The voice comes back again, "Confirmed. All traffic shall be halted while you make your descent. Please begin your descent to the coordinates previously provided by the general. You have clearance to touch down at your discretion."

Ted replies, "Excellent, tower, if you find any issues please advise."

The voice acknowledges, "Affirmative, Parche I. Your vessel is indeed capable of a vertical descent upon touchdown?"

"Affirmative, tower."

The voice comes back, "This enormous vessel can sit down vertically? This is impressive, and there shall be no issue with a vertical descent at these coordinates, Novaraca tower over."

Jake feels the vessel slowing and walks to the bridge. Upon entering, Dean hands him a device that appears to be an electronic tablet and says, "The translation application, as well as the time program, is on this device, sir."

"Thank you, Dean." Jake looks at Ted. "Ted, do not shut her off. Keep the engines at 30% and listen for me to come on with a warning. If talks go badly, I want the shields up and this craft safely back in orbit as soon as possible, and you bring force to get me out of here."

"Understood, sir."

Ted then brings the ship to a slow descent and eventually to a stop as he positions the vessel into the coordinates the general provided. He sits the ship down onto a large vacant parking area and speaks, "Earth vessel WRC Parche I is now on the ground and our commander, Jake, is prepared to meet with your representatives." Ted then pushes a button on his control panel and opens the hatch and a large metal plank lowers from the side of the ship.

Jake walks toward the hatch and takes a deep breath. "Okay, you guys wish me luck." The crew all says, "Good luck, Commander." Dean speaks up and says, "Prayers that all goes well, Commander."

Jake walks off of the spacecraft to be greeted by General Zelicwi and his aide. The general shakes Jake's hand and says, "Please, come with me." Jake secretly, and without the general's knowledge, takes a small red dot that was in the palm of his hand when they shook hands and places it into his jumpsuit pocket. They walk away from the area and the noise from the engines roaring at 30% grows quieter with every step. They reach a great building that is white on the exterior, with huge doors and a pedestrian door. It appears big enough to be a hanger for an airship or blimp. The general swipes his finger and the door opens. They enter a large room with ceilings that must be 150' high. A large formal table sits in the center of the room, with two men and two women sitting around it. At the head of the table sits President Haulk, to his right is Vice President Haulk, then two additional seats are occupied by Governor Grainta Tasilhan of Daringranka and Governor Veliama Cariaolkia of Longenthros. Two security details consisting of four people in black, with earpieces, stand near this very large, bare conference table.

Jake speaks up, and his universal translator speaks shortly following his words, "Greetings, gentlemen, and ladies." Jake extends his hand and shakes hands with the president, vice president, and all others seated at the table. They each introduce themselves.

President Haulk replies in a language that sounds much more like the Japanese language than his own. "Hello, and greetings from Malpeada," radiates from the device. The president continues, "I thought it strange for you to know our language so fluently. Please have a seat at our table. How far have you traveled to visit our great nation, Commander Conley?"

"We have traveled for six months at a speed of 20/1 light years to be with you today."

The president says, "That is quite some distance. How many crafts do you have with you today?"

Jake wonders if he should be honest, indicating there are more ships than just his one in case things go badly. He decides honesty is the best policy, to an extent. "We have but one ship. We are a reconnaissance class vessel."

The table is immediately silent as the security detail moves in as if to protect Malpeada's officials from Jake. All eyes are on him as if he may pull a weapon, some with fear, others obviously enraged. Jake's heart rate quickens as he sees the response from his type of ship.

The president exclaims, "Reconnaissance vessel! You come to my world with a vessel that is gathering intelligence for war?"

Jake is thinking their info could be remarkably accurate. He is surprised by the response and calmly says, "Sir, my apologies, as our language translator has worked so well that I have not experienced any missed translations up until now. I believe that we have discovered a misconception of what a reconnaissance class ship is. On our world, this ship has many uses. It is used for exploration as much as to research, and it has been used for fact gathering during wartime. My apologies if I have confused or misrepresented our intentions. We simply refer to a vessel of this class as reconnaissance." The group appears to relax a bit, but they are still on edge.

The president speaks, "On our world, if a reconnaissance vessel comes to your shores, then warships and troops are sure to follow."

"No, sir, we have no plan or wish of invasion of your soil, however, there is a reason why I am standing upon your beautiful planet. We have a planet and people that are very much like your own and we have determined that our planet's nearest star, our sun, is dying. This is very much like your sun. We wish to find a new world where we can relocate."

The president looks at Jake and considers what does this mean. *Do they want to live by our rule, would they attempt to overtake our*

world by force? Would they try to put us into slavery or kill us all?
He speaks, "What does your government have in mind?" He then looks at his general. "Alert Longenthros and call the secretary of defense and put the militaries of our world at a level two threat at once!"

Jake speaks up, "Sir, there is no reason for raising your country's defense level. We have no warships, every one of our vessels are back home except ours, and they shall be six months or more before they can reach us."

The president does not believe Jake. The president speaks again, "How many individuals do you have a need to relocate?"

"Well, sir, less than the population of your world initially." Vice President Haulk then speaks, with a very authoritative voice, "We want to know totals, not initially or not how many are in your craft! How…many…crafts…are…with…you…now?"

Jake, with a soft voice, says, "One."

She continues, "How many populate your world?"

Jake responds, "Seven billion." The group grows quiet once again.

The president asks, "How many total do you wish our world to accommodate?"

Jake looks around the room and says in an unwavering stern voice, "We shall relocate three billion people and one billion animals."

The governor of Daringranka speaks up, "What do you gentlemen propose?"

Jake says, "We do not know. I am not the leader of my world. I am but a representative that has been directed to speak with you and explain that in the next two years, we will be relocating people and animals to your planet."

The president shakes his head. "This is an impasse and you must leave to give us time to consider everything."

91

Jake says, "There is no option, we shall inhabit Longenthros with our own government laws and rules. We don't intend to run your people out, but shall occupy your abundance of uninhabited land in this territory. We shall declare **Eminent Domain** by Earth over Longenthros."

Longenthros' governor shouts, "This is an outrage!"

The president says, "I will be in contact with your vessel within twenty-four Malpeada hours."

The general, with a commanding tone to his voice, speaks, "This way!" as they make the journey back through this large installation and out into the bright sunshine, to once more hear the rumbling of the Parche's engines. Jake stops and turns back to the general and extends his hand. The general just looks at Jake and says, "It is customary for us to lock wrists, but you shall not receive this welcoming response from myself now that I know of your world's intentions."

Jake says, "Very well."

He walks up the ramp back into the Parche I and says, "Ted, Greg, get us the hell out of here!" as he has a seat at his station.

Ted speaks into his headset, "Novaraca tower, the Earth vessel WRC Parche I requesting permission to take flight." A voice comes on and says, "Permission granted." Ted starts a vertical lift, again very much like a helicopter, then throttles up the engines, and with a loud roar and a flash, they are up and away from the base and take off into orbit.

Chapter 12

Charles Phillip's Arc

Back on Earth, Charles Phillips stands beside of an air traffic controller in the small tower room that he stood in just days previous with the members of the WRC steering committee. Woody, his assistant, and Brenda Smith, his administrative assistant, all stand watching the sky as a huge shadow passes along the ground in the distance, large brown plateaus can also be seen in the distance. The controller has headphones on and Charles hears him speaking with Arc 0. He says, "You have clearance to land on runway number one." He watches as this winged vessel, seemingly the size of an aircraft carrier, makes its descent to the ground. The craft lands with the tires screeching and sliding as the weight of the craft sets down on them, and it shakes the floor of the tower, feeling as if artillery is going off in the distance. The roar of the engines makes it difficult to speak over the sound, even in the sound dampening walls of the tower. The craft passes by at what looks like take-off speed and the engines reverse. The booming sound and roar become even louder, then swiftly, the enormous vessel comes to a stop. It taxies around to an area of about a half-mile away from the terminal. The controller speaks up, "The WRC Arc 0's test flight is complete."

Charles asks, "Do I have clearance to approach?"

The controller responds, "Yes, sir."

Woody, Charles, and Brenda all climb into the big truck and drive out to the craft. The hatch door is open and the first one to appear is Pilot Dalton Coleman. He is shortly followed by the other crew members, Bill Hogan and Jeff Briscoe.

Charles says, "Greetings, and welcome back to Earth."

The crew looks fairly well rested and in great spirits as Jeff speaks, "Flawless test flight."

Charles asks, "Not a blip on the instrument panel? Not a button that is inoperable?"

Dalton boasts, "Flawless flight, not a flawless craft." He goes on to say, "We have several enhancements to make, but she handled with ease."

Jeff agrees, "We always have to debug a new design. Some of the air make-up systems had to be placed on manual override. The hologram shielding had an issue and it iced up during reentry, and the calibration of the cabin pressure was a little off, causing our ears to pop a little. We can correct everything that we see in a fairly fast pace and be ready for a second run and time trials next week. The craft seems to be adequately powered. We will have mock passengers in the form of sandbags next week."

Charles says, "That is absolutely awesome! We shall tell our replicator programmers to expect design parameters and complex models for three-dimensional printing within two weeks?"

"I believe that is accurate," acknowledges Jeff.

Charles explains that he is heading back into his office, but he tells them, "I want all of you to know that I believe you guys are doing one hell of a job."

Jeff smiles. "Commander, this means a great deal to my team that you are pleased with our progress."

Charles, Woody, and Brenda all get into the truck and head back into the city. They arrive at WRC World Headquarters located in Las Vegas, Nevada. It is about a three-hour drive. They get back to the office and Brenda gets back at her station and has received a correspondence from Jake.

Dear Brenda,

Today I am traveling to the planet's surface. I must meet with the leaders of Alpha Kantabury I—Goldilocks. I have to explain to them that we are relocating to their planet rather they approve this or not. I am uncertain of how they will respond to this action, and it is possible that I may not be free to come home to the Parche I following this. I fear that I may never get a chance to tell you how I have felt all of these years while working side-by-side with you. I want you to know that I LOVE YOU. Not like a friend or like I love my sister, but as a lover. I remember the trip that we took to New York together and I went to your room in the middle of the night. This is my favorite memory that I have had in my life, with a woman. I want you to know this as I fear that I may never get to tell you in person. If you do not feel the same, then I can live without you and I hope this doesn't make you uncomfortable, but right now, I want you like I have never wanted a woman, simply to hold and have someone to be waiting for me.

With my Love!

Jacob Conley

Commander WRC Parche I

Somewhere in orbit of Alpha Kantabury I

Brenda is blown away by Jake's email. She wonders if he has perished. She immediately drafts a response to Jake and contemplates hitting send for a long time. She reads the correspondence several times, pondering the way that he will take it. Charles calls on the intercom, she presses Send, then says, "Yes, Commander."

"Brenda, please forward the packet from the Arc 0's logbook."

"Sir, is someone emailing this information to me? I have not received this."

"No, Brenda. Jeff Briscoe handed you a packet and it contains a log from the controls onboard the ship. It should be in the form of either a flash card or a thumb drive."

"Oh, yes, sir. I have the thumb drive right here. Do you want the physical media or do you want me to send the information to you?"

"Brenda? Is your mind elsewhere? I asked that you forward the information to me. I need you to archive it on the network and save the file in my common folder, please. You know, young lady, as we always do with external files such as these."

"Of course, sir, sorry for my inattention."

Charles brings up the files and finds that every key aspect of the voyage was successful. He is dying to give the order for this $850 trillion dollar project to begin. He receives a correspondence in an email from Jake Conley.

Dear Charles,

We have made contact with President Gryntha Haulk. I am preparing to meet with him and his advisors. I shall tell him that we are coming in large numbers to their planet, like it or not. I pray that they don't imprison me, or worse. I am going to order the crew to keep the engines of the Parche I at 30% so that the ship will be protected by the shields and they can leave the surface immediately if necessary. Sir, I will send you any additional correspondence once this meeting is complete, to inform you of the outcome with the leaders of this world. Please wish me luck, and a prayer would be in order.

Sincerely,

Jacob Conley

Commander WRC Parche I

In Alpha Kantabury I's Atmosphere

Traveling to Coordinates: 35°00'21.82"North and 92°08'38.01" West

Charles places his hands together and asks his Lord and Savior to be with his friend, Jake. He then says, "Amen." He gets Brenda on the intercom and asks that she set up a meeting of the steering committee for tomorrow at 2:00 pm in the WRC Headquarters and a conference call for members that can't be present in person. Charles soon receives an email with a meeting notification for the steering committee for 1400 hrs on August 18, 2116, then a new email from Jake and the Parche I shows up. He reads it and understands that essentially the government is considering the options and repercussions of not helping us and that more shall follow after a day or so. Charles forwards this email to Brenda.

He then calls Jeff Briscoe. "Jeff, how are things progressing, have you all made additional evaluations of the flight?"

"Very well, Commander. Our evaluation has dictated that we correct several small issues and will make a second test flight in the morning."

"Excellent. We must move forward as rapidly as is humanly possible in order to get our people off of the planet Earth."

Jeff inquires, "Sir, do we have a place to go?"

"Affirmative. You keep this information confidential, though, my old friend."

"Indeed, Commander."

"Jeff, do we have enough to begin building the superstructure for the spacecrafts?"

"Yes, sir, if you don't want to wait for the formalities. I don't see a reason why this ship's airframe isn't the master for all others to be built from." Charles decides that this is a very good topic to bring up during the board meeting.

It is now 1:00 pm—1300 hours—on August 18 and Charles is reviewing his agenda with Brenda. They cover all of the updates and make sure everything sounds reasonable, informative, and professional. Brenda does remind Charles that trying to be professional around some of the committee is impossible, as some are morons. Charles agrees and they both have a good chuckle.

He and Brenda walk into the boardroom to take his seat at the table's end and her to his right. Charles starts the meeting. "Welcome, ladies and gentlemen, the reason for our meeting here today is to update you all on the efforts being made to find our new homeland.

"First, I would like to ensure that all of the members of our committee received and trust the contents of the time capsule that we retrieved from the orbit of the planet, from the discussions of last time." He pauses and no one speaks up. "On to updates and new business. Our vessel, Parche I, has not only made contact with the leaders of our Goldilocks planet but have sat and discussed the fact that we shall be relocating there." The room immediately fills with talk among each group. Charles gives them a few moments. "Our commander has explained to their world leader that we shall have three billion Earth beings on their soil within the next two years."

The Korean President turns his triangle with the point up and shortly following, without being called on, says, "Do you people not understand any tactics of warfare? You must meet them and become friendly, learn what it takes to defeat their army, and then, only then, when you have their last army defeated and your combat boot on their throat do you explain your intentions!"

The room becomes silent. Charles looks at this man in disbelief. Charles then says, "Do you and your country wish to continue to be a part of this coalition?"

The Korean President answers, "Yes."

"Then we shall do things my way! My way shall be diplomatic if at all possible. This world of 3.5 billion individuals must realize that they do not stand a chance against three billion technologically advanced individuals of Earth. Commander Conley declared *Eminent Domain* over a landmass that is larger than all of our countries combined. Please believe that if it becomes necessary, the WRC is prepared to use force." Charles looks around the room and there are no other triangles that are pointed upward. He continues, "The test on our prototype ship–the Arc 0–was successful in that the ship operated correctly. The crew found a few items that require enhancements in the ship's programs, but the basic superstructure is sound and works as necessary. I move that we release the plans for the space frame of the vessel to our replicators of the world to begin reproduction. The ship begins a second trial mission tomorrow to finalize the improved programs and to carry a load of passengers in the form of sand bags for a mock-up of the mission."

The United States President, Robert Lynch, agrees, "I second this."

Charles continues, "Please be aware that we will be expecting a final list of individuals from each country to finalize plans for the flights to the new world. We have but the initial approximated lists and require detailed names for evaluation and to ensure that everyone is accommodated.

"During our last meeting, we discussed allowing underdeveloped nations an opportunity to ride along with us. I announced that we would vote on it during this meeting. We have considered this and determined that we shall all offer some additional space for these doomed souls. We have so many that are in need of transport, I believe that different committee members should provide one extra transport for this purpose in each fleet. This shall be the rule. We shall plan for a meeting again in three days. If there are no objections, then we shall dismiss." The group disperses.

Charles and Brenda go back to their offices and Charles checks mail, with no correspondence from Jake and the Parche I.

Chapter 13

Malpeada in a Giving Spirit

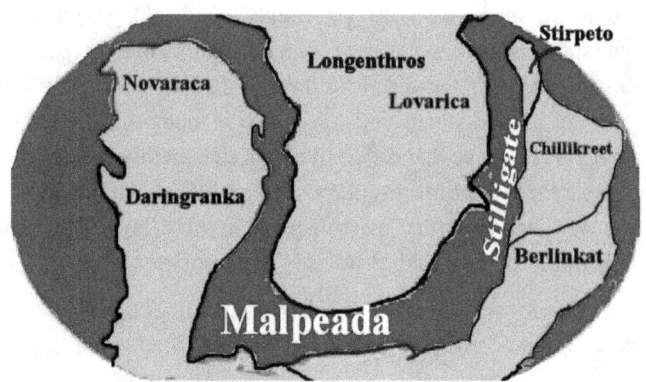

In a conference room on Goldilocks' surface in Novaraca, night has fallen. President Haulk and his team of advisors sit around a large table. Each member engulfed in heated conversations concerning their options.

President Haulk speaks. "They must live under our rule if we are to cohabitate with the aliens."

Governor Tasilhan of Daringranka says, "Longenthros is sparsely populated and the obvious decision between our two lands. We should give them this state if the choice is between our two states. They have even claimed *Eminent Domain* upon this land."

The female governor of Longenthros, Cariaolkia, replies, "The people of our state will not release our land without a war."

Suddenly, Vice President Haulk says, "No one is seeing the obvious answer to this."

President Haulk replies, "If there is some obvious answer, please enlighten the room, my love."

She nods. "Give them the landmass of Stilligate. The countries within this land are foreign countries that the barbarians occupy, such as Berlinkat and Chilkreet, even Stirpeto, that we occupy, could be released if necessary to avoid a war that we may very well lose with these aliens. They can have their war with this very sparsely populated area and deal with the Torntauks. The aliens will undoubtedly overthrow these uncivilized, unruly beasts on that continent. Who knows? They may modernize this land and become good neighbors that can help contribute to our own civilization."

A landmass known as Stilligate is located between their two countries. Even though this continent is smaller than Daringranka or Longenthros, it is large enough at nearly 125 million sq kms to accommodate the massive amounts of individuals that are relocating from Earth. It is undeveloped and has jungles and a few Wild West style towns, as well as a king that rules over some portions of the land. The people of this land do not have very many modern automobiles. The people of Malpeada do not mingle with this society as they have very different levels of inhabitants and Stilligate's stage of development is way behind Malpeada's.

President Haulk speaks, "We have the embassy for our prime minister of the area, an Air Force base, and a prison in the providence of Stirpeto at the very northern tip, but other than that, it is mostly undeveloped. The earthlings will have to clear land, develop their nation, and defend themselves against the savages and animals in this region. It is still a much better option than giving up our land or waging war against possibly three billion beings with an unknown technological edge. They have faster than light travel and if they do not care for these provisions, then they must use this for a home base and venture deeper into outer space to find themselves a new world to inhabit. Does anyone have any objections?"

The group is deathly quiet. The governor of Longenthros, Cariaolkia, speaks, "What if they come, settle in, and then wage their war upon our nations? We have many resources that are mined from this land. Do we simply give this continent to them?"

President Haulk shakes his head. "This land is not ours to give or to sell. It belongs to the people of Stilligate. It is true that we have some interest in some small portions of the land, however, there are not any resources there that we can't supplement within our two nations. The people there must defend it. They will have rights to whatever they take. I strongly recommend that if Longenthros has claims to Stirpeto, they are present during our talks and give their recommendations to this landmass for specifics. It is simple to me. These people are desperate, and it is my belief that we will be at war with them if we don't show support to their needs. I will invite our new guests to the surface again, and we will give our blessings on this landmass, explain that this could mean war with these individuals, and denounce their claim to Longenthros or it shall be war!"

Back on the Parche I, Jake briefs the crew of the results of his meeting with the leaders of Malpeada. He explains that they weren't very receptive to our claim of *Eminent Domain* over Longenthros.

Dean says, "Can you blame them? Suppose an alien showed up on Earth and says that they are going to invade and take over North America?"

Jake does not see this in the same light. He goes on to detail that the WRC is near complete with exploratory voyages with the prototype transport ship and shall be sending crafts within weeks. He decides to go to his quarters and reflect on the meeting and think about the things that have transpired.

Greg stretches. "Man, I am beat!"

Ted looks at Greg with a puzzled look. "You? I am the one that has piloted the craft down and back up again."

Dean agrees, "We are all beat and stressed. I have had plenty of rest as I have just sat back and been an observer, and truthfully, I nodded off while Jake was at the meeting. If you guys want to go, then I will take the helm for a while."

Ted doesn't hesitate. "Transferring control."

It doesn't take them long to abandon their posts. Then Dean sits there and looks over at his sleepy-eyed little girlfriend. "Why don't you go hit the hay, my sweets?"

Heather yawns. "Nope, I'm not that tired."

"Yeah, right."

"I'm not going without you, Dean. How is that?"

"Well, I will be along in about four hours. One of the guys will be back up by then."

"Maybe you didn't understand. I can't sleep well without you now."

"Heather, this is not the best trait for a well trained WRC crew member."

"It isn't that I *can't,* I just don't want to."

Dean shrugs. "Suit yourself."

Jake sits in his office and he sees two emails. One is from Brenda.Smith@WRC.com.

Dear Jake,

I find you to be a very interesting and attractive man. I have had a fondness of you since that night as well. I never understood why we didn't pursue some type of a relationship following that night. I was disappointed and considered that perhaps we were just caught up in the moment and maybe you thought I was just on the rebound from Dale. Yes, I have feelings for you as well, but you can't expect me to sit idly by and wait for you to come around without giving me some indication that there can be a potential relationship between us. That night was and is very special to me. Dale is completely out of the picture now. I know at that time we were in the middle of the divorce and we slipped and got back together a couple of times, but at this time, it is over and I very much look forward to seeing you on Goldilocks. We shall see how it goes. I am not comfortable with telling you that my feelings are strong enough to be called "Love" at this point. It very well could

be at some point in the future, from all that I know and from the feelings that I have for you.

Sincerely,

Brenda Smith

Administrative Assistant to WRC Commander-in-Chief Charles Phillips

Jake sits alone, silently thinking to himself. What an absolutely classy lady. I hope that I haven't overdone it and made her feel uncomfortable with me. I do love this woman. I hope that I can make her feel the same and we can find that we are as compatible as it has seemed. She was undoubtedly the best woman I have ever had!

He continues in his email account and sees another from Charles.Phillips@WRC.com. He essentially gives Jake an update on the trials of the Arc 0 and that they expect to have replicators building airframes within a week.

Heather comes over the intercom, "Commander Conley."

"Yes, Heather?"

"I have President Haulk's aide on the line for you."

Jake looks at the time. "They are early. Please find out what they need and if the president shall be able to speak with me." It goes quiet.

After some period of time, she comes back on the line. "Commander, I now have Vice President Haulk to speak with you."

"Ask her to hold long enough for me to reach the bridge."

A few moments later, Jake walks through the door and sits at his station. "Okay, Heather, please put her on comm."

"Mrs. Vice President Haulk, you are now being connected with the Commander."

Jake asks, "Vice President Haulk, what can I do for you?"

She replies, "We have decided on a solution for accommodating your needs."

104

"Okay, ma'am, is this decision something that we can discuss openly or shall we sit and meet once more?"

"President Haulk will now speak with you."

Jake looks around at the others as if to say what is going on down there? "Okay, ma'am."

Suddenly, a very authoritative-sounding President Haulk can be heard. "Commander, you clearly must rescind your claim to Longenthros or we shall not discuss this any further and our world shall prepare for war!"

Jake replies, "One moment please, Mr. President."

Heather mutes the line. Jake says, "I am getting tired of screwing with these beings. Dean, if I gave you a DNA sample from the group below, could you create a bio-weapon that could be placed in their water supply that would annihilate them but be harmless to us?"

Dean looks at the commander as if he has lost his damn mind and responds, "No!"

Commander Conley speaks once more, "You cannot or will not?"

Dean says, "I am not a medical professional or chemical engineer. If you want some type of bio-weapon, then this is someone else's field. Hell, I could kill all of us. I believe in the right hands that a weapon could be built, but not here, and certainly not by me or a man of my education in engineering."

Jake nods. "Understood. Heather, put him back on, please." Jake continues his conversation with the president. "President Haulk, I am not at liberty to rescind this unless there is some other compromise. We shall all perish either way, and we shall fight you to attempt survival."

The president comes back on the line, in just as stern of a voice as before, and speaks, "You shall rescind this or we shall destroy your ship."

Jake replies, "This ship is protected in such a manner that you have no weapons that can damage our ship."

Heather says, "He disconnected the transmission."

Jake looks at Dean, and shouts, "Where the fuck are Ted and Greg!"

"I relieved them, Commander."

"I do not have a pilot and copilot on the vessel to have my engineer piloting my ship!"

"Understood, Commander, however, I authorized this. I will get them both on the bridge at once if this is your order."

Commander Conley says, "Wait, they have to sleep like the rest of us. You must realize that I have been in difficult situations side-by-side with Ted, and he is a phenomenal pilot. This is why he is at the helm of this vessel. Dean, are our shields at maximum?"

"Yes, Commander, they are now."

Jake says, "Give me ten minutes and I will require President Haulk back on the damn line!" Jake leaves the bridge and heads straight to his quarters to the replicator and says, "Kentucky Bourbon straight, on ice!" A glass of Jack Daniels appears, he then says, ".5mg of Xanax, tablet." The replicator comes back and says, "Authorization code required." Jake speaks, "Conley Ibfx0321." A small orange pill appears. He snatches up the nerve pill and swallows it down with a gulp of the drink. He stands in front of the replicator to catch his breath and walks into his dining area and says, "Okay, so you cocksuckers want a damn war, then you shall have it!"

He walks back onto the bridge and finds that Ted and Greg are both at their posts. He says, "Heather, call that sorry prick back again!"

She looks at him, then at Dean. "Are you sure, Commander?"

Dean speaks up, "Commander, can we discuss this within our group before we wage a war against this world?"

The commander says, "Absolutely, Dean. You can't kill them, but you can mediate our discussions?"

Dean remarks, "Better than I can build a bio-weapon." Ted and Greg both focus on Dean as if to say what did we miss?

"You have about fifteen minutes, Dean."

"The vice president said they have a compromise. Is it not prudent to hear a compromise? You can rescind and claim Eminent Domain again if it isn't an appropriate compromise."

Jake responds, "All I could hear was 'rescind your statement'."

Heather says, "Sir, please allow them to tell us of the compromise before we declare war."

Jake considers what his crew is saying and says, "Heather, get President Haulk back on the line, please."

A few minutes pass, and a voice comes over the comms and says, "Hello, this is Vice President Haulk."

"Hello, ma'am. This is Commander Jake Conley."

She responds, "I know who this is, the question is…are you calmed down?"

"Yes ma'am, could I please speak with the president?"

"As long as you two mad schoolhouse bullies can speak as adults before bloodshed."

"I can't promise that, ma'am, but I can promise that I will hear him out for the compromise."

"Very well, Commander."

A few moments pass, and a voice comes on just as firm and as stern as before. "This is President Haulk. I need to know if you are now ready to rescind your claim to our land in Longenthros."

Jake speaks with a stern voice as well. "Yes, sir, I officially rescind my claim of Eminent Domain, however, please be aware that these are merely words. If there is not some accommodation that is agreeable, another claim is imminent!"

President Haulk says with a great deal of sincerity, "You have now retracted your claim to our land?"

Jake says, "Yes!"

President Haulk says, "Very well. We have another landmass that we have not spoken about. It is 2/3 the size of Longenthros. I have asked that they bring me statistics on this land, and we have found that it is slightly less than 125 million square kilometers. This is comparable to about 1/3 of our entire landmass here on our planet."

Jake is totally amazed. He and President Haulk discuss the other statistics of the landmass. Jake asks as many questions as he can think of so he has a clear idea of just what exactly they are offering, and to make sure they are not trying to pull one over on them. He finds out that it does have an inhabitable climate and there are natural resources that could sustain the people from Earth. But that was all the information the president was willing to give him.

"Commander, it is necessary for us to sit down face-to-face and discuss this land. If this is acceptable and you can tentatively accept this agreement, then we shall welcome you and your craft back to our homeland. We shall then sit down and discuss what is on this land and what must be done to develop it to a point so that your world can inhabit it."

"Very well, the same location, President?"

"We shall discuss the location and be back in touch. Tomorrow at 1300 East Daringranka time?"

"That shall give me the time I need to prepare for a meeting."

"No hard feelings, Commander?"

"No, sir, President. I feel that you have made a proposal that will be beneficial to our relations and perhaps will accommodate the people of my world. We shall see you tomorrow." Heather closes the comm link.

Jake looks at the others. "Okay, I'm headed to my quarters."

Dean looks over at Ted. "You guys got this?"

"Yeah, we got it, Dean."

Jake looks at Dean and Heather, both with red, tired eyes, and says, "You two are relieved for seven hours." They both walk off the bridge with Jake.

Chapter 14

Determining a Heading

Back on Earth, the first replicated transport frame is coming off of a replicator that is the size of three city blocks. They roll this enormous ship's carcass out of a gigantic doorway on fifteen individual dual wheel Buckingham Dollies. It is a rainy day in rural Arkansas where the first ship is being constructed. Charles, Woody, and Brenda flew out to see the first unit come off the replicators.

Charles Phillips, Brenda, and Woody all stand in the rain, each wearing WRC blue and white striped, hooded rain attire, watching the crew remove the big unit out of its 3D printing facility. Brenda inquires about how much is done as it leaves this stage of manufacturing. Charles responds, "It has the outer shell, interior with floor coverings, quarters, bathrooms, and beds."

Brenda is shocked. "They can print steel and cloth?" Charles explains that it requires a very sophisticated process and multiple systems within other systems. She says, "Wow, I didn't realize that they have come that far with three-dimensional printing. Can they also print the electrical and electronic components?"

Charles replies, "They do replicate most of those devices as well, but in another specialized facility. The new three-dimensional systems are no longer considered printers, they are replicators. The technology is truly amazing when all of the countries of Earth set aside their differences and released military secrets." The huge ship is outside of the building now and everyone just looks in awe. From wing to wing is like the distance across the Golden Gate Bridge.

A man comes walking over to them and asks for their IDs and Charles shows him his and the man says, "Oh, hello, sir. Do any of you have any questions, Commander Phillips, sir?"

Charles asks, "What is your position with our team, how long before the next one starts?" The man explains that he is the foreman over the crew and the next one is already being fabricated and will be rolling out by midnight tonight. "How long does fabrication take for one?"

The foreman explains, "The primary replication requires sixteen hours, then another eight hours is spent on installing and removing gates and bridges that are temporary items used to support different areas while they are printed and removing it from the Buckingham Dollies to rest on its own landing gear."

Charles asks, "One ship every twenty-four hours?"

The foreman says, "For now, but in three weeks we will double up and be able to produce two airframes every thirty-two hours." Charles knows there are hundreds of these facilities scattered across the US and many more abroad. He feels very confident that transportation is coming together. They complete their visit and travel back to home base.

The second test for the prototype craft is underway. They are finding the program modifications have corrected the issues that were noted on the first trip and all systems are functioning as intended. The power of the engines is adequate to lift the mock passengers–sand bags–that were placed into the fuselage. Charles sneaks a quick peek at his email, on his tablet, to see that all systems are green and no bio-signs indicating any anomalies in the crew. He smiles as he remembers the initial voyage and the apprehension that Bill Hogan had. Everything that is necessary for the trips is shaping up very nicely on Earth.

On Goldilocks' surface, the leaders are meeting yet once again. They are discussing what to do about Stilligate and deciding rather to allow their guests to go unannounced or to speak with the leaders of the nation. The countries have had strained relations ever since Malpeada was formed. They didn't overthrow the leaders or change the layout of Stilligate but claimed the northern most country of Stirpeto for a prison, embassy, and military base. They basically wanted to have a presence on this continent. The decision from the meeting is made to hold a meeting on Stilligate at Stirpeto's Air Force base. They have decided to inform the people of Earth and allow them to handle informing the people of the continent in the same way they informed them of their intentions. They will not have the luxury of speaking via electronic devices and when they meet with the leaders of these countries, they have decided to give them an armed protection detail.

Dean and Heather wake up at about 0300 and they are sitting around the bar in Dean's quarters. Dean speaks, "So, what do you think of the compromise?"

"I think the president passed us off on another continent. What do you think they will think of our desires?"

"We will probably have to have a war if there is some civilized society there." They sip their coffee and talk about making a life together in the new world.

Commander Conley is up early as well. He is reading over articles from the capsule to see if there is any mention of this continent that has been proposed. He drafts an email to WRC headquarters.

Dear Charles,

We have made contact with the president, President Gryntha Haulk, and his Vice President, Seltico Haulk. They have confirmed that they shall make accommodations for our world's relocation. It may not necessarily be ideal due to there are inhabitants on the continent they have offered. We may face the same challenge as a war, or some type of a compromise with these individuals. I have another meeting at 1300 East Daringranka time. I will make additional communications once we find what they have offered. This may not be an acceptable option and the president insisted that I recant the statement of claiming Eminent Domain over Longenthros. It ended with him nearly declaring war with me if I didn't retract this. They are not very similar to the people of our world as it pertains to negotiations, as they seem very stern on issues. We shall learn to deal with them, just as we have with dissimilar societies on Earth, I am sure.

Sincerely,

Jacob Conley

Commander WRC Parche I

In Alpha Kantabury I's Atmosphere

Jake sits and sips his morning coffee, wondering what the day holds. He finds two different articles in the package that was derived from research from the surface. Both regarded Stilligate as being uncivilized and a nation made up of wild men and outcast businessmen from the previous society. It sounds very much like an early North America, complete with Indians, con-artists, and royalty.

He decides that it is time to go to the bridge to inquire about the proper time to start the descent to the surface. He arrives at the bridge to find Ted at the helm and sits at his workstation, setting his coffee on the counter. "Ted, have you had any communications with the surface? Do you know how long our trek to the surface will be this time?"

"Commander, no one has given me coordinates, but if it is the same as before, then the travel time will be very similar."

"Can you speak with them and find out if they can release this information to us? Isn't it getting about time to begin our reentry?" It is 0400 East Daringranka time.

"It is somewhat irregular for me to run the comms, sir."

"Yeah, sorry. I am just getting somewhat anxious. How long before Heather returns to her post? Do you know?"

"It should be any time now, sir."

Just then, Dean and Heather walk in hand-in-hand. Dean sits down at his station with a yogurt and a cup of coffee, and Heather sits down carrying a replicated Pepsi. Jake says, "I am happy to see you two."

Heather asks, "What can we do for you, Commander?"

"I need to know the coordinates that we are heading to."

"Commander, they sent correspondence late last night indicating the coordinates would be on the continent of Stilligate at their air base in Stirpeto at the coordinates of 61 deg 32'51.24"N and

113

105 deg 22'33.94 E, with the code of <u>EARTH – Zelicwi – CODE EX1.</u>"

"They want to meet up north, huh? Will President Haulk be present, Heather?"

"I believe so, sir, however, the communication was from General Zelicwi and he didn't give many details. He is a very direct and to the point man."

"Well, excellent. Perhaps we can get a good look at the country and have some clue as to what kind of land we will be acquiring."

Ted says, "Sir, these coordinates should only take about four hours Alfa Kantabury I time."

"Well, if we have some time, then I shall go back to my quarters and try to get a few items prepared."

Dean says, "We may as well go prepare a few things, too," as he smiles at Heather.

Ted nods. "It will probably be somewhat boring here for the next few hours." Heather, Jake, and Dean all leave the bridge.

Dean asks Heather for a game of racquetball, and she happily responds, "I am surprised you want to play again considering the way that I shamed you the last time." She chuckles.

"Funny, that isn't how I remember it." They head on off to the rec. area, still joking with one another and laughing.

Jake gets back to his quarters and drafts another email to Charles to update him on the meeting coordinates. He also emails Brenda to let her know he was thinking of her and he wanted to spend some time with her when she arrived. He begins looking at video from a search for Stilligate from the information acquired and sees men and women with dark complexions, and beads in their hair and around their necks. He thinks of how much it reminds him of Indians that he studied in history books. He mutters to himself, "Year 2116 and we shall play cowboys and Indians again."

Greg is up and checks in with Ted. He enters the bridge and says, "Ted, if you need me to relieve you, I can, but I would like to have a little alone time if it is okay."

"Getting homesick, Greg?" Greg explains that today is his sister's birthday. Ted says, "Sure, ole buddy, I completely understand."

"Thanks, Ted, when is reentry scheduled for?"

"Preflight checklist should begin at 0930 East Daringranka time." Greg looks at his console and it shows that it is currently 0503 East Daringranka time.

"That will be great, Ted! Thanks!"

Greg takes off to the observation deck, opens the big hatch and pulls out a chair. He pulls out a bunch of glossy, paper pictures and sets them around. He goes through the pictures one at a time, looking at himself with a military style buzz haircut, holding his little baby sister's bottle for her. Others appear to be professionally done, she is sitting in a cute, little dress, between his legs, and he has his arms around her from behind. He remembers the day that each picture was taken, how protective he was of his little, real-life babydoll Shelly. His main concern for the mission is about her and his family. The future of mankind is also at stake. He is an ambitious man, but must consider what the ambition is for. The future of his race is near its end if this mission is not successful. He speaks and says a prayer to God concerning the situation that he finds himself in.

At the racquetball court, Dean has beat Heather three games to one. She asks, "You getting tired?"

"Well, I don't want to be called an old man, but I have had a very good workout."

"Well, I am tired."

As he grabs her and pulls her close to him, Dean asks, "Oh yeah? How tired? 'Cause I am never too tired to spend a little quality time with you." They begin a long passionate kiss, then exit the court and walk down the corridor to Dean's quarters.

The time is passing very slowly for Ted as he sits staring at the monitors, pilots the ship, and reminisces about big parties on his personal yacht back on Earth. He remembers all of the fun and women that he had. He imagines that he will have to rebuild all of his wealth and obtain new toys on the new world.

Chapter 15
Welcome to the Jungle

0900 East Daringranka time rolls around and in walks Greg. He asks, "Ted, how about a break before we get underway to the surface?" Then in walks Jake, and he asks, "Are we about ready to go down?"

Ted says, "Well, Greg has offered me a break, so I will be ready for our preflight checklist in about thirty minutes."

The commander responds with, "Very well."

Dean and Heather are laying arm-in-arm asleep and Heather opens her eyes to find Dean laying there watching her sleep. He says, "Creepy, huh? Old man lying here staring at you when you wake?"

"Not in the slightest. It is very sexy that such a sexy gentleman would gaze upon me and protect me while I sleep. I sleep with no worries knowing that you are watching over me. I lov…" Dean puts his lips to hers and cuts her off in mid-speech and gives her a long passionate kiss. They complete the kiss and he looks into her beautiful green eyes and says, "I want you to understand I have no misconception of the fact we both have been on this little craft, with very few members of the opposite sex. I know when the others come, it is very unlikely you will always find me the hunk that you now envision me to be."

She looks back with "fire" in her eyes and replies, "You think I am somehow under some misconception and showing judgment I would not if we weren't together on this ship?" She continues, "I want you to know I have always found you to be attractive, Dean! If I didn't, I would not have this romance with you that we are both enjoying. If I didn't feel this way and I only wanted a one night stand, then I would have Greg in my quarters. He is a young, attractive man, but he is still but a child in my eyes compared to you. The question from me at this point is will your perspective be changed when these other women are in the picture?"

"Listen, Heather, I would marry you right now if you would. I think that you are the most beautiful, honest, fun, and fulfilling woman I have ever met, and you are more compatible to me than anyone I have ever known."

"Is that a proposal, Dean?"

Dean thinks for a minute and pauses. "Do you want it to be? Is this the right way for me to do that? I am pretty old fashioned and that is not a proposal." Dean rolls off of the bed and drops to his knees. He reaches across and grabs her beautiful, little, tanned ankle and drags her across the bed, the bedding draping across her bare body. He looks at her gorgeous long legs, then into her eyes and says, "Heather, will you take my hand in marriage?"

She gazes back at him and replies, "Of course I will. I love you, Dean Stinson. I want so very badly to be Mrs. Dean Stinson. I don't care if it is on this ship, Malpeada, Earth, in a shelter, or a tent in the woods. I want to be in your arms until the end." Just then they hear the thrusters come on and feel a jerk of the preflight torque check on the engines.

Dean looks at the clock and says, "We are late!"

"Let's call in sick."

Dean thinks for a minute. "I could talk to the commander. They will not need us at our stations for the flight down."

"Could you? I would very much like to spend our trip down in the observation lounge with you."

"I will, but please understand that if the commander feels that he needs us, we shall accommodate his wishes."

"Of course," she replies.

Dean goes to the bridge and says, "Jake, can I see you for a moment?" The commander gets up from his post and walks out into the corridor just outside the bridge. Dean says, "I asked Heather to marry me."

Jake looks very surprised. He says, "I didn't realize that she was a minister." Dean looks at him with a 'that's not funny look'.

Jake continues, "You both have been cooped up in this tin can for months, are you sure this is what you two want?"

"She is all I have ever wanted. Is it possible for you guys to navigate to the surface without us today?"

"You two haven't had any off time in weeks. We can get there, but it may become necessary to call on one or both of you. You two can spend the day together until we get to the surface, then I would like for you both to be on the bridge. If something comes up, then I would very much like to be able to call on you."

"Absolutely, Commander. Would you do the honors and marry us when things settle down, as commander of our vessel?"

"Of course, Dean. I would be honored."

Dean returns to his quarters to Heather who is waiting with a sparkle in her eyes. Dean says, "Nope, Commander says 'At our posts immediately!'"

"Really?"

"No, not really, Heather. He asked that he could call on us if it was necessary and he felt it was necessary for us to join the party when we land."

"Absolutely, I would not want to miss the party!"

Meanwhile, on the bridge, Jake settles back in at his post. Ted turns back to look at Jake and asks, "Are our lovebirds not going to make it?"

Jake scoffs back at Ted. "No, those two haven't had a day off in several weeks and there is no reason for them to be present during our descent. They will be up here once we land."

Ted says, "Not many of us have had much down time lately," in a snooty sounding voice.

The commander cuts his eyes back at Ted and says, "You and Greg both have had at least one to two days off each for each of the past three weeks. Those two have taken none."

Ted says, "Understood, sir."

"Are we ready to get underway?" asks Greg.

The commander says, "Let's go. Ted, I would like to enter on the south end of Stilligate and travel as slow as possible to survey the landscape until we arrive at our destination of Stirpeto."

"Aye aye, Commander," responds Ted.

They begin to descent out of their orbit. The craft moves in a southern direction as Ted positions the spacecraft to enter the surface over the southern region of the planet. They see brilliant lights dancing around the lower pole that appear to be similar to the Earth's northern lights as they get closer. They then begin to break through the surface and the hologram shows arcs and sparks all down the sides of the craft as they break through the surface. They all sit comfortably, without even a seatbelt. They enter the surface and plane out with the wings at a high rate of speed. Ted begins to slow the craft and turn it to the north toward Stirpeto.

Jake says, "Greg, could you give us an image of the landscape below on our holograph so that we may view what we will need to conquer?"

"Certainly, Commander."

The image shows a very snowy landscape of mountains and frozen lakebeds. Jake says, "It must be pretty cold here."

Ted says, "We are really deep in the southern hemisphere. I wondered how deep to go, Commander."

"This is fine, Ted. The landmass shall be ours all the way until it ends both north and south."

"Will? Aren't we negotiating with the people of this land, Commander?"

"We will try, but ultimately, we will declare Eminent Domain over this land. I don't think they will want to acknowledge our authority without force. We will try to do this in a peaceful fashion initially."

"I understand, sir."

Jake says, "Greg, take the helm, Ted, you have about three hours. I want you back on the bridge when we land."

Ted says, "Sir, I am fine, really."

Jake replies, "I didn't ask." Ted then gets up and exits the bridge.

Jake and Greg continue watching the hologram and the white ground turns green and blue with the familiar image of trees and lakes. They see fires and tribes with teepees and communities with makeshift cabins. They see so many images that remind them of an early Earth. They pass a very large animal that for appearance sake appears to be a dinosaur. Greg speaks up and says, "Dinosaurs?"

Jake says, "I saw some things about them from the research and found they have something similar. They were nearly extinct at the time the capsule was launched due to the inhabitants hunting them, but it sounded as if they had made a comeback on Stilligate. They are herbivores and carnivores. They could be a force to deal with as we relocate here."

"Interesting, a whole new world to explore and to learn about."

They continue on their journey as they are glued to the images on the monitor. They pass what looks like a hot spring area. It has small pools and large plumes of steam rises from them. A large village is located very near there. They also come upon a volcano that is active, with lava slowly pouring down one side.

Jake says, "No traffic control this time, Greg?"

"No, sir, this area is very rural and behind in the times. I don't think there will be a frequency that we shall find these natives communicating across the airwaves."

"Indeed, I just thought the civilized nation would reach out to us, but perhaps we are out of their reach for detection or at least for communications."

"Sir, I could attempt to reach someone up north if it is your wish."

"No, I just would kind of like to know how well they could keep tabs on us from Malpeada."

Greg is viewing a TOPO map created by Heather. "I see, Commander. We are currently passing the border between Berlinkat and Chilkreet." They see what appears to be a very small landmass that looks like a mini desert.

Meanwhile, Dean and Heather are in the observation deck, with a view of the sky out of the porthole. They are sitting in lawn chairs, drinking sweet tea, enjoying each other's company like never before, and talking about the future. Dean says, "We should have first dibs on claiming land with us being the first ones to land."

"It is likely the corporations will try to push to reclaim the same amount of space as was necessary for them to operate on Earth," Heather responds.

"Well, there haven't been any rules established on that as of yet. I think since we found it and are negotiating for our world, we should be allowed to have what we want first." They begin to feel the spacecraft slow.

Greg is preparing to arrive at Stilligate at the time of the meeting and he adjusts the speed of the spacecraft. A voice comes over the comm, "Air traffic control Stilligate requesting identification of unknown aircraft."

Greg replies, "Our clearance code is EARTH – Zelicwi – CODE EX1."

The voice comes back on and says, "Very well Earth vessel, continue on your heading and you are cleared to land on runway number one."

"I understand and will do," Greg replies.

They then set the big ship down on Daringranka's air base in Stilligate. They are greeted by a small group of officials.

Ted walks onto the bridge and asks, "Any problems?"

Greg says, "Not at all."

A few minutes pass and Dean, with Heather in tow, enters the room.

The large door opens to reveal General Zelicwi awaiting his arrival. Jake tells Ted to bring the ship to an idle in a show of good faith. He grabs his universal translator and tells the group that he doesn't know how long he will be and they should all be prepared to join discussions if necessary. Jake then walks down the ramp to meet the welcoming party. He joins the general with his entourage close behind. They take off to a nearby hangar for their meeting.

Chapter 16

Welcome Wagon

General Zelicwi leads Jake into a large room that has a modest meeting table and an excess of ten fully-suited armed guards, complete with battle helmets, padded suits that are assumed to be some type of Kevlar, and what appear to be submachine guns. They stand along the outside of the table. The table has some colorful characters sitting around it. Jake looks at the general and the general says, "These are the leaders of the communities that you all hope to occupy."

He begins with a gentleman who has a red beret and a highly decorated military uniform, and the general says, "This is Daringranka's leader of the country of Stirpeto and his cabinet, his name is Prime Minister Jimelclay." Jake shakes his hand and greets him and his group. The general then says, "The first man to his left is Chief Greybird, and his top leaders." Three other men sit beside him. "He is the leader of Chilkreet's largest tribe, the Gargaliks," General Zelicwi explains. Jake extends his hand to greet Chief Greybird. He is dressed in a crude pelt outfit that exposes his chest and upper body that is very muscular, as well as displaying several different colors of face paint and darkened skin from exposure to the sun. No one within his entourage moves a muscle and only glares at Jake as if they would kill him and the general, given the chance.

The general says in an amused tone of voice, "Moving on to the left side of the table is the largest group within the Berlinkat region." This group looks more civilized than Chief Greybird's group. They have beards and basic cotton looking clothing. "This is King Sedimo and his entourage." Jake again extends his hand and the king and his men all rise, the king shakes hands with him. Jake says, "Pleased to make your acquaintance." The king speaks and an interpreter repeats what he is saying in the Malpeada language, the universal translator says, "Nice to meet you." They both exchange smiles and the room gets very quiet.

The general and Jake both walk to the front of the room and the general begins to speak to the members around the table. "This is Commander Jacob Conley. He is the leader of a spacecraft that has come here from another planet named Earth. His planet is dying and he has three billion people that must be relocated." The armed guards step near the general on one side and near Jake on the other, as if to show support and to dissuade anyone from attacking the two as the group begins to look outraged. The general then says, "I would like to now allow Commander Conley to speak and give you a synopsis of what he and his people have in mind for a plan to bring his people into your land."

Jake speaks, "Gentlemen, we are in a dire situation on our world. We have come to your world to find a place for a portion of the inhabitants of our planet. Our planet's sun is dying and our planet will perish within the next two years. I have seen the layout of the land here in Stilligate, and I find that it is sparsely populated compared to many places of my homeland of Earth. I feel that we can both occupy this land if we work together, find some new borders, and we respect one another's needs."

King Sedimo speaks up, "What if we are happy with our land just as it is and we don't feel a need or desire to share?"

Jake replies, "Perhaps we could avoid moving into your area. How do the others around the table feel about working out a peaceful solution to our needs?"

Prime Minister Jimelclay speaks up, "We in Stirpeto realize that you have needs and we will do all that we can to accommodate the needs of your people. We have an Air Force base and a prison that is within this region. We are spread out across this land, but we are willing to consolidate and release the majority of our region to accommodate your needs. We would respectfully request that a common government is formed that will allow for our members to have a voice within this region."

Jake says, "This is exactly the type of accommodations we would very much like to have with all of the people of your lands."

Chief Greybird stands. "We shall not share, we shall not surrender, and we will view it as an act of war if you step foot on our soil." His entourage stands up in near unison and General Zelicwi's guards ready their weapons as the chief leaves the room.

Jake looks somewhat nervous over this turn of events and says, "Damn, I thought there was going to be a knife fight right here!" He continues, "Seriously, that scared the shit out of me." The general smirks. Jake then gazes upon King Sedimo and asks, "How do you feel about our needs, King?"

King Sedimo stands and says, "We will allow some portion of your people upon our world, but they will have to contribute to our society and live by our rules. We will not bow to the requests of the likes of you. We have ways that members of our country join our society, and you all will be expected to apply and be chosen, or else you shall not be welcomed. What of Malpeada and their vast land and humanitarian ways? Perhaps if each of us received some of your people, it would not be a travesty on any one nation of our world?"

Jake responds, "I will bring this news to my people. I am certainly not the final word of the choices that my society will make. I must tell you, and word needs to go out to Chief Greybird, that we claim *Eminent Domain* over this entire landmass referred to as Stilligate, with the exception being small portions of the northern most country of Stirpeto. We shall work with this society to find a peaceful solution. We will do what we can to work with the society in the land of Berlinkat, but I must advise you to prepare to make accommodations for my people, as we are technologically advanced and will take this area with force if we can't come to a peaceful resolution to our needs."

King Sedimo says, "Eminent Domain you say? There is no chance to be offered some of Longenthros or Daringranka's land to ease the sole burden on us? You are basically telling me to prepare to be invaded. Thank you for the warning, and you better have some very strong forces if you and your planet intend to force your way onto our land! We shall declare war on your society when the first individual places their foot on our land without our consent!"

Jake replies, "I do not mean to create difficulties with our future relationship with your people, but I would advise you to work with us to help accommodate our needs, as we have no other option but to occupy this land or perish."

The king continues, "What about all of the land in Malpeada? They have three times the landmass as us. If you are so technically advanced, why don't you force them to accommodate your people?"

Jake says, "I have said all that I need to say. Please prepare to work with us over the coming months and years. We shall be back in touch."

The king and his entourage exit the room with strong scowls on their faces. Jake looks at the general. "Well, that was better than it could have gone."

The prime minister walks up. "Our country realizes that there is no choice. I could leave and move back to Malpeada without any difficulties for me or my people."

"We really don't want to force our position, but we have no other choice. I hope that you gentlemen realize that if your world faced the same fate as ours, you likely would be making the same accommodations if possible."

The general speaks up, "If we had some type of FTL propulsion, we would probably be out prospecting, even without the need."

Jake looks at the prime minister and explains that they could very well orbit the planet in the Parche I for the next few months, awaiting the arrival of the first transport ships from Earth, but would like to have an area to settle on and begin to build or inhabit a home base on Stirpeto with the land they have offered.

The prime minister says, "We have a compound that is currently occupied, but we can encourage the people to relocate. We will not go and run them out with force, but we will offer them a place in Daringranka, or near the prison, and encourage the group to accept this. I feel that until we get these accommodations in place, you should probably stick to orbit unless sitting here on our runway or in some open area within our base is agreeable to you."

Jake says, "No, within orbit is a comfortable place for us until we have a place to build or a compound that we can occupy."

"Give me a week and contact me through my mobile device. We also have several embassies here that accommodate visitors. We will likely be able to contribute these items in a gesture of good will."

Jake says, "Very well." He thanks these two gentlemen for their graciousness and help with the meeting, as well as their protection. He and the general make their way back out to the waiting Parche I, they pause at the door and Jake says, "General, I am very grateful for your support with this meeting and your willingness to work with us at this difficult time. I found it strange that the president or the governors didn't make the meeting."

The general looks at Jake. "Well, your presence doesn't give us many options. The leaders of Malpeada determined that this could be hostile and dangerous for them and decided to not attend.

"I am very interested in your spacecraft. I have led the Air Force base in Novaraca and have worked with designers to develop spacecraft and aircraft, but none with your technological advances. Would it be acceptable for me to tour the craft?"

"It will be acceptable to come onto our bridge, however, before I could give you a proper tour, I would have to have approval from my home base. Please understand that I believe this to only be a formality as I consider us allies, but upon my return, if acceptable, I will show you everything about our spacecraft."

"Okay, Commander." He follows Jake up the ramp into the ship. They enter the door and everyone looks somewhat surprised that he has boarded their vessel. Jake says, "General Zelicwi, allow me to introduce my crew. To the far left is Heather Lawson, she is our Sr. Research Navigator, to the front is Ted Snider, our Pilot, to the right of him is Greg Compton, our CoPilot, and last but certainly not least is Dean Stinson, our Design Engineer. His efforts afforded us the engine that we use to travel at FTL speeds."

General Zelicwi looks around and takes a step forward. "May I?"

Jake says, "By all means, be my guest."

The general then walks to the front of the cabin, looking at the hologram and reaches to touch it as if it is a solid object. His hand passes through it and he looks at Dean and asks, "Your work?"

Dean replies, "Not the original, and I did not invent it, but that one is."

The general then steps to Ted's control console and looks at the touch screen display and asks, "You touch each of the devices to control the ship?" Ted says, "Yes," and he changes the screen to show the current status of the temperature of the engines, and scrolls through others to show the general its many uses.

The general asks, "Will you partner with us to develop this type of technology in Malpeada?" as he looks at Jake.

Jake says, "If your country assists us with survival and forgives us for the war that may be inevitable with the people of this land, then we will undoubtedly share a great deal of our technology with you."

"I have no way to know how strong our support can or will be, but I wish you all well. I look forward to working with you in the future. I would very much like to call you friends."

"We would very much like to call you friend and ally as well. When we return, I will be ready to give you the grand tour if our leaders allow it." Jake extends his hand and the general shakes it as if they are life-long friends.

"Until next time, my new friends. No dot on your hand to prick me this time?"

Jake chuckles. "I'm sorry if my DNA swab was uncomfortable. Goodbye, friend."

Chapter 17

The Production Race Is On!

Charles Phillips is now in Moscow, Russia, to visit with a scientist that claims to have a way to determine precisely when the sun will begin its red giant phase. He has one of WRC's top scientists, Randy Green, traveling with him to speak with the Russian scientists. They meet in the lobby of a Russian hotel. They step out of the nice warm hotel to walk to the facility, and the air is very cold and dry, the sidewalks are covered from a fresh Russian snowstorm. It is bright white in the sunlight and the reflection almost appears blue in some areas from the reflection of the sky. It is mid-September and it is very cold. The trip has two purposes. They intend on confirming the information is accurate for the sun analysis and to review the replicator that is building Russia's transports.

As they walk, they pass people in wool hats and drab, bland colored clothing. They themselves are wearing long leather coats, long, thick woven scarves, and wool hats. They walk about nine blocks and find the facility where the meeting is to take place. It is a gray and dingy off-colored white with a stucco texture. The building is about three stories tall. They ring a buzzer on the front of the building and a lady comes over an intercom and says, "Good morning," in Russian–Доброе утро. The scientist that is traveling with Charles responds in Russian and explains they are there by invitation to see the Russian scientist Andrei Yolkin. A buzzer sounds and the door releases. They enter a small lobby area that is also a dingy white in color, but it is finished in what appears to be white stone with green and blue streaks through it, there is an old style pane type window trimmed with crown molding that needed repainting ten years ago, a ceramic tile floor that is multi-colored but dingy, with a marked path where people have walked in the door and through another large wooden door that leads into the facility. The smell is of butane and weathered wood from the heating stoves used to keep the cold out. The lady is sitting behind the window and the sill has a small ledge. She raises the window slightly and puts a clipboard on a chain up on the ledge and tells Randy to sign in. Randy puts his and Charles' name down, and they sit down by an open front radiant gas heater in need of cleaning. Charles pulls his gloves off, revealing red, cold hands and rubs them together by the heater.

The lady speaks to Randy, seemingly something about Charles. Charles asks, "What did she say?"

He replies, "She more or less called you a wimp, a weak American."

Charles laughs. "She has no idea who she is dogging out, does she?"

"Not at all."

About five minutes pass, and a Russian man opens the door. In English, with a thick Russian accent, says, "Charles, Charles Phillips and Randy Green?"

Charles speaks up, "Yes?"

"Come in please," he replies. They go through the large wooden door and it creaks as they pull the door shut after them, closing with a thud. They walk down a hallway that looks more like an old medical facility than a modern scientific laboratory. They get to the end of the hallway and Andrei presses a button to call the elevator. They hear an old-timey bell ding a couple of times and the old metallic door rattles and shakes as it slides open. Charles looks at Randy and they follow the Russian in. They start up and the elevator makes creaking and popping noises and shakes slightly side to side and up and down as it begins to travel upward. They get to the top floor and it stops. The door has a clicking sound but nothing happens. The Russian hits it a couple of times and presses a Door Open button and it begins to open slowly while he growls with obvious displeasure.

They step out to a clean, modern looking laboratory. It has large, clean windows, with fresh earth tone paint on the walls, a new shiny ceramic tile floor, and a retina scanner for security. Compared to the rest of the facility, it is certainly a very professional looking atmosphere for the scientist to work in. The room has skylights and telescopes affixed to a mezzanine about eight feet from the floor. The telescopes are of varying sizes. One is connected to a sophisticated looking servo-driven mechanism with approximately twelve axes. Each has the name BOSCH REXROTH in red, bold letters across them.

He walks over to the big fancy one and explains that it has a laser array which is projected out and into our dying sun. A thick red beam of light is protruding from this one. It returns data to the exact spot that it is sent and is decoded to reveal the heat from the core, the diameter, and essentially the health of the sun. Randy inquires if he can see the software that he uses. The scientist brings up a computer screen that is near the telescope. Randy and the Russian go through several different screens and look at quite a bit of code. Charles doesn't follow exactly what the line of thought is on how everything works. The servo software opens with the label Indraworks Engineering. Randy says, "A German servo system, eh? I am familiar with their servos." They spend several hours there discussing different concepts and ways that could be used to obtain this data. In the end, Randy is convinced that the Russian has a valid way of determining the health of the sun. His forecast is different than what Randy has believed to be true. They request the data to bring back to America for analysis and the Russian agrees. Randy hands him a thumb drive and the data is transferred to it. They follow the Russian back out of the room and down the hallway to the elevator.

Charles asks, "Do you have a stairway? I need the exercise."

The Russian says, "Don't be afraid, my friends," as he summons the elevator using the Down Call button. Charles grimaces at Randy and they follow the Russian back into the elevator. They leave the facility and travel back to the dingy lobby.

They leave the building and begin their trek back to the hotel. Randy looks over at Charles. "I am impressed, Charles!"

"He knows his business, huh?"

"Well, not just that, but they have had a method of measuring the sun since the sixties."

"The 1960s?" Charles asks.

"Yeah, the 1960s, sorry. It was crude and may have been questionable for accuracy, but the fact that the records and methods exist gives us a basis to find a way to track the decay if the data set proves viable."

Charles replies, "Could the predictions be wrong? It has long been believed that our sun has millions of years left, not hundreds of years or months and days left."

"Well, no one can say with one-hundred percent certainty, as we can't predict exactly when the end will occur. The characteristics that the sun has been showing are pretty clear signs of a star that is running out of hydrogen. We have better ways of tracking the amount of hydrogen available within its core than ever before, and it can be compared to a fuel tank in a car that is running on fumes. The more data and different perspectives that we have to evaluate, the better so we can predict the end date. Something we all agree upon in the astrological and scientific community is, we have years, months, and days; not millions, thousands, hundreds of years, or perhaps not even years."

Charles ponders the thought for a few minutes and replies, "The time is now to take action. There is no doubt about that and there has been no doubt in all that we are doing to prepare. I just hope God forgives us for what we may have to resort to in order to save the human race."

They return to the hotel, entering the front door and passing a stand of maps with writing on them in Russian. They walk up to the counter and Charles asks for the key for rooms 116 and 127. The man behind the counter hands Charles the keys. They walk to the hallway past the clerk. The floor is covered with red aged carpet with a gray faded diamond pattern, and there is dated wallpaper on the walls. It is a fairly clean, Russian five-star facility, but not exactly what he would expect of a five-star hotel back in the states. They

133

walk down the adequately lit hallway and stop at the end of the hall, as the arrow says 100 – 125 to the left and 126 – 150 to the right.

Charles says, "I guess this is where we part trails for now. You did intend on attending the tour of the transport 3D replication facility down south in Lipetsk, didn't you?" Lipetsk is a southern industrial Russian city known for its steel and metal fabrication.

"Yes, my itinerary should be identical to yours. We will be traveling via a limousine, my itinerary says?"

"Yes." Charles chuckles a bit. "I will see you in the morning." Randy looks a little confused about why Charles would think the limousine idea was funny.

The next morning they both meet in the lobby as breakfast is served at 8 am. They have toasted bread, what appears to be pancakes, cream cheese, and dark bread, with coffee. The coffee is very strong and is kind of bitter, but it is coffee. They eat with a bit of trepidation as it is much different than what they have become accustomed to in Nevada. They finish eating and Randy asks, "Charles, why the amusement yesterday about the limousine that is taking us to Lipetsk today?"

"You will see. The car will be here to get us at 9 am. I will head to my room, grab my bag, and meet you back here in ten minutes."

"I will be here," states Randy. As he has already brought his luggage with him.

They meet in the lobby just before nine. Charles steps out the front door and an older, black, Mercedes looking, Russian-made four door car is waiting, with a man wearing a limo driver's hat standing by the back. Randy looks at Charles and remarks, "This is their version of a limo?"

"Yeah, not exactly what you were expecting, huh?"

"Not really!"

They both climb in and the driver puts their luggage in the trunk, and they start down the busy ice cleared road. They travel through the Russian countryside, passing nearby towns with huge smokestacks billowing smoke up to the sky. The snow looks very deep on the sides of the roads, but the road has been plowed and treated. It is clear enough for them to travel at a fairly high rate of speed.

They arrive in Lipetsk to find a very industrialized town. Smokestacks on every block, it seems. They pass gate after locked gate, with guard shacks at nearly every entrance to each factory. The smell reminds Charles of Pittsburg. They arrive at a very large, more modern hotel, and the driver pulls to the front of the hotel. The driver comes around and opens Charles' door, then opens the trunk and grabs their luggage. Randy hands the man a tip of a few rubles, they grab their bags and go check into the hotel. They find a very similar interior as the other hotel, but it is newer and less worn. Their rooms are on the fifth floor. They take off and put their bags in their room. Charles goes into his room to find a typical foreign hotel room, and sets his bags down but opens his personal bag and removes his toothbrush and puts it in the inside pocket of his coat. He then heads back to the reception area to meet with Randy. A short time later Randy arrives and they speak to the hotel clerk to find the location of the replication factory. The clerk explains they have a shuttle to the airport that can drop them off and pick them up at the facility. Charles says, "Man, that would be fantastic." A few minutes pass and they hop on a shuttle and travel a fairly short distance.

They go to a large manufacturing facility, and it has a big runway with several ships sitting along the tarmac. They can see through an old chain link fence that runs along behind it. They walk up to the guard shack and the guard looks at their credentials and calls someone to come and meet them. They are in a small room about the size of a storage shed but built from red bricks. They are sitting on a light blue, metal bench beside a radiator style heater. The guard says, "Americans, huh?" Charles says, "Yeah, Americans." They just sit and wait until a man dressed in a suit and a long leather coat walks in, and the guard seems to stand at attention. The man says, "Commander Phillips?"

"Yes, well, Charles, please."

"Very well, Charles. My name is Igor. Please follow me and I will show you our facility here."

They follow him into a gigantic factory with large, dirty, yellow, overhead cranes that stretch from end to end, with cabins for the operators. They walk for a long distance to find an area where the crane track ends and a replicator is busy printing a ship. The Russians don't have the same safety rules as the US, and there are people walking around while these massive arms, protruding from the roof, violently swipe back and forth. The arms have a gigantic cake decorating tip looking end, with several rolls of smaller ones in a circle along the outside of the large nozzle that appear to rotate on a turret, depositing composite material and metals that make the ship.

Charles asks, "Do you have one that is completed?"

Randy says, "This area looks a bit hazardous!"

Igor grunts. "This way." They walk along a yellow line on the floor, alongside the large printer tip that is swiping rapidly beside them. They feel heat and wind off of the arm as it passes by depositing layers of molten material to the airframe.

They finally arrive at the end of the facility to find an exact replica of the ship that Charles first saw back in Arkansas. It appears as big as two city blocks. They gaze upon the marvel of our world's engineering and Charles asks, "Is this one complete?"

Igor answers, "No, it is ready for the fuel rods."

"Do you install those here?"

"Nyet! The fuel rods must be inserted in a controlled environment. They will kill the workers if they aren't in a protected area."

Charles is thinking that he is glad they have a greater respect for the plutonium and uranium than they do physical exposure.

"Do you have one that is completed?" asks Charles.

"Yes, it is." Igor points to the sky.

"You have one that is currently in flight?"

"Yes, it is on its first test run."

"We were not aware. Have you coordinated with the WRC concerning this?"

Igor says in a thick Russian accent, "But of course. We have worked with your controller in Nyeavadia (Nevada) US of A."

Charles says, "We have much going on and I don't hear everything, but since we were coming here, I would have expected someone with the WRC would have let me know that you all had released one for tests."

Igor says, "One? No, nyet, we have ten that are currently being tested."

"Have any completed the trials? How are the trials going?"

"No issues, but none have returned yet. The first one left five days ago. It is expected to return tomorrow."

"Excellent. Perhaps we should have no fears concerning Russia's progress."

Igor responds, in a challenging sounding tone, "How many has the America completed?"

"I am unsure. I feel there have been near fifty airframes complete, but only two are underway with tests."

"Mother Russia is dominate! We need parameters and design criteria so that we may replicate a warship."

"You all are doing a very fine job. We will have design criteria very soon for military and supply ships that are necessary to support the transports."

Chapter 18

It's So On Now

Back on the Parche I, Jake asks that the door be closed and they return to orbit. Ted closes the door. Jake takes a seat at his station and everyone is curious about how the talks went, but they all remain silent thinking he will speak of it when he is ready. Ted throttles up the engines, lifts off, and rotates the craft to the south, and they blast off. They travel for a short period of time, fifteen minutes perhaps, and they hear a loud boom that sounds like fireworks outside of the spacecraft. Greg pushes a few buttons on his display and the holograph shows a streak of fire and an explosion from the surface that travels up toward the craft. Jake exclaims, "What the hell? These idiots are firing on us? Ted, what are the shields set at?"

"Fifty percent is what we travel through the atmosphere with, and that is what I had them set to until I heard what sounded like fireworks. They have now been set at seventy-five percent, sir."

"Ted, let's slow the craft and give them a taste of the laser defenses that our little reconnaissance craft has."

"Very well, sir. What should I target?"

"Only the source of the attack, for now."

The holograph is now showing a space-age looking anti-aircraft installment that is attached to a fortress or a castle. It appears the facility has in excess of ten of these types of installments. Each of them begins firing on their craft when they turn around, with a few deflecting and exploding on the outer edges of the shields.

Jake asks, "Are you freaking kidding me? Ted, give them full 750 Megajoule laser bursts at each of the installments that are firing on us."

Ted then presses a couple of buttons and the holograph turns red, with multiple blue Xs in the area of the weapons and a small white label that reads "Threat" beside each one. A large label appears at the top of the image, "FIRING TWO FULL SPREAD LASER BURSTS AT 750 MEGAJOULES". A very quick and sharp laser sound radiates from beneath the spacecraft and a bright light, similar to a blue lightning bolt, travels from the ship. The holograph shows each of the weapon sights turning red, like molten metal being poured from a ladle, and portions of them melting. What appear to be weapon storages, beneath and behind the weapons, begin exploding. Large fireballs, plumes, and narrow individual streams of smoke streak across the horizon. Large clouds billow up from all ten anti-aircraft guns. The walls collapse on some of the installations in the front of the fortress and the entire facility is on fire.

Jake says, "I wouldn't have shot at us if I were them. *They really won't like me when I am angry.*

"Ted, do you have the ability to release a message in the sky?"

Dean speaks up, "Yes, Jake, we equipped the spacecraft with a special communications ability that is referred to as skywriters. You type in a message, send it to the system, and it releases phosphorus in the sky that can spell out words, and even show a film if we maintain a position and project it to the night sky."

Jake says, "It's better at night, though?"

"Yes, it really should be done at night. You can see it during the daylight hours, but it looks like old skywriters or clouds that blow away quickly. It doesn't have the best graphics during the day."

"We will not leave a message this time, but we will likely do a little skywriting to ensure they understand that this is our weakest ship. Hopefully, we can get an opportunity to convey that warships will be en route soon. I hope these beings realize that we are here to stay.

"Heather, I want research done on these coordinates to find who lives here. What the significance of the facility is and if there are others that we should buzz on our way back down."

"Aye aye, sir."

139

He then looks over at Dean. "Dean, does the ship have the ability to skywrite from the ground?"

"Yes, Jake, it does."

"Once we get settled in our new home, we shall set up some communications using this utility."

They then pass through the barrier between space and the world's atmosphere and put the spacecraft back in orbit.

Jake speaks up, "The meetings went quite well with General Zelicwi. He and the others from Malpeada are being very accommodating. They will empty some installations to allow living quarters for us. Also, they are going to allow us to take over their base here in Stirpeto, from what I gathered."

Dean says, "Really? I guess they decided that we weren't prepared to take no for an answer and agreed to release this land."

Jake says, "Yeah that, or they believe it would be easier to kill us all in one place. I so fear a biological attack, but I like our odds much better than an Earth that is sure to be an ice land and being stuck in some shelter, waiting for Earth to leave orbit…if you even survive."

Ted becomes vocal, "We saw Indians and what appeared to be a king and his entourage come storming out while you were in the facility. Judging by the attack and the look on their faces as they exited the facility, they don't plan to be quite as accommodating, do they?"

Jake looks at Ted and responds, "Not in the slightest. They wish us death, as they clearly demonstrated. I see no choice but to expect to be at war with these inhabitants. I feel like it is morally and politically incorrect to come in here and run these people out, but modernized society did it to the Indians on Earth. We have no choice. We would like to find some negotiation without overthrowing their society, but we have clearly claimed this land for the greater good of our people."

Heather speaks up, "Such a large curiosity here, Commander!"

Jake says, "Lay it on me."

"I am doing research on this facility. I find that the religion of the people of Malpeada has them worshiping Jesus Christ and they have what appears to be a copy of our Bible that is interpreted into their language. I first believed that our translation device was in error and referred to their supreme being as the Lord and Savior Jesus Christ, but after further reading, the book of Matthew, Mark, Luke, they are all here. The stories tell of a world far away where many of the facts of the book take place."

Dean remarks, "I feel a little faint. You seriously have a copy of the Bible, New or Old Testament?"

"Both." The room becomes deathly silent.

Jake says, "We should all say a prayer." He bows his head. "Lord, please guide us as we move forward in this endeavor and forgive us for what we do, Amen. Are there other Christians among us?" Dean, Heather, and Ted all raise their hands. Greg looks on and says, "I am not a Christian, but I now believe if that means anything to you all."

Jake says, "The king's name is King Sedimo and he has a kingdom within Chilkreet, but they didn't elaborate where. I assume it is near the anti-aircraft installations. It is strange that the general didn't warn us of these." He continues, "And the chief is Chief Greybird. He is the leader of the largest tribe in Chilkreet. I believe they are probably scattered throughout the mild environment of this area of the country. They seem to be very limited with their weapons. They could kill you, but it will likely be with a bow and arrow, spear, or knife. Needless to say, none of these groups care for our presence, so we must be cautious when we settle there and travel into the wilderness or begin to expand." Jake explains that he must return to his quarters to report the meeting to headquarters. Dean and Heather are due for a break, so they leave as the commander leaves the room. All three walk down the hallway to the cafeteria while Greg and Ted continue piloting the ship in what seems to them as another boring orbit of Alpha Kantabury I.

Heather and Dean make their way back to the observation deck and enjoy one another's company while stargazing. Dean says, "Just think, we can create new constellations in the sky here if they haven't already done so. That could be a major endeavor for some of our newcomers when they arrive."

"Yeah, and theology will find a whole new validation when finding the religion of Malpeada and we can expect a strong, if not an exclusive, movement to Christianity."

Dean says, "I never had any doubt once I was saved. I am a scientist and I understand many of the scientist's perspectives when it comes to our Lord and Savior, but I have never doubted. The one thing that I have a need to know and far be it for me as a humble follower of Jesus Christ, but what I would like to ask him is, where did he come from? I may not get an answer and this may be wrong of me to question, but isn't it a fair question? Would I understand if he explained it?"

"Dean, that is such a unique thought! I now would like to know the answer to that question. I have always been a strong believer. I may not have been the best Christian, but I have always had a strong belief in him."

"Well, I don't want to spend the rest of the day explaining how I found the Lord. That may bore you to tears."

Back at the helm, Ted is watching TV shows. This time it is a western movie with none other than Malpeada's version of John Wayne going after the Indians within Longenthros. Ted speaks up, "It's uncanny how they have their movie stars just like we have back on Earth. I wonder if they have super heroes like Superman. I would like to discover if there is horse racing or the equivalent, gambling, drinking, and partying. We could have a very negative effect on this world."

Greg shakes his head. "Man, I hope they already have it, otherwise, it would be a pretty dull place!"

Jake begins to draft an email to Charles.

Dear Charles,

I had a meeting with the inhabitants of our new world. It was a very intense meeting. The people that live here don't have any desire to have guests. We were even attacked while leaving. The shields of our ship protected us from sustaining any damage. We did turn around and give them a rebuttal. The laser defensive systems on the Parche I are pretty impressive. It destroyed an installment of anti-aircraft weapons pretty easily. I certainly was impressed, as I have not had any reason to use the ship's weapons. We have struck an agreement that the Malpeadans will vacate the land they possess to relinquish it to us. Currently, they are preparing an embassy to accommodate a place for our crew and will release an Air Force base that is here. This should serve as a receiving center for the transport ships. We shall now plan to travel to the surface when the embassy is ready and begin research on the natural resources that our people can use to sustain our existence. I look forward to hearing an update from you personally, sir, especially since I have not had a communication from you within a few days.

Sincerely,

Jacob Conley

Commander WRC Parche I

On the surface, the people awake to a new day in Stirpeto. They have all evacuated the embassy, with exception of a small support staff and security. Prime Minister Jimelclay stands in front of his home and shakes his head, thinking that at the height of his career he is having to abandon his post, his office, and the home that he has come to love. He is remorseful that he is forced to leave. The convoy of large trucks pulling trailers with all of their belongings inside leave to go to the air base, and they have prepared the Parche I a home.

Chapter 19

Packing To Move

Charles Phillips sits at a large conference table with his staff. There is an early morning meeting concerning the goals and progress they have to relocate Earth's inhabitants. He goes around the table discussing everyone's status. General Brett Silvers–the top USA General that is planning the relocation for the troops and essentially the move to Goldilocks–is sitting to his right. Charles asks, "General Silvers, what stage are you at in planning for the move?"

"We have plans, but the ships that are being built, ones I have gotten to review, are primarily transports. We must also move equipment, replicators, and we require defenses of some type in the event that we run into opposition somewhere along the way."

"We have specialty replicators that are producing the complement of one thousand military ships for each voyage. The top military design engineers around the world designed them. There shall be four thousand transport ships that will transport twenty million souls per Armada, five hundred supply ships that will serve to keep the food replicators fueled and will provide in-flight filling so that everyone can eat, and five hundred ships used for defenses, transportation of supplies, and equipment for what may be needed on the surface. All of the items that you recommended when we had our initial meeting for what was necessary for this endeavor."

The general is astonished. He asks, "These ships are being built at this time?"

Charles replies, "Yes. Each one hundred ships of each style have gone through the same test flights as the others. Would you like to review the designs? They were all taken almost precisely from your description."

"I would love to see the designs, but if you have the top engineers of the world, who have designed our military transport aircraft and spacecraft, they will know what is necessary for transportation of the list of equipment and supplies that we suggested."

"Every item that you proposed is being adopted. Please plan a trip to Area 51 in Nevada so that you can review the designs and the actual ships that have been built. The first groups of ships are kept there."

General Silvers replies, "Yes, I would very much like to see them. It has only been a couple of months since I submitted these plans, you are sure these ships are currently being replicated?"

"I gave the order myself and have no doubt that this has been done and tested. There should be thousands of these ships across the United States and over a hundred at Area 51. Sir, we are desperately trying to move forward and the leaders of our world have given me the authority to do anything necessary. I have nearly unlimited resources on this end and it is taking every resource the United States has to complete this endeavor. You are my advisor and you provided a plan that I have adopted. I didn't care to bog you down on the details of each ship, but I believe you will find them adequate per your description. I need a detailed plan for every step of the evacuation utilizing these ships."

"Brenda, have all of the countries provided a list of people that will be going?" asks Charles

"Yes, sir. I have them from all of the countries of the coalition and it is broken down by their rules for determining who is going, military as well as each one's administration and leadership members that will be attending the journeys. They all fall within the three billion individuals that we have planned to accommodate."

He then speaks to the next person on his staff and it is the first of five planners. Her name is Glenette Lowery, she is responsible for coordinating the trips. "Glenette, do you have the plan and date for the first voyage?"

"Yes, sir. We have all of the other planners of the world set up, with ships leaving from the US, South America, China, Japan, Taiwan, England, Belgium, Germany, Italy, Egypt, Israel, and

Russia. The initial voyage will consist of military personnel, supplies, and twenty million individuals."

"Do you have a date?"

She sighs and takes a big, deep breath. With a bit of trepidation in her voice, she says, "No, sir."

"Okay, why don't we have a date? Do we have enough information and a good enough plan to put these ships in the sky and move out?" asks Charles.

"Yes, sir, but we have issues with Japan and Russia deciding when they will be ready."

"When will the others be ready?"

She replies, "Three weeks from today's date and the first voyage for all the others will be ready."

"If they can't produce a date, could we send additional ships from other regions to make up the four thousand ships that are planned in the same time frame?"

"Yes, sir. The only reason these areas are sending five hundred ships each is because every coalition member, eight in total, are promised this. The eight that make up this group are North America, South America, Eastern Europe, Western Europe, Russia, Eastern Asia, Western Asia, and Australia."

Charles responds, "You tell them that they will be ready to leave in *three weeks* or we will send others in their place."

Glenette says, "Absolutely, sir."

Charles then goes through details of the preparation for enough food and amenities such as sleeping arrangements, the estimated supplies that would be needed such as tents, food replicator fuel, and transportation on the surface, etc.. that is required to accompany the fleet for their voyage. He gets an adequate answer from the others. He then gets to the final planners, Virgil Russell, along with the ground coordinator, Joe Bennett.

146

Virgil is an older gentleman who has had several years planning for military movements and support for supplies throughout the world for humanitarian aid support, etc. He is the top planner in the world for movements of troops and supplies.

Charles asks, "Will we be ready in three weeks?"

Virgil says, "We are ready right now with the plan. It will take quite a bit of coordination on the ground." Joe Bennett speaks up, "We will be ready."

He then goes back to Virgil and asks for the schedule. Virgil then gives him a comprehensive schedule that includes military and supplies, and a schedule of five thousand ships per week for a year pending the first launch date. A return voyage should then be seen from the original fleet. The remainder will be transported through the continued manufacturing of the four thousand transports and one thousand military ships until these return ships leave for a second voyage. This will then put the capacity at eight thousand transports per week, with fifteen hundred support vessels. This second transport chain will continue for slightly over a year, and everyone should be on or en route to the new world on or around December 15, 2118. Charles is content and feels like a plan is set to begin in three weeks.

He addresses the group. "This is monumental. It is without question the saving grace of Earth's human race. Please let each of us pray that two years is enough time to get everyone off of this planet before our sun fails. Please do not let me and society down, ladies and gentlemen." He then adjourns the meeting and he and Brenda leave the conference room following everyone else.

They go to his office and he sits down. "Brenda, what do you make of these countries not being ready?"

"I think it is comprehension of what is actually planned here. There has to be disbelief in the world ending and our technology taking us to another planet."

"It is unbelievable that Russia isn't ready. I was just there and they boasted of how ahead they were. They better prepare themselves or be left behind to die."

"I agree, sir."

Charles then goes into his office and finds an email from Jake Conley explaining the meeting with Stilligate. He reads it and says out loud, "If they don't care for a little reconnaissance ship, they will be deeply disheartened in about six months." He drafts a response to Jake.

Dear Jake,

I am very encouraged that you have had an opportunity to at least know who we are moving in on. I regret that the war has already begun. We shall give them fair warning and eradicate the inhabitants if we must. The ship has very strong weapons for a reconnaissance ship. I am also encouraged about the agreement that was reached with Malpeada in order to inhabit an existing establishment. Will it be possible to send details of the base? It is very desirable to have blueprints of the facility so that we can begin to decipher accommodations for the people we are bringing. I wish you well with traveling to the surface and remember that you are responsible for the welfare of your ship and shipmates. If defensive measures become necessary, do not hesitate to act. We can declare war at this time with the inhabitants if they have fired on our vessel.

We will have the first voyage of five thousand ships leaving three weeks from today. There will be four thousand transport vessels containing five thousand souls each and a complement of one thousand supply and military ships. I will confirm their departure when this occurs. We will then plan for the departure of this number of ships each week for one year. The first ships sent will be returning at some time during this time and we will load them and send them for another journey, along with the newly replicated ships that will be nonstop. We will continue this for about two years. You all will not be alone for long!

Sincerely,

Charles Phillips

Commander-in-Chief WRC

He then sends the email and prepares to leave the office for the day. He steps in and tells Brenda to have a good evening as he walks out the door.

The crew are all at their posts on the Parche I and a light comes on Heather's panel. Heather says, "Commander, we are getting a transmission from the surface. It is the general's mobile phone."

"Put him on speaker."

Heather then presses a button and says, "Hello."

The translation device pauses for a second and speaks in his native tongue. The general greets them and requests the commander. Commander Jake says, "This is Commander Conley. Please go ahead, General."

The general then speaks, "The embassy that I spoke of is now ready for your crew. It shall be somewhat large for only five people. I would be willing to provide some security forces and perhaps servants that can prepare meals and keep up with the facilities if you like."

"That would be wonderful, sir. When can we come?"

"As soon as you are ready. I have not released the grounds crew, as the facility will require upkeep regardless of your choice."

"We will plan to be on-site in seven hours, sir, and help would definitely be desired until we have additional people and support here. Will there be a place to land our ship at this location?"

"Yes, there is a very large parking lot at the side of the property. It will accommodate your ship and if not, it is joined by the embassy's meadows. No vehicles will be parked there except for the grounds crew and I will have them park at one end. I will plan to meet you to ensure that you get in and settled and introduce you to the servants and security forces. I have a new security clearance code, EARTH – Zelicwi – CODE WELCOME."

"We all look forward to sitting down on solid ground and getting off of this ship. I will see you in approximately seven hours."

The general inquires, "You may have mentioned this, but how long have you all been calling the ship your home?"

"It has been over seven months since any of us have settled into a bed that doesn't move. The ship has many amenities that are desired, though, a recreational room, first class quarters, and a nice cafeteria. We all miss some place to call home." They both say their goodbyes and Heather turns off the communications link. Jake tells everyone to prepare to go to the surface.

They are all too excited to sleep, so Ted turns to the commander and says, "We are ready now, sir."

"How long will it take to reach these coordinates?"

"About four hours if we start at the south again and trek north and about thirty minutes for the checklist."

Jake says, "Perhaps they won't mind us being a little early. I would like to begin at the south and travel north again, only perhaps near the eastern border this time since we have seen much of the western side. Ted, submit your flight plan, begin your checklist in an hour, and make plans for this eastern route."

Ted answers, "Aye aye, sir!"

Chapter 20

Goldilocks Came Upon a Cabin in the Woods

The time actually seems to pass very quickly. Dean and Heather ask to be excused as Ted and Greg prepare to go through their checklist. The commander questions, "What do you two do to pass the time as we travel to the surface?"

As they are leaving the bridge, Dean turns back and says, "Wouldn't you guys like to know." Heather and Dean just kind of chuckle as they make their way through the automatic sliding door and down the hallway. They again find themselves on the observation deck, with the hatch open, awaiting the trek through the ionosphere. They have a makeshift bed made from a large sleeping bag that was stored in the closet, along with pillows. They lay arm-in-arm in the darkened room, looking up at the window to the greatest light show they have ever seen. Suddenly, it begins, the craft shakes a little and the window reveals blue and silver lights streaking by, with patches of complete darkness. In a flash, it is over. The spectacular light show is through and the dark side of the planet is now a brilliant blue sky. The craft smoothes out as if they were sitting on the ground. The excitement is over for a few hours and they fall asleep.

On the bridge, the commander, Ted, and Greg are all looking at the holograph of the land beneath the ship. They see an occasional cabin, with very large fields of vegetation that appear to be vineyards and orchards, very remote cabins on hillsides, a crystal clear blue ocean is to the right of them, with a sandy white beach that seems to go on forever. It all reminds them of home except it is very sparsely populated.

Ted says, "Commander, we are coming up on a fortress that is very similar to the one that fired on us near the west coast."

"Shields ready?"

Greg says, "Yes, sir, they are at seventy-five percent. This is the same strength that was used last time."

Jake nods in affirmation. "Very well."

They begin seeing large fields of vegetation in rows miles before they get to the castle. The fields and orchards seem to go on forever. Each farm seems to have a small cabin at each end and they look very clean and well-kept. They get near the fortress and slow the vessel to get a good look. It is a mammoth sized home sitting in a deep cove that extends to the ocean, this allows it to have a beach that ends at the back of the home. It has what appear to be gold covered arches and gold lined drives, with three helipads and a double bladed helicopter sitting on each. Fancy looking vehicles are parked in the circle drive. Jake says, "Gee, it looks like God could live here."

Ted says, "Perhaps it is the king's castle."

"More likely," Jake replies. They circle the installation and continue north to arrive at their destination.

Ted slows the craft and they all look at the landing site on the holograph. Jake says, "There is our parking lot."

Ted says, "I fear that I may warm that surface up with the engines, setting it down." He converses with the control tower at the nearby military base. They then land. Ted inquires to Jake, "Shut it down?"

Jake replies, "No, we should leave everything up at idle for now until we figure out what we need to do. We may need to stay in the craft if we must provide our own protection." Dean and Heather walk onto the bridge as Ted is opening the outer door to reveal a beautiful, large gray brick home with golden trim work and craftsmanship that is second to none.

Jake gets up from his station. "Well, without further ado, let's get off this little flying saucer and see what this world is about." Everyone but Greg makes their way down the walkway to see a complement of armed guards, along with General Zelicwi. The general speaks in a foreign tongue and the handheld translator says, "Welcome to Stirpeto. You are a bit early."

Jake says, "Thank you, sir. Yes, everyone was a bit anxious to get to their new home."

The general replies, "How was your trip? Did you blow up any castles?"

Jake looks back at the general. "You heard about our little skirmish when we left?"

"Yes, King Sedimo voiced his displeasure by declaring war on anyone on Stilligate land. He does this every couple of years when he is upset with us. He can be a dangerous adversary, and I would definitely look out for him. When he knows that you are here, he will come after you. He has some pretty ruthless Special Forces units. We have lost people to him before."

"This all sounds like we are in danger," says Jake.

"I would be ready to defend yourself, Commander. Our security forces here in Stirpeto are good, but not exactly our top guns. If there is some way to be prepared, then I would take measures."

Dean speaks up, "I designed the ship and configured the force field. It can withstand a great deal of opposition. I can and will relocate the repeaters from the outer shell of the ship and place a protective force field around this compound."

Jake asks, "Will the force field be safe to us?"

"No, it is energized by using air as a conductor and operates at a very high energy level. It isn't something that you would want to touch, as it would vaporize the part of your body that touches it. I can configure it so that it resides just within the fence around the compound and we can put up warning signs."

Jake says, "That shall not be enough. I would feel better if we built another fence that contained the field within it. We are seeing great hospitality, and it would be tragic to vaporize someone's hand or worse!"

"That will be fine with me, just so long as you are okay without protection while the fence is being built."

The general speaks up, "We have very few craftsmen that can perform these duties here."

Jake says, "We must have signs every ten feet. You can replicate the signs and some type of a barrier. If nothing else, use orange cones and a rope."

Dean says, "Very well. I will get busy."

Ted asks, "Need some help?"

Dean says, "I would very much like some help." Dean continues, "Heather, can you replicate our signs? They should say extremely high voltage in Malpeada's native language, as well as in English. I will need about two hundred orange cones, with signs and a yellow rope between each to start with. Ted, we must install repeaters around the compound and extend the ship's force field out to the fence line."

They go to the spacecraft and tell Greg to place the ship in shelter mode. Dean says, "Put the shields in maintenance mode." Greg replies, "Done and locked." They proceed to remove silver, rectangular stations, with black boxes at the top, from around the ship. Greg comes out and begins to assist with removing the devices. A few hours later they have them all removed and begin to install them around the inside of the twelve-foot-tall stone fence that circles the entire property, including the parking lot and helipad.

Jake and the general walk through a great outer door and into what appears to be a castle. The building has a large receiving area with shiny marble floors and two grand staircases that make a half circular arc up and to the left and right. The staircase is all made of marble or a similar surface and inlaid with a substance that resembles gold. At the center is a broad walkway to an area behind the stairs, with the ceiling reaching a great distance up. It appears as though there are several doors through that area. To the left and right of the stairways are large walls of rounded glass that contain rooms that resemble large curio cabinets. They walk through this area and ladies

154

are standing on either side of the entrance to the stairways, they appear to be the maids. They aren't wearing any special uniforms, just jeans and t-shirts, and are very attractive.

The general says, "This area is a commons and reception area, where visitors are typically greeted and allowed to wait on their hosts. These ladies are caretakers of the property. They will greet guests and help administer the cleaning staff. They will serve primarily as liaisons to the other staff. They are maids as well, but this facility has a staff of about thirty for cleaning, gardening, electricians, and mechanics, for upkeep."

They walk toward the stairway to the right and begin walking up. Jake while looking at a gold inlay on the banister that is about two inches wide and embedded into the four-inch wide marble and appears to go the entire length of the staircase on each side, says, "What is this golden substance that is incorporated into much of the building?"

"It is what we call gold. It is an ore much like iron but is very shiny and pretty. Women use it for adornments, and many upper-class homes use it for building materials. It is very plentiful; our world has millions of tons of this substance. It is also a wonderful conductor of electricity."

Jake wonders what something like that would be worth back home. He says, "I am familiar with this substance, but it is very scarce on our planet and is very valuable."

"It is of less value than other building materials. It is not as strong as an alloy that we create from iron and other ores that are mined. It is about as valuable as another substance that we use that we call lead. Lead is not as shiny or pretty, but it is useful for ammunition in weapons." They reach the top of the stairs to reveal another open commons with the same marble floor and one large staircase of the same design that seems to get wider at the top. It has a grand, golden chandelier in the center of the large room and there are many doors all around the outside of the room. They walk to the first door and the general explains that this would likely be crew quarters. They walk in and it is a very nice office, with a gold

155

insignia in the floor that appears to be a Malpeada symbol, a fine large oak and gold custom built desk, and empty bookshelves that are also made of oak, with gold inlays. They extend all the way up to the ceiling. A ladder that slides across resides at one end that is comparable to the other furniture. They walk through the office area into living quarters complete with a big screen projector screen and a projector that is protruding from the ceiling. It contains large brown and blue leather couches, two recliners, and end tables to the side that is of the same construction. It is all very similar to what he would expect from a modern home back on Earth, except for the gold. They walk through this area to reveal a kitchen, with a clear glass refrigerator, a cook stove with a clear glass front, an oven, and a bar with bar stools.

Jake says, "This is very similar to home. What is the clear glass box for?"

The general says, "We cool our food so that it will stay fresh longer."

Jake replies, "A refrigerator, why is it clear?"

"This is so that you can see what is in it without having to open it and lose the cool air."

They walk on through this area into a small outlet that has a bathroom to the left, with a toilet and urinal, like Jake is accustomed to, and a bedroom with a queen sized bed, dresser, and nightstands. The floor is covered with carpet and all of the furniture looks brand new, with the same finish as the office.

Jake speaks up, "This will be fine for our crew members. I only worry about our security."

"As do I, my friend. I feel that if your crew can get the barrier up that you speak of, we may be able to leave you and feel you are safe until others arrive."

They walk back through the office/quarters and Jake looks along the wall. The doors are identical to this one. He says, "Are all of these the same?"

"Yes, I believe so. Some have different colored walls, a variety of woodwork, and different types of flooring. It depended upon the preferences of the individuals that stayed in the quarters."

Jake then says, "What about my quarters?"

"But of course, my friend. You will have the ambassador's suite. It is the entire next floor." They begin to walk up the center set of stairs to find a room that reminded Jake of a penthouse suite in the finest hotel that he ever stayed at. There were earth tone colors, fine thick white carpet throughout, large windows all the way around the outer rooms, with large blinds that extended the full length of the windows, a huge office with a large fine desk made from a wood that looked similar to mahogany and some others that would be exotic wood back on Earth, and gold inlays throughout the entire facility.

Jake asks, "Is this the top floor?"

"No. The top floor is reserved for military forces and tactical installations against threats."

They walk to a narrow dimly lit hallway and walk a short distance and at the end they find an elevator. The general keys in a series of characters into a keypad and the door opens. They get in and he presses "Security" and the elevator moves upward a short distance and stops. The door opens to reveal an entire arsenal of weapons behind glass cabinets on each side of the entrance. The room has several large protruding servo driven barrels that protrude through the outer walls of the facility. They appear to be very large battleship guns, a battery of what appears to be missiles sit beneath doors that appear to open for access to the outside roof. All around the outer walls of the room have large mounted rocket propelled grenade launchers and machine gun installments, with doors that open so they have full access to outside.

A man walks up in a black military uniform that appears to be a tactical uniform and he extends his hand to Jake. Jake shakes the man's hand, and says, "I am Commander Jake Conley from Earth."

The man says, "I am Major Eaton Murdock from Malpeada. I am to lead your security detail for the next six months."

Jake thinks man this place is set up and ready! He says, "Hopefully, we can protect ourselves very soon and be allowed to relieve you of your duties here." Murdock looks at the general and nods his head as if it is some type of a salute and returns to the room at the middle of the floor. They walk back to the elevator and travel back down to check on progress with Dean and Ted.

"How are things coming along?" asks Commander Jake.

Dean says, "We have all of the repeaters in place, there were only about twenty. We are ready to power the system up and program it so that it works for this configuration."

"What is necessary for you to perform the tests?"

"Everyone must evacuate the structure so that if it is energized, no one is injured."

"Dean, I've never seen a force field configured in this way. How do we enter and exit while it is on?"

"You can't. It must be turned off and on for anyone to pass through it."

"Very well, not much for visitors," remarks Jake. The general grimaces and goes to order everyone out of the building.

Dean says, "The problem will be with Heather. There are only twenty repeaters, but there are four hundred signs and cones."

Jake asks, "Can you all help her in her duties?" Ted and Greg both nod and take off into the spacecraft to find Heather. The general returns with a group of people in tow. He decides it is a good time for them all to meet their new boss. It is a very mild and comfortable day outside, so they walk to a shaded area of the parking lot and the general introduces Jake and explains that he will be the one that they report to after he leaves. He has each one say their name and explain what role they play.

Greg emerges from the craft carrying an armload of signs and orange cones. He takes off toward the furthest corner of the fence and begins to set them out. Heather built the cones with a holder for the sign so that it sticks down into the top of the cone. He begins to set them out. The maids ask if they should assist them. Jake says, "Yes, please." They had all of the warning signs out in no time. Jake explains to the group about the force field and how it will harm them if they touch it when it is on.

Dean comes out from the craft after a short while and explains that he is ready to try the force field. They all gather near the front of the craft as Dean instructs them. A very high pitched ringing is heard and lightning bolts shoot from the top of the craft over the top of the building. A buzzing noise is heard and a blue hue appears all around the fence and green well-defined streaks that connect the spacecraft to each repeater and from each of them, as Dean adjusts the strength and frequency. It is transparent and you can see through it, but it is obvious that there is something there.

The general explains that he is ready to leave and if they need anything that the support staff can accommodate them. Jake thanks him for his time and helping them get settled in. Dean turns off the barrier and the general climbs into a vehicle that is very similar to a Humvee and leaves the compound. The barrier is then raised again and everyone feels very safe. They begin to meet one another and go into the compound to find suitable quarters and to relax, as it was a long day.

Chapter 21

Exit Strategy

Back on Earth, Charles Phillips sits at the WRC Headquarters in a meeting with the world leaders. Two weeks has passed since the meeting with his staff concerning the preparation of the ships and Russia has committed to the three-week deadline, but Eastern Asia–Japan specifically–still was holding back on being ready. Korea had shown displeasure that they weren't chosen for the first voyage and was upset that Japan wasn't ready and they still weren't being invited.

Charles begins the meeting. "Once again, we must discuss progress on our relocation efforts." He calls on Eastern Asian representatives to provide explanations of why Japan will not commit to the date. The man speaks, "He says the first ship that we tested is not completed. We have issues with the FTL drive. Our scientist decided to improve upon the basic design that the USA has provided and our ships will not achieve the speed."

Charles responds, "We can fix your issue, but it is regretful that you haven't divulged this information so that we had additional planning time to fill your slot. We will have a team at your facility from the USA as soon as possible. My guess will be in the morning. We will not plan for Japan–representing Eastern Asia–to join the voyage for at least one month."

The man humbly replies, "We understand. We will welcome the assistance."

The Korean President raises his triangle, indicating he wants to address Charles. Charles says, "I know what you are interested in, Mr. President," as he looks at the Korean President. "You wish to have Japan's spot in the Armada."

The president speaks and says, "We not only want it, we demand these five hundred ships be ours."

"I regret that I must tell you frankly that Korea is not willing to work with our other countries, as well as the countries that we are sending for the initial voyage. Korea will not have any ships until the eighth Armada. If this is unacceptable, then Korea will not be welcome to come at all."

The Korean President *slams* his triangle down on the table, making a gouge mark on the fine dark wooden conference table in front of him. He jumps from his seat and leaves the meeting.

The dimly lit room is deathly quiet as Charles speaks, "Was it something I said?" Low tone laughter is heard from a portion of the group. Charles continues, "The five hundred additional ships will be made up of USA and Russia. The United States is ready with two hundred and fifty additional transports and Russia is ready as well. South America has ships prepared to go, but they don't have any additional ready. Russia or Western Asia can consider inviting some of the Koreans as their guests, but USA will only be sending USA and Canadian citizens."

The Russian leader speaks up, "We have sent the list of our Russian citizens that will be aboard these vessels."

Charles continues, "We continue to have positive results on the outcome of the construction of the ships. We will be able to support the five thousand ships weekly with current production around the world. The first transports will be North America, South America, Eastern Europe, Western Europe, Russia, West Asia, and Australia."

He then asks for any additional business and no triangles are raised. He says, "Gentlemen, we are adjourned."

Charles returns to the penthouse, with Brenda just outside of his office. He has an email from the US scientist, Randy Green, assigned to researching the data from the laser. The email is dated September 14, 2116.

Dear Commander,

I have now made a full review of the data received from our Russian trip. I find the following:

161

- *The profile they have developed over a number of years appears valid.*

- *Using their method of gauging the life of our star, it appears the date is going to be on or around July 15, 2118, that our sun begins to morph into a red giant.*

  - *This date is contingent on the data being accurate from the monitoring that has been derived by this device.*

  - *I give this particular credence as they have accurately predicted ninety percent of major solar storms on the sun since the year 2035.*

  - *It isn't likely that Earth will be destroyed overnight. It shall be a very difficult winter that is never ending. I don't believe that life as we know it will be sustained following this due to the harsh cold that will be cast over Earth.*

  - *It will be a never ending ice age until the sun burns out in thousands of years from now and then Earth shall be released from the sun's gravitational pull and will float uncontrollably through the solar system. It will likely then collide with another celestial body, causing its complete destruction.*

I wish the news was better. This is the best that I can interpret from the data I have received. I am sending my findings to others in my area of expertise for their opinions. I am considered the world's foremost expert at this time, though.

Sincerely,

Randy Green

Chief Solar Physicist WRC

Charles now has the all-important drop dead timeline. He now knows everyone who is going, to ensure their survival, must be evacuated by Jan 1, 2118. This will provide a six-month window in hopes that it will be enough.

Charles calls Brenda into his office. She comes in and he says, "When do you want to go to the planet?"

"Wow! I knew this day would come, but it is going to be hard. We really are going, aren't we, Charles?"

"Yes, and sometime prior to January 1, 2118. The doomsday date is July 15, 2118. We will treat it like January 1, 2118."

Brenda replies, "When do you want to go? Shall we travel together?"

Charles says, "Brenda, the Commander-in-Chief of the WRC gets his own personal craft for him, his family, and his personal staff."

"So my family and I will be allowed to travel with you?"

"Obviously. I need to know how many and who will be coming along. There is your mom, Dale, and your father?"

Brenda says, "Dale and I are divorced."

Charles speaks up, "Brenda? You are a single lady? Have you been seeing anyone?"

"I am very fond of Jake."

"Jake who?"

"Jake Conley, Commander of the Parche I."

"I see, I had no idea. Brenda, let's set a date to travel fairly quickly. I want to depart in five weeks. Will that work with you and your family?" asks Charles.

"Yes, I will inform everyone to be ready and coordinate our plans with Virgil Russell and Joe Bennett."

Charles then says, "Set up our next meeting with the committee for Wednesday and each Wednesday at 10 am after that for the next four weeks. That should give everyone four days to review the data that was derived from the Russian's laser and understand the timeline that must be followed in order for us to be successful. Please forward the email from Randy Green to all committee members, including the Parche I."

Brenda says, "Aye aye, Commander."

Charles says, "Jake, huh?" Brenda nods her head yes and leaves the room. Charles says out loud, "She is such a very fine woman, and damn, not even a shot at her." And he shakes his head.

Brenda forwards the information as Charles requested to the committee members and sends Jake the message with a personal note.

Dear Jake,

Attached, please find a communication from Physicist Randy Green. Due to these developments, I will be leaving in five weeks, along with Commander Phillips. I will be traveling with my family and we will obviously need provisions. The WRC is providing temporary lodging for the incoming people, but I know you have settled into a state house there. Will you be staying there? Is there enough room for me? I will be very interested in finding out your answer to these questions and look forward to seeing you when I arrive. Please do not take this as desperation, as I am certain that Commander Phillips will have fine provisions for us, "his cabinet". But remembering our time in New York and the years that we worked together make me long to see you and spend time with you.

Sincerely,

Brenda Smith

Administrative Assistant to Commander-in-Chief of the WRC

Brenda also sets up the meetings with the WRC officials for the dates requested by the commander.

The next morning, Brenda arrives at work to find Charles in his office. The only light on is a desk light and the light of his computer monitor. She asks, "Sir, have you been here all night?" She makes her way to the coffee pot.

Charles replies, "No, not all night, but I woke around 3 am and couldn't sleep. We get to tour our new home for the next six months today." A young, beautiful blonde walks from the sleeping area of Charles' quarters, straightening her shirt. Brenda looks pretty surprised. She brushes her hand across the commander's back as he sits at his desk and says, "Call me later?" She then gives Brenda a *you're missing out look* and boards the elevator to leave the room.

Brenda asks, "Who was that?"

Charles says, "Not important."

Brenda continues unscathed, "I didn't think our ship would be ready until next week."

"Our ship was not going to be ready but others were. I run the show, and guess what? Ours is ready now. Please cancel any appointments and meetings that we have today and be ready to take a drive to Area 51."

"Very well, sir. Have you made all of the necessary arrangements?"

"We will just jump in the pickup with ole Woody and have him take us."

"Sir, are they expecting us?"

"Of course," says Charles.

A short time later, Brenda and Charles come walking out of the front of the building and climb into the truck with Woody. Charles sits on the passenger side and Brenda sits in the back seat of this rather large pickup truck. They take off into the busy traffic, headed toward downtown Las Vegas, driving south to Area 51. They travel for about two and a half hours. They arrive at a large gate with a guard shack that has large tinted glass windows. It is set in a way that half of the building is within the inside of a large chain link fence with razor wire along the top. The building has large columns and a lookout tower located on top of it and the front wall is aligned with the fence. There are large plateaus and mountains off in the distance and they are in the middle of the desert. A guard in a military uniform comes out through a door on the outside of the fence and comes up to Woody. Charles hands his credentials to Woody, then Woody hands them to the guard. He looks at them and says, "Sir, I am surprised to see you riding in a work truck. Most high ranking officials arrive in limousines and with a convoy of security in tow."

Charles says, "I'm not that important."

The guard replies, "Sir, you are in charge of saving the people of our world. No one is more important than you right now."

"That is flattering, thanks. Is General Brett Silvers expecting us?"

"Yes sir, he will be at the gate momentarily to escort you to the base, sir."

Charles says, "Thank you very much." The guard steps back into the guard shack and the gate opens. The guard appears again and hands Woody a pass to place on his windshield. Woody pulls to the side of the road until a Jeep arrives. It circles, pulling a U-turn in front of the WRC pickup, and parks. General Brett Silvers then steps out of the driver's seat and walks back and greets everyone and asks Woody to follow him.

They travel for about ten minutes, passing old buildings and old airplanes, like the SR-71 Black Bird and the U2 that are on display along the road, until they reach a huge runway that goes out of sight on both sides. The runway has a long line of spacecrafts sitting along it. They go on for as far as you can see down the runway. They are all colored with the dark gray and black outer covering that is similar to the Arc 0 they watched during the tests. Each has the enormous engines and swept wings, as well as multi-levels. Each ship takes up the space of an aircraft carrier.

The general stops near the first mammoth ship and everyone gets out of the truck. Commander Charles walks up to General Silvers, wearing BDUs, and they shake hands. The general then shakes Woody's hand and the commander introduces them. Woody and the commander are both dressed in their typical casual dress, jeans and a WRC blue and single white striped polo shirt. The general looks at Brenda in her yellow summer blouse, tanned skin, and tight blue jeans, and asks, "How has this beautiful young lady been?"

Brenda answers, "I have been good. I am very apprehensive about traveling on a spacecraft for six months, though. I don't even like to fly."

The general says, "Shoot, sugar, that little flying saucer you guys have to travel in will be like a cruise ship. You will not want the trip to be over. The replicators are even set up with all of the cruise ship buffet food."

"I only expected to see our dignitary transport. It looks like there is much more here than just our ship, General," says Charles.

"Well, we have many, but at least one of each style. They are officially supposed to be in storage until next week when we prepare them to join the first Armada, but I thought you would like to see them all."

"You are absolutely right! I am happy to see them all sitting out here like this for us to tour."

The general says, "Well, what are we waiting for?"

They follow him to the first of four ships. The general says, "This ship is the dignitary transport. It is for you and your cabinet. The US President will ride on one like this, as well as leaders of the other countries. The dignitary ships and the military transport ships are the only ones that are planned for only one trip. The personnel carrying transports will make two trips. If necessary, you and your cabinet could live on this ship, on the planet, for up to five years before you will require refueling. It will require restocking the food replicators within about a year, though."

He pulls a key ring out of his pocket and presses a button on a fob; a door begins to lower from the side of the large vessel. A staircase leading into the ship is affixed to the top side of the door. The general begins to walk up, followed by Brenda, the commander, and Woody. When they reach the top of the stairs, they are at a foyer. To the left it appears to lead into the cockpit, straight goes into a dining area, and to the right are the living areas. The ship has what appears to be ceramic tile on the floor in this area and the walls are finished with a covering that looks like sheetrock with trendy colors.

167

It looks as though an interior decorator spent a great deal of time inside the ship. The foyer has abstract paintings of the Golden Gate Bridge and the Whitehouse on the wall, also a golden plaque that lists Commander-in-Chief Charles Phillips, then all of the members of his cabinet who will be making the voyage on this ship.

The general says, "Let's have a look at the mid-level deck first. It is the lookout deck." He opens the large heavy metal door to reveal what appears to be a wooden plank deck that is about twenty feet wide and extends through the end of the ship. A handrail is on the right side and a hologram is projected to the right that makes it appear to be the ocean. There is a large blue sky above them and an occasional cloud that passes. Brenda asks, "Can you get a suntan out here?"

The commander says, "Yes, the hologram is designed so that UV is projected from the top. We felt a need for our passengers to be able to supplement a little vitamin D and this was a creative way to do it." To the left there are glass-faced rooms, many have awnings and lawn chairs along the way as they walk, and an occasional hallway between them. They take a left at one of these hallways. They pass by a glass front room.

Woody asks, "What is in the glass rooms?"

The commander answers, "Have you ever gone on a pleasure cruise ship?"

"Not on a ship. I am a little claustrophobic."

The commander says, "Well, those glass rooms open up into different amenities. Some are spas, hot tubs, buffets, reading rooms, and even viewing rooms where you can go and watch a movie."

Woody says, "Well, I will need a map or maybe even a GPS, I suppose. It seems awful fancy for a transport. I have caught a ride on a C-130 and you're lucky to have a seat to sit down."

The commander says, "You weren't on that C-130 for six months, though. Woody, one of our fears is people with claustrophobia. Do you feel comfortable with the holograms and the wide hallways?"

"Yes, it is fine. It tricks your mind into believing that it is larger than it actually is."

They continue on and walk along a hallway to a place that has doors on each side. The commander opens the one to the right to reveal a suite that is like a presidential suite at a fancy hotel. It has gold light fixtures, thick carpet, and is fit for a king. They walk through the room to find a kitchenette, a separate bedroom, living quarters with a flat-screen television, and a special room that has a hologram projector that can be used to project any image that you want to view. Brenda asks, "This viewing room has preloaded images?"

The commander says, "Yes, it has quite a large library. You can sit here and have the beach in front of you, Times Square at New Years, or even a quiet snowfall at your house if you have recorded it."

Brenda says, "That will help a lot with cabin fever."

The commander remarks, "Indeed."

They leave and walk down the hallway and turn right at a four-way intersection. They follow the general for a few steps and there is a big beautiful staircase, they begin to walk down to a large room below. The room has a swimming pool, a bar with alcohol, and palm trees. It is quite a sight. Brenda asks, "How many decks are there on the dignitary vessel?"

The commander says, "There are six decks total."

Brenda asks, "How many on the personnel transport?"

The general speaks up and says, "Ten decks on those ships."

Brenda asks the commander, "Do we have enough time to tour everything today?"

"No, I didn't realize they would have all these ships to review." He looks at Woody and Brenda. "Do you two have any plans for tomorrow?"

Woody says, "I'm good."

Brenda says, "Well, I did have a dinner date with a girlfriend, but I can postpone that."

The commander then looks at the general and asks, "Any problem with us staying the night?"

The general says, "Not at all. Try out your ship if you like. You are the boss. The only issue is, we don't have a soul to staff it, so you will have to work the replicators and any amenities that you care for."

Commander Charles says, "No issue with that. If there is, we will just have our little southern gal cook for us." Brenda just kind of cuts her eyes over toward the commander, thinking, *you won't see me as one of your little whores, pal.*

They continue on and walk through this large open area with lawn chairs and holographic projections of the sky and water in locations that would be windows on a cruise ship. They continue to each level. Each level is nearly identical to a modern day cruise ship and with what seems to be every amenity including bars, hot tubs, dining areas, recreational areas, and a running track around the outer edge of the grand deck suspended above the walkways. They have viewed just about every area of the ship when the commander asks, "How about the office area and my quarters?"

"That is on the top level, sir." They walk to an elevator and go up five floors. It opens to reveal a modern office area that looks very much like the offices in Las Vegas. They walk into the main entrance and a glass front office is off to the left. The commander says, "Brenda's office is over to the left." She smiles, they walk past it, and to the right down a wide open area is a large conference table that can be seen through a doorway. Then straight ahead is a plaque beside the door that reads: Charles Phillips, Commander-in-Chief WRC. They walk through this door to find a fine office with a real wood finish of mahogany and oak, a large bookcase is behind the large office desk, and two thirty-inch computer monitors sit on the desk. There is a doorway behind and to the left of the large desk. They pass through this entrance to find a modern split level condominium style apartment, complete with a Jacuzzi, small personal swimming pool, a pool table room, and a personal gym. Charles smiles and says, "I think I could stand to live here for six months."

The following day they tour the other ships. They begin with the civilian transport to find that it is very similar to the dignitary transport, only much larger and many more decks. The grand room is like a city park, literally. The ship is the finest looking, best quality, largest vessel they have ever been on.

They end the tour late in the day with the military and cargo transports. They have a setup very similar to an aircraft carrier but with some amenities to help the crew cope with the long journey. It has a rec. room, pool, a jogging area, and a swimming pool, but nothing in the order of the other civilian and dignitary transports.

Chapter 22

The New Frontier

It is the dawn of a new day on Alpha Kantabury I. Dean and Heather are sitting out on the top level of a dimly lit deck. The deck has wide handrails covered in thick marble, with a strip of gold inlay, and the floor is made of white marble to match the handrails, with a violet pattern that looks like paint was dribbled all over it. It appears to be brand new. There are no scuffs or wear marks that can be seen. They sit watching the sunrise. They are both drinking coffee and sitting in padded lawn chairs that are white leather with a violet striped pattern and white metallic frame. The chairs are placed around a fixed round table of marble and it has a fire that dances around in the middle of it to help with the chilly mornings or evenings while enjoying the deck. Dean has on leisure clothes that are similar to pajamas but made of a thick material that is blue and similar to terry cloth. Heather is sitting in a nice thick pink robe that she has fastened tightly, as the crisp morning air has a bit of a chill to it. The sky above is a deep violet color and they can see what looks like faint aurora borealis lights that dance around above the snow capped mountains off in the distance.

After a short while, Goldilocks' sun beams across the sky in the colors of the rainbow. Dean speaks and says, "I think I could get used to this!"

Heather agrees, "No question about it. It definitely beats the lil flying saucer as you call it."

"I hope that Teegarden's star has a lot of life left in it."

"At least a hundred years or so. I don't want to have to go through this again." She kind of chuckles.

Dean replies, "It is actually a young star from what I can tell."

Jake comes walking onto the veranda. "Good morning, Dean and Heather. I am disappointed that I missed the sunrise. It has been quite some time since I have seen one."

Dean says, "You didn't miss much. Just the light from the northern lights and a rainbow-colored prism-like sky before the large yellow blinding light."

Jake says, "Yeah, that sounds disappointing." He chuckles. "I will not miss it tomorrow. I guess it was good for you two to enjoy the first morning here alone. That will be a nice memory for you two to share. I trust you two found adequate quarters." He shivers as his large unrobed chest appears to have chill bumps and his nipples are pointing in their direction. He is obviously cold. He is only wearing gym shorts and crocs.

Dean says, "Sit down here by the fire," as he cranks up the knob that controls the flame. Jake sits down and rubs his hands together over the fire. Jake says, "Beautiful sunrise was it?"

Heather replies, "Prettier than any I have ever seen on Earth."

Jake says, "That could be because Dean is here."

She smiles, and says, "Could be."

Jake, with a smile, looks over at Dean. "Have you guys set a date for the marriage yet?"

Dean replies, "Not yet. Is your schedule open?"

"To tie the knot for you two? Just tell me when. This looks like a wonderful place to do it and it appears to be fall here. The backdrop of the lake and the beautiful fall foliage would be nice." Heather smiles with sparkling eyes.

Dean smiles. "We will consider it, Commander. Thanks for such a gracious offer."

A short time passes as they relax, enjoying the warmth of the sun and one another's company, and Greg comes walking out. He says, "I wondered where you all went. I thought everyone was sleeping in." The commander looks over at Greg and smirks, "Yeah

173

right, someone was sleeping in." Greg says, "Maybe, but where is Ted?" He gets no response.

Heather asks, "Dean, is the force field still up? I thought there would be something that you could see."

Dean responds, "No, it is perfectly clear, except for the blue hue that is emitted near the repeaters, and it is still up." He pulls an ink pen out of his pocket and draws back and throws it up in the air. A blue arc is seen and the pen falls back to the deck. Heather says, "I see."

Dean replies, "That is why it is so important to put up a barrier so that none of us walk into it. That would be a third-degree burn or amputated limb."

Jake asks, "What is the extent of the barrier? Is it a bubble or a fence?"

Dean says, "It is more like a roof. It protrudes upward in a vertical fashion from the repeaters, then turns about one hundred twenty degrees and extends horizontally to the center."

Heather questions, "Nothing below ground?"

Dean replies, "Nope. It could be just like the ship has, but I don't believe we want the underwater services to our new home energized. That may make for a difficult time in the restroom."

Ted comes walking out on the deck, with a pretty little maid following close behind, and a smile on his face like a cat that ate the canary. They all look abruptly at him as he makes his way to the table in a gray sweat suit. Greg says, "Introduce us to your friend there, you rude bastard." He chuckles.

Ted says, "You all met her when you toured the facility. Her name is Gwentalapie. I call her Gwen for short." She is dressed in a French maid's outfit, complete with a short skirt and white stockings. She has blonde hair and blue eyes. She is around five foot eight and a hundred and ten pounds, perhaps. She speaks and the translator kicks in and says, "Nice to make your acquaintance."

Greg immediately responds, "The pleasure is all mine, ma'am!"

Ted looks at Greg and scoffs, "Slow your roll there, horn dog!" Heather and Gwen both snicker.

Gwen asks, "Is there anything that I can get for you, perhaps a nice homemade Stirpeto breakfast, or some more of your blackened drink?"

Jake speaks up and says, "We wouldn't want to impose."

She replies, "It is no trouble at all. The chef is in the kitchen making breakfast for the staff already."

Jake says, "Well, in that case. What would you recommend?"

She says, "I will bring you back some eggs, sausage, and bacon."

Dean speaks up, "That could be a glitch in translation. This will be their version of it." Everyone pretty much agrees to try it.

After a short while, she returns with several empty plates and a few bowls of food. They all dig in and find that it actually has a very good flavor. It tastes almost like taco meat and the eggs taste a little like Braunschweiger. They also were served fresh fruit that was similar to kiwi and watermelon. They all make favorable comments about the food and say that it is a little bit different than their typical breakfast food, but it is edible and not undesirable.

Gwen speaks, "Is there anything more that I can do for you all?"

Jake says, "I have to admit that our tour was a little less than ideal. It seemed like the general was ready to get through that and move on."

"I would be proud to show you all around."

They all leave the porch and go through each area of the estate. They find that they have a form of television, as well as a system that is similar to the Internet but to the crew, it is all gibberish. They will have to learn the language, or at least have some app to make sense of it.

Jake returns to the ship to check for communications from back home. Dean and Heather go there for a little racquetball. Ted and Greg both return to the bridge to check the logs. Greg is sitting at his console and says, "Hey, Ted, this is interesting." Ted looks on and Greg starts a video from the side of the ship, showing a group of people dressed in somewhat tattered-looking uniforms, walking up to the fence during the night. They stop at the fence and stealthily walk around the outer perimeter of the property. They do not try to cross the fence, they only observe for a couple of hours. Ted gets on the intercom and says, "Ted Snyder to the commander."

Jake responds, "Go ahead, Ted."

Ted continues, "Commander, we had visitors last night. You should come to the bridge to review our log."

"I'm on my way."

Dean and Heather hear this in the court and towel off and make their way to the bridge as well. They arrive and Greg has the holograph up of the people, outside of the fence, attempting to spy on them. They all watch the video for a period of time and the group takes turns climbing on top of a bin for trash that is just outside of the fence. They take what appears to be pictures of the area and spend a great deal of time trying to learn what they can, seemingly to plan an attack on the vessel.

Dean says, "Fortunately for them, they didn't get curious enough to cross the fence. That would be a life lesson for the rest of them."

Heather asks, "Ink pen?"

Dean responds, "Yep, ink pen." Jake asks that the recording be emailed to him so that he can review it with the security staff.

Jake finds his way back to his quarters and wakes up his computer monitor to find emails from Commander Charles and Brenda.

Dear Jake,

Attached, please find a communication from Physicist Randy Green. Due to these developments, I will be leaving in five weeks, along with Commander Phillips. I will be traveling with my family and we will obviously need provisions. The WRC is providing temporary lodging for the incoming people, but I know you have settled into a state house there. Will you be staying there? Is there enough room for me? I will be very interested in finding out your answer to these questions and look forward to seeing you when I arrive. Please do not take this as desperation, as I am certain that Commander Phillips will have fine provisions for us, "his cabinet". But remembering our time in New York and the years that we worked together make me long to see you and spend time with you.

Sincerely,

Brenda Smith

Administrative Assistant to Commander-in-Chief of the WRC

Jake sits in front of his monitor studying every single word for quite some time. He feels speechless. He wants to scream at the monitor to tell them to get his family on a transport immediately. He wants Brenda there immediately, but this strong man will have to wait and allow it all to run its course. He drafts a reply.

Dear Brenda,

I hope this email finds you well. I am fine. I find the attachment very disturbing to know that the end is defined for us. I fear they have miscalculated by a year. I will convey to Commander Charles that my family needs to be on the first craft out. I would very much like to see you on that craft as well. I understand that you must wait and travel with your family and the commander. This embassy/statehouse is within a military base. All of the people have gone and it will accommodate a lot of people. Perhaps your family would be more comfortable there. I am very happy to accommodate you and perhaps your family if they would like, they are welcome. You can even bunk with me if you so desire. I will draft a correspondence to Commander Charles later today. Thank you very much for the information. I look forward to hearing back from you.

177

Sincerely,

Jake Conley Commander WRC Parche 1

On the bridge, Heather and Dean have taken their posts and are reviewing information gathered so far. Heather says, "Gosh, are we on the surface? Isn't this everyone's position on the ship in orbit?"

Dean looks up, and replies, "I thought this felt familiar."

Jake's voice comes over the intercom, "Heather."

Heather replies, "Yes, sir."

"Could you get in touch with General Zelicwi and patch him through to me?"

"Right away, sir." A short time passes and Heather has her headphones on. She gets on the intercom once more, and says, "Heather Lawson to the commander. Sir, I have the general on the line for you."

Jake's voice comes back and says, "Please put him through."

Jake sits in his quarters in his large recliner when he takes the call. He says, "General Zelicwi?"

The voice on the other end says, "Zelicwi here."

Jake continues, "We had visitors last night. We have holograms of the ones that came to the embassy."

Zelicwi responds, "Well, we knew they would find out you were here sooner or later. Did you get the force field working properly?"

"Yes, we did."

"They didn't do any damage, did they?" the general inquires.

"No, they were scouting our facility."

The general comes back and asks, "Have you talked to Murdock, the security chief there?"

Jake says, "No, that was one of the things I needed to know. What is protocol with contacting him?"

"Protocol my ass! That is your security detail, put them on guard near the fence if you like. They haven't told you different?"

Jake says, "No, nothing like that. I was just uncertain on how to approach them."

"Don't be shy and let me know if they give you any grief!"

"Very well, sir. Thank you greatly."

"I am leaving back to Malpeada later today. Do I need to stop in there, Commander?"

"No, sir, but how long do I have this security detail for?"

"They work for you, along with the grounds staff, until you decide you don't need them. They have pledged alliance to you prior to your arrival. I don't know how your army is, but they will fight until the death for you with this understanding, and the grounds staff will go to any extent to ensure you are well cared for."

"Very well and thank you so much, General!"

"Goodbye." The general's line goes silent.

Jake wants to drop a short note to Commander Charles to inform him that they now have accommodations on the surface secured.

Dear Commander,

We have now settled on the planet's surface. In fact, they have been very gracious hosts. They provided us with a luxurious mansion with servants. We have extended the Parche I's shields around the perimeter of the grounds to protect us from unwanted visitors. I suspect we will have to face this threat very soon. They also left us with security forces that seem to be looking out for us. They stay in their area and do not interact with us. I hope everyone there is well.

I feel sure it is very hectic now that we have a deadline we can't meet. I don't have a great deal of time, as we had visitors last

179

night performing reconnaissance, and I need to meet with our
security staff. Please plan for the Parche I's family members to be
among the first couple of groups to be transported. I will send
additional correspondences when we discover the length of their
runways here at this facility and determine how many people it can
house. Malpeada has abandoned the facility with the exception of
guards and maintenance staff to keep it up until others arrive.

   Sincerely,

   Jake Conley Commander Parche I WRC

   Jake heads to the bridge, with his tablet, and explains that he
is going up to the house to speak with the security detail. Ted asks if
he needs some company. Jake replies, "I think that I shall take Dean
to look over their installment."

   Dean is still at his workstation and looks back and inquires,
"Now, Commander?"

   "Yes, if you are ready, let's head over."

   They enter the front door of the embassy and Gwen and her
coworker are sitting in a small glass front room to the right of the
foyer. It has an arched shaped front made of arched glass panes fitted
within fine mahogany strips. It is similar to a front on a curio cabinet,
only much larger. They are both dressed in typical Belgium or
French maid attire. Either lady could easily be models back on Earth.
There is the blonde haired Gwen that Ted seemingly claimed last
night, and this young lady. She appears to be about the same age as
Gwen at twenty-five-years-old, brown hair with a reddish tint, and a
build that would make every dignified man turn his head. They both
hop up and come out to greet Dean and the commander.

   Gwen says, "Commander Conley, this is Detsyl." She then
speaks and the interpreting device says, "Detty, this is the leader of
the spacecraft, Commander Jake Conley and Dean Stinson."

   She speaks, "Pleased to make your acquaintance, gentlemen.
What may we do for you?" Both Dean and Jake return the greeting
and Jake continues, "We need to go to security and speak with the
group leader, Murdock."

Gwen inquires, "Would you like for Murdock to come down and meet with you or do you desire to go to their area, Commander?"

"We would very much like to go into their area and have a closer look at their resources."

"Very well." She then leads them to an elevator and they travel up to the top floor of the facility. It stops and the door opens to reveal a dimly lit room and several men dressed in black uniforms, monitoring displays. Murdock comes walking toward the group and greets Jake. "Commander Conley. Pleased to see that you have found your way to our facility. Welcome."

"Thank you. Thanks very much for the warm welcome. On our world, the security staff isn't usually so happy to welcome visitors."

Murdock answers, "Sir, you are no visitor here. You are our leader for the foreseeable future."

"It is not a typical situation for me to have someone accept our presence so willingly."

"I am a soldier and I have taken an oath to follow my leaders of Malpeada, and they requested that I support you and keep your group safe. To help you in any way that I can to ensure you feel comfortable. This is my directive and shall be my goal."

"That is great. The reason we are here is that we had visitors that very well could have been intruders if we hadn't had our shields around the facility."

Murdock responds, "Yes, sir. I have full footage of the king's soldiers spying on our facility. Trust that we are and were aware at the time they arrived. They made no hostile advances, so we let them look. Our facility is no different today than it was when they were welcome to visit, with the exception of your spacecraft with its shield of death. I don't believe they could have gathered any tangible intelligence."

Somewhat surprised, Jake responds, "So you all were aware of the whole situation?"

Murdock says, "Yes, sir. I don't know what kind of technology you have on your world or what you have in your craft, but if you will follow me over to this monitoring and defense cell, I will demonstrate what our capabilities are." He walks over to a long table with four security guards sitting in front of dimly lit television monitors. Jake and Dean can barely make out the images.

Jake says, "Murdock, how can you all see this and why do you all keep everything so dimly lit?"

Dean interrupts, "Commander, do you recall when we monitored the world and we couldn't tell that any light existed except for what we believed to be campfires?"

"Yes, what of it?"

Dean continues, "Their sight is slightly different than the spectrum that we see at. This room is likely well lit. Their monitors are all adequate for their vision. It is at an ultraviolet frequency that we can see, but it isn't our normal light."

Murdock shrugs, and responds, "The room is bright to me."

Dean smiles, and says, "See?"

Jake responds, "I see."

Dean continues, "I will replicate some additional glasses and perhaps some contact lenses that will help us with this frequency if you would like, Commander."

"Are the glasses you are wearing filtered to see the light normally?"

"Yes, sir."

Jake replies, "Well, if it will get my ass out of the dark! No wonder everything has seemed dim."

Dean says, "Very well, sir."

They continue the tour of the facility and find a state of the art monitoring and defense cell that is set up to protect the compound. They have remotely fired weapons that are stationed along the fence. They possess drones that can fire weapons that can be deployed along the top of the facility. Escape routes are through tunnels beneath the facility and soldiers that are seemingly trained similar to Earth's Special Forces unit.

When the tour is ended, Jake looks at Murdock and asks, "Could I have some way to reach you in the event that we need to drop the shields, or that we discover some problem?"

Murdock hands him a business card that has his contact information. The three men shake hands and Jake and Dean find their way down the elevator and back on the ship, to join back up with the others.

Chapter 23

The Departure

Back on the doomed planet, in Las Vegas, Wednesday's first meeting with the board comes pretty quickly for Commander Charles and Brenda. He walks into the meeting and sits at his usual chair, Brenda by his side. He looks out over all of the world leaders, welcomes everyone, and brings the meeting to order by a firm clap of his gavel.

Charles starts the meeting. "First, I want to ensure that everyone received the communication that provides information as to the believed health of our sun. If anyone did not receive this data, please speak now." Nothing is raised by the members. He continues, "Due to this information, we have stepped up efforts even more than we had. I plan to leave on the week following the second Armada, along with immediate members of my staff. I will be taking Brenda Smith, Woody Jamison, General Brett Silvers, Virgil Russell, and Joe Bennett, along with their families. We have support staff that will be left to coordinate the remainder of the move, and once the third Armada is released, it should be a replication of departures. Does anyone have any comments or questions concerning my decision to leave at this timeline for myself and my staff members?"

The US President, Robert Lynch's triangle, as well as multiple others flip up, pointing to the ceiling. The commander says, "President Lynch, please go ahead with your questions."

The president stands. "My cabinet is so large that a standard dignitary ship will not be large enough. We have discussed the issue with Joe Bennett and he explained that we could use two dignitary ships. I believe that we should have a large transport for my people."

Charles responds, "Do you have five thousand people on your staff?"

The president comes back and says, "No, we have near eight hundred, including their families."

Charles responds, "You are the President of the United States of America. You have enough power and money within your means that you can do anything you wish with the vessels allotted to you. Is it wise to leave four thousand, two hundred of your countrymen behind and exposed to the potential of their lives being extinguished because you want extraordinary treatment? Do you propose that you have forty-two hundred commoners riding along in your vessel? Sir, I would also like to point out that the amenities on a dignitary ship extend well beyond the regular transports. The dignitary transport has greater maneuverability, escape pods, and more sophisticated communications systems. They have finer quality facilities, with superior pilots, and one very important aspect is that it can make a vertical descent like a helicopter. This could be key when arriving at the new world. All of these points were pointed out in the evacuation plan that was sent exclusively to each member of our committee."

The president responds, "I was not made aware of all of these points. I have toured each of the ships located at NORAD. The personnel transport ships seemed the nicest of the group, and I assumed that was what the WRC would have me and my group traveling in. I had no idea there were additional reasons why it was planned using this dignitary ship. This being the case, if my cabinet is not cramped and packed in like sardines, then this will be fine. I want three, though."

Virgil Bennett speaks up, "Sir, we have three scheduled for you. Commander Phillips, I would also like to leave with your Armada." The rumble of other members is heard around the room.

Charles explains, "We have not planned to have any of the world leaders to travel in the same Armada. This is reckless due to the possibility of a catastrophic event. It is possible that an entire Armada could be destroyed due to reasons beyond our comprehension at this time."

The president says, "Very well. Plan as you wish."

Charles continues, "Everyone should have a schedule for every last ship that is leaving based upon the production rate and the quantity of people you have selected, as well as a contingency plan.

Please review this plan and give me your feedback if anyone has an issue. Any additional comments or questions?" Triangles go up again.

He continues, "Let me see if I can answer some of these questions prior to calling on anyone. The schedule is set. We will not change the order of departure for anyone. I refuse to have any other group leaders traveling with my Armada, and we must set order and continue on this path. I would also recommend that high ranking cabinet members be scheduled on different Armadas for each government, but this is each group's preference." Most of the triangles go down following this announcement, with the exception of the Mexican and Korean Presidents' triangles.

Charles considers closing the meeting because he doesn't want to put everyone through this bitch session. Charles closes his eyes, and says, "President Kim Sun Pang of Korea, go ahead, sir."

The Korean President responds, "It is a travesty that you will allow my people to stay behind for such a long period of time while everyone else's army is allowed to arrive and establish their positions."

Charles replies, "This relocation shall be peaceful and the only offenses that may begin shall be against resistance on the world. Sir, if you do not agree to this, or if you bring up this resistance toward your fellow Earth brothers and sisters, then we shall ban you from the coalition. Do I make myself clear, President Pang?" Charles has a very strong tone to his voice as he asks the last question. The Korean lays his triangle down softly and looks away.

Charles states, "President Vasquez of Mexico, did you have a comment or question?"

The Mexican president stands. "Yes sir, Commander. We have trusted your group to handle the space exploration, designing and manufacturing ships, and this evacuation schedule. Sir, we have not seen anything as it pertains to the distribution of land. Who will determine this?"

"A valid question. This is good information. We have only just recently received maps of Goldilocks, and we will need to take a strong look at this once we arrive. I intend to try to accommodate everyone with the same amount of land as they have had on Earth, however, we must consider the inhabitants geographical location and everyone's desires. We will put together a comprehensive plan while en route and propose it. We will then determine what works best for everyone. Please remember that I have been granted the power for these decisions and ultimately, I will decide who gets what. The flow of people onto this land will be at a rate of twenty million plus a week and this decision will come swiftly once it is determined."

"Understood," replies the Mexican President.

Charles addresses the group once more, "Is there any issue with being ready to load our ships and leave on our first Armada in two weeks?" No triangles are raised. He continues, "Has any of the governments had an outcry from the older members of our society that want to go?" Triangles raise for the US, Russia, and Western Europe.

"President Marco Bilabio from Italy, we have heard very little from Western Europe. I am interested in what you have to add," states Charles.

President Bilabio stands. "We have made provisions for anyone who cares to go from our country. I realize the coalition determined that it was only people that were under a certain age, but we found that many of our young people didn't believe the news and their wishes were to stay in a shelter in Italy. We have approximately one hundred thousand fewer evacuees than we proposed from our original count of the young people. So many that we offered it to the older generation."

Commander Charles replies, "That is interesting. Are these older individuals that you mention in good health?"

"Yes, they are all in very good health."

Charles adds, "The young people didn't do this as a showing of respect to their elders, did they?"

The president again responds to add, "This is not out of the question in some instances, but none that we, as their government, are aware of. The young people know what is to come, and they have noted they do not want to miss our Savior's appearance."

Charles pauses. He thinks of the belief that these people have and if he should mention the religious material that was found, in the capsule Heather discovered, concerning the Lord. He decides to keep it to himself and not mention it, as this could turn into an all-out boycott of the evacuation by Christians. He speaks, "Mr. President, as long as you have the number of individuals that are planned and they are not a major hindrance to all other members of the coalition, then I believe this is acceptable. Other countries have given passes to older individuals for various reasons as well, but you are the only group that has offered it freely."

The president responds once more, "We have enough shelters to accommodate everyone who is staying in Italy. They will be able to live the rest of their lives in these shelters, and who knows, God could pull these people in as they believe, or the scientists could be in error. God could perform a miracle."

Charles says, "Perhaps."

He looks around the room and two triangles remain for the US President and Russia. Charles says, "President Skuratov of Russia, what is it that is on your mind?"

He stands. "We have made the announcement and everyone who is going is currently preparing to board the vessels, but I have not heard when they should be launched. Is there a launch schedule for each?"

Commander Charles looks over at Joe Bennett. "Joe, I understood that all of these details had been covered."

Joe stands. "It is simply miscommunications on this country's part. We have given them all detailed instructions, sir. They all must be in orbit above our world in two weeks. They can launch now if they like. This is their choice, but at midnight on the fifteenth of October, the first Armada leaves from the orbit of the Earth, nonstop to Alpha Kantabury I. The lead ships and military ships have explicit orders to go regardless if there is only one transport from other countries there or if all five thousand ships are present."

Charles clears his throat and looks angrily at the Russian. "Have you not been informed of the protocol and plans, Mr. President?"

President Skuratov looks at the others within his group, with a flame in his eyes and responds, "Nyet! No, I have not been told of this. My sincerest apologies to the group for wasting our time."

Charles then looks at the US President, with optimism, hoping he has something tangible to say. He says, "Mr. Lynch of the USA, please let me have your questions or comments."

President Lynch says, "I believe the thousand pound gorilla in the room has not been mentioned. So our plan puts our evacuation short of the sun failing?"

Charles' face turns a shade of red. He is pretty emotional concerning this and hoped it wouldn't have been tabled for discussion. He replies with trepidation in his voice, "Yes, sir." He pauses. "Yes, sir, we now have information that appears that we shall come up short of the timeframe due to the laser monitor the Russian scientists have submitted. I have no answers for this. I can only offer the following, we have set our plan on two years in hopes that it will be enough time.

"It is too late for our resources to build any additional replication factories. There is no way that we can move the people any faster than the path we are on, and if we retool and change direction, it is possible we will not hold to the obligations that we currently have. The only words that I can offer are, send your dignitaries and young people as early as possible. If there are ways that we can prioritize whose life is more valuable than another's, then we have to do what is necessary for the good of our new society.

"Hope and pray that the six-month window that is assumed on the date from Russia falls in December of 2118 instead of in January. I was aware of this but have not wanted to discuss it, as I honestly

189

have no answers other than we will stick to our plan and get as many to Goldilocks as is humanly or godly possible." A silence fell over the room.

Charles speaks with glassy eyes once more, "We are much more successful than we would have been without the coalition, or my decisions and my group's planning. Something that should be considered is that celestial bodies rarely act quickly, and one of the things we can hope for is that when the sun fails, it isn't something that causes catastrophic destruction overnight. Perhaps it will take six months to lose the heat that is within our soil. It was described to me as the coldest winter anyone ever seen and one that will not end.

"The majority of our facilities have the capability to continue producing through temperatures of ten degrees below, maybe colder, so let's keep hope that we can still make it with everyone, and if not, perhaps that is how it is meant to be. Are there any other questions from the group?" No triangles go up and there is a hush in the room. Charles says, "We shall convene again this time next Wednesday, you ladies and gentlemen, are adjourned."

Charles, Brenda, and Woody all go to the penthouse. They look exhausted. Charles goes into his office and without saying a word tells Brenda that is a wrap for today.

She says, "No visitors?"

He replies, "Depends on the visitor. No Koreans."

"I understand, sir."

Charles calls Brenda and asks that their staff have a special meeting for Thursday, October 1.

He drafts an email to the Parche I.

Dear Jake,

The steering committee discussed the fact that the sun will perish prior to everyone's evacuation. That wasn't pretty! I can't change everything in the middle of all that is going on, though. We have developed this plan using all resources possible and as expeditiously as is viable. We must stick to the plan and get as many people out as we can. We will have the first five thousand ships leaving our orbit in two weeks. This will be on Thursday, at midnight, October 16, 2116. You should see this Armada arrive at Alpha Kantabury I on or around April 15, 2117, and they will be tired of the cruise. There will be planners that were trained by Joe Bennett and Virgil Russell that will serve to assist in the logistics.

The transport ships will be the only ones that will require a conventional landing site. This must be a very large runway. The specifications should have been communicated. If one doesn't exist, I suggest you begin work to make accommodations for one if at all possible. Otherwise, we will have to build one once the military and supply vessels land. If a runway must be constructed, it could postpone the flow of ships. We desperately need to avoid this if at all possible. All of the other ships are capable of a vertical descent, so they will be able to provide immediate assistance when they arrive. I will confirm their departure and put them in touch with you. The military and dignitary vessels will have the same communication systems as the Parche I.

On a personal note: Brenda Smith, eh? You old dog you!

Jake, keep safe and begin to prepare for their arrival.

Sincerely,

Charles Phillips Commander-in-Chief WRC

The commander has trouble with the fact that they could still lose over half of the population and they haven't even accommodated for the people in a shelter. He is the king of this coalition, appointed by the leaders of all of the countries of the world, and he has made a decision. He will put together temporary shelters and find suitable transportation, no matter what the winter weather forecast looks like. He phones his scientist, Randy Green, and asks about conditions on Earth immediately following the sun's failure.

Randy replies, "The Earth will not die immediately. It will take several years for this entire metamorphosis to occur. It will begin, as I said before, with the worst winter in the history of record keeping.

191

The oceans will begin to freeze over due to the extreme cold. It will be coldest in Antarctica and ten below at the equator."

Charles speaks on his speakerphone as Brenda enters his office and he motions her to come on in, "So, what kind of heater would be required to warm a facility at absolute zero?"

Randy replies, "A damn good one, but absolute zero isn't really expected for years to come! In actuality, you can create an environment that will sustain life for up to a couple of years. The gas bill will be quite high, but shelters could be built for the evacuees. It is in the second and third year that wildlife will have no natural resources and freeze to death. When vegetation is no longer dormant but dead is when insurmountable odds are against our inhabitants."

"Who, who could design these shelters and transportation within our coalition to sustain our people for a year?"

Randy replies, "Doug Long with the United States Air force's CE–Civil Engineering–division could help with the shelter. If he can't design and build them, then I believe he could point you toward the people that can. The transportation is tricky. What do you have in mind?"

"You tell me. What would make it through this ice age planet? What could we use to de-ice the runways?"

"All I can picture is a Greyhound bus with monster truck tires."

"Fire up the tire plants is all I know."

"Sir, I don't know if that is practical or even possible, but currently, the world is business as usual. You could build a lot in a year. Give General Brett Silvers a call. He can assist with finding a supplier. He used to handle quite a bit of the specifications and testing for the military transports and vehicles. I am sure he has some contacts."

"Thanks a great deal for the information! Goodbye, Randy." They hang up.

He then looks over at the clock. It is 4 pm. He looks at Brenda. "Do I have an opportunity for our planners tomorrow?"

Brenda responds, "You have figured out a way to keep our people safe until they leave? I knew you would. That is why our leaders picked you!"

He says, "You are such an attractive woman, did you know that?"

She says, "Gotta go!" as she chuckles. She actually finds the commander to be a very handsome and super guy, but she knows that he is somewhat of a playboy. He likes to wine and dine and have a good time with the ladies. She is not looking for a one night stand. She knows there is potential there, but Jake is a very settled down and serious man, who will likely be there for her on the new planet, and hopefully, make a life for them that is long lasting and sincere. Unless of course they don't work out, in that case, she may spend some time with Commander Charles, but will not anticipate a serious relationship.

The next day, Charles meets with his group and explains the situation and asks Virgil to do research installing adequate heat in the existing facilities around the world and coordinate this change with the administrators. He asks Joe to get in touch with the men that Randy Green mentioned and put together shelter for the evacuees after July 15, 2118. He also asks Joe to inquire about all-terrain types of transportation to and from the facility for them. He received a positive response from both of these men. He releases them with the authority to do whatever is necessary to accommodate this directive.

Chapter 24

The Explorers

On Goldilocks, the group has gone through all of the normal day to day duties on the ship. Jake sits in his quarters, looking over past emails and thinking about Brenda when a musical note signals that he has new mail. It is from Charles Phillips.

Dear Jake,

The steering committee discussed the fact that the sun will perish prior to everyone's evacuation. That wasn't pretty! I can't change everything in the middle of all that is going on, though. We have developed this plan using all resources possible and as expeditiously as is viable. We must stick to the plan and get as many people out as we can. We will have the first five thousand ships leaving our orbit in two weeks. This will be on Thursday, at midnight, October 16, 2116. You should see this Armada arrive at Alpha Kantabury I on or around April 15, 2117, and they will be tired of the cruise. There will be planners that were trained by Joe Bennett and Virgil Russell that will serve to assist in the logistics.

The transport ships will be the only ones that will require a conventional landing site. This must be a very large runway. The specifications should have been communicated. If one doesn't exist, I suggest you begin work to make accommodations for one if at all possible. Otherwise, we will have to build one once the military and supply vessels land. If a runway must be constructed, it could postpone the flow of ships. We desperately need to avoid this if at all possible. All of the other ships are capable of a vertical descent, so they will be able to provide immediate assistance when they arrive. I will confirm their departure and put them in touch with you. The military and dignitary vessels will have the same communication systems as the Parche I.

On a personal note: Brenda Smith, eh? You old dog you!

Jake, keep safe and begin to prepare for their arrival.

Sincerely,

Charles Phillips Commander-in-Chief WRC

Dean is getting a little restless with their accommodations. He goes to the commander's quarters. Jake welcomes him in. They sit in Jake's living area and begin discussing their plan. Dean asks, "What is our next move?"

Jake responds, "Well, we have much to do, but the first group of people isn't due to arrive until April. We need to find a runway that will accommodate the transport ships. We need to scout the area and find areas that are suitable to set up shelters and build towns."

"How do you feel about personal weapons, Jake?"

"I believe they will be necessary if we travel anywhere and must go without the protection of the shields. We have the armory in the bridge if it is necessary."

"I want to go exploring through the base. To see what housing is there. If they have food stores and things like we have back on Earth."

Jake asks, "What mode of transportation will you use?"

"I don't know. I suppose I will walk if need be, but I bet the guards don't walk."

"I imagine they have a garage around here somewhere and there are a couple of cars in the parking lot. I will get in touch with Murdock later today and you and Heather can go sightseeing tomorrow."

Dean was looking forward to getting away from the compound. He was a little disappointed that the commander wasn't ready to turn him loose right then. Dean says, "Very well. What do you want me to do for the rest of the day, Commander?" It is about noon on the planet and Dean has finished his duties for the day.

"Help Heather finish hers and you two take the rest of the day off. Go explore the grounds, play some racquetball, get back some of that sleep that I have taken from you. What time will you be ready tomorrow for your trip?"

195

"I am ready now." He smiles and gets a sour serious look back from the commander. Dean quickly says, "I will be ready by 10 am Alpha Kantabury I time."

"I will get with Murdock and if he can't accommodate that time, then I will let you know."

"Excellent!" Dean exclaims.

Greg sits beside Ted on the bridge. With a smile on his face, he asks, "Ted, did you score with Gwen?"

"When you say score?" He chuckles.

Greg responds, "Did you do the nasty, jump her bones?"

"Well, a gentleman never tells."

"I know you, you ole horn dog, and you have never been considered a gentleman, a wild thang, maybe. You forget the times we went clubbing, ole buddy? What is her assistant's name?"

Ted inquires, "How do you even know about her assistant? Who is actually the same as she is. She is no assistant. Her name is Detsyl, or Detty as Gwen called her when she was screaming at her last night 'cause she spanked a little too hard."

Greg exclaims, "No shit!"

Ted starts to reply and they hear Commander Jake enter the bridge. He explains with a bit of disappointment, "Your comms channel is open, guys!"

Ted says, "Do what? That is not possible. I checked when I heard Greg start this conversation."

Jake looks over at Dean's console. "Looks like the old man got you. Your mic is open to my quarters."

Ted says, "That evil old fucker. Will you turn it off, please?"

Jake laughs. "Absolutely, but I want to hear about this sex party with the maids last night, Ted!"

"Commander, I was putting Greg on."

"Don't bullshit your commander."

"I wouldn't do that, sir."

Greg interrupts, "You lying sack of shit!"

Ted asks, "Commander, we are about done for this morning. May we take off the rest of the day?"

"You both still have some PMI–preventative maintenance inspections–that I haven't seen come across my desk yet."

"Yes, sir, but the craft is on the ground and these inspections typically get lax during this time," speaks Ted.

"Have you done your checklist for flight?"

"Per protocol, and we have run diagnostics on the shields. Sir, we will not get lax to a point that is reckless."

Jake says, "Very well, but PMIs don't go over a day past, regardless. We could be in space in an hour if the situation dictates it."

"Understood," reply Ted and Greg in unison.

"You two are excused, don't you come back with some new STD that will rot your tallywacker off."

"Aye aye, sir," they both reply.

Ted and Greg enter the front door of the estate. Gwen and Detty are both sitting in their little glass room, drinking what appears to be wine, laughing, and chatting. Greg thinks they are talking about Ted from last night. Ted carries his interpreting device up to the entry to their room as they sit there, not even noticing the men have entered the foyer. Ted speaks, "What does a man have to do to get a drink around here?"

Clearly startled, Gwen looks up with surprise on her face that obviously turned to joy when seeing the pilot. She replies and the interpreting device speaks as she talks in a foreign tongue, "What would you like to have for a beverage?"

He replies, "The beer we had last night was a little stout for my taste. Do you have any beer that is not brown in color, perhaps a blond beer?"

Gwen thinks about what he said. "Yes, in the bar."

Greg speaks up, "You have a bar?"

"Yes, however, without our usual complement of officers from the military base and our ambassador not entertaining, I expect that it is pretty empty and we will probably have to obtain our own drinks. I haven't seen the server down there since the others left. I believe she was related to the ambassador. She probably left with him. It all happened so quickly that I didn't get to take roll call. We are still deciding who we still have."

Greg says, "Awesome, are there other females like y'all?" Ted rolls his eyes as the girls look on.

Detty speaks up, "No other females are like us."

Greg realizing his error, *even with Alpha Kantabury I women,* he says, "Not *like* you two, but other girls?"

Detty says, "Yes, there are still a number of females that work to maintain the facilities."

"Let's get to the bar!" exclaims Greg. Ted kind of glances in his direction and nods, like okay.

They take a short walk, following these two beautiful women to a staircase that is behind the grand stairs that leads up to the second level. They turn to the right and there is a door. They open the door and walk down this small narrow flight of stairs into a kitchen. Stainless steel pans hang on hooks and the facility resembles one on Earth to almost a "T" except there is also quite a bit of gold-colored utensils and serving platters lying around, neatly stored. They walk through this area, past a swinging door, and into a dimly lit room with tables and chairs. They see some guys that appear to be security guards from the penthouse. One of them in a black jumpsuit and black hat looks back with surprise on his face and scowls toward the men with these ladies. Gwen speaks to a young lady that is sitting with this group. The interpreter repeats her words in English. "Jelk, I need you to monitor the front for a while." This beautiful, young dark haired lady gets up from her group and walks out of the room, with particular focus on Greg. Gwen says, "Take a seat and I will see

198

if I can find you that blond…beer." Ted and Greg both get a kick out of that, and they have a seat on the opposite end of the bar from the military men.

Greg says, "So, Detty, are you currently seeing anyone?"

"I see you, I see Ted."

"Excuse me. The interpreter is not always so well at interpreting my words. What I mean is, are you in a relationship with a member of the opposite sex?"

"No, no one exclusive," she replies.

"Do you have anything against earthlings?" Greg asks.

"I don't know. You are the first that I have met." She glances at Ted and says, "If you all are anything like Ted was last night, then I like earthlings." They get a look from a couple of the military group. Greg looks over at Ted like you SOB!

Greg says, "You guys aren't dating any of the guards, are you?"

Detty smiles. "No, I have, but currently, I am not."

"That is good because they don't look that friendly to me."

"Are they making you feel uncomfortable or scared?"

Greg looks at her as if she had called him a coward and replies, "Scared? I rode a bottle rocket faster than light for the past six months. I am far from scared."

She realizes that she has said something wrong. She wants to be sure that she isn't offending him. He is a vibrant man, so she says, "The interpreter must change around my words, too. What I mean is, these people are here to keep you and me safe. You should not have any trepidation toward them." She then calls out, "Jerdek, come over, meet my friends." Three of the large men dressed in black get up and make their way across the bar. He gets to their table and asks, "Who are these strange men that you sit with? Are they the earthlings?"

Detty replies, "Yes, this is Greg and Ted." She then introduces the military men. "Ted, Greg, this is Jerdek, Rekote or Reko, and Senkio or Senk." The men exchange kind gestures, but then they all become silent. It is a little awkward as none of these men have any idea what to say or not say to each other.

Gwen then returns with Ted's beer. Ted says, "Aw Michelob. That would be nice if you brought me a nice cold Michelob Light."

Gwen says, "Try it." Ted takes a sip and is absolutely astonished. It is Michelob or as close as it is possible to one. It could have a slight bit more flavor, but they just about nailed his favorite beer. He asks, "What is the name of this ale?"

She replies, "I believe it is…" she speaks without the aid of the interpreter and says, "…Mike Ale Olbe."

He responds, "You actually have a beer here on Alpha Kantabury that is called Michelob?"

"I have to be honest. I went to your ship and asked Commander Jake if he had your favorite ale. He went to a funny looking sink and said 'Michelob' and it filled this mug for you."

Ted thinks of how awesome this lady is to do that for him. He says, "I see, you sneaky little lady!"

Jerdek speaks up and says, "You have no idea." Gwen cuts her eyes at him. He says, "A little Malpeadan humor. I didn't mean anything by that."

"Okay," Gwen says. She returns to behind the bar and comes back with a pitcher of the beer that Ted likes so much and sits it on the counter.

Greg says, "Man, I should have asked for some Bud Light." Gwen returns to the bar and returns with a second pitcher. Greg says, "I could get used to this! You asked the commander for me, too?"

"Certainly. He had no issue and kind of laughed when he figured out what I was doing. I am your host and if I can please you, that is my desire."

"Damn!" exclaimed Greg. Jerdek looks on with a little hint of envy. They have a few drinks and Jerdek and the others give this ale a try, and before you know it, they strike up a conversation.

200

Jerdek says, "So the planet Earth, is that correct?"

Ted replies, "Yes, that is where we are from."

Reko inquires, "How far away is this planet?"

Ted says, "Twelve light years. That is six months at a speed of twenty times the speed of light." They all have a sigh and a bit of a wow in response to this news. "How did you all obtain propulsion that can do this?" asks Jerdek.

Greg answers, "We designed it. Actually, the scientists of our world built this. The head man is riding with us. Dean Stinson is the smartest guy I know."

Ted then responds, "So we gathered information from your capsule in orbit of the planet. Your society is very stringent on crime?"

Jerdek answers. "Yes, since the war. We used to be ruled by corrupt politicians and kept in debt by businesses. We had a war and ejected all of these people. In our country, you can't have a job that isn't providing a service or a product. No job is based on obtaining currency from wealth that you have. This is against the law. Does your technologically advanced society have these rules?"

Ted is feeling the beer and isn't that comfortable discussing these things in very much depth but has to give some explanation. He explains, "Our world is dying. We are currently in such a state of panic that there is a world order called the WRC. WRC stands for World Relocation Coalition. This group has all of the leaders of our world banding together to find some way to save our civilization's inhabitants. This has put a very different face on our world in the past few years, however, we do have bankers that collect money for the sake of allowing others to use this money. We have lawyers that convince others that someone is at fault and they earn money by arguing and proving that this was unjust, or the person was doing wrong."

Jerdek replies, "We have lawyers but they are paid for by the government. We use them for no cost. They are simply there to investigate and help the judges decide if someone was treated unfairly."

Ted asks, "Free to you, huh? These people in our world are considered evil by many because they cost so much to use their service."

Jerdek says "Gentlemen, we all have to be on point at 0500. Please excuse us." The three men then get up and exit the bar. The others at the table they previously sat at were already gone.

Greg looks over at Ted and says, "That is very interesting. I don't understand how any of that would work for our people." Ted has made up his mind that it may not be a choice depending upon the requirements that Malpeada places upon the castaways. He simply replies, "I suppose we shall see, Greg. I suppose we shall see."

Since the military guys have left, Greg feels a little more relaxed and starts teasing around with the girls. He boasts of his position with WRC and how he is the youngest of his crew. The girls seem to be entertained by his antics until it starts getting late. Gwen says, "Gentlemen, I hate to put an end to our fun, but we both need to get up early ourselves."

Greg looks somewhat surprised. He quickly asks, "Detty, would you like to come to my room for a little music, maybe some coffee, or TV?"

Detty smiles contently and says, "Not tonight. Gwen is right, we should get some rest." Greg is very persistent to the point that Ted, in an authoritative voice, says, "Greg, the ladies are tired. Give them a break. There is always tomorrow and many other ladies around this complex." Without saying much more, Greg gets up and leaves the bar through the kitchen and as he passes through you can hear pots and pans clanging around as his drunk ass staggers through there. He gets to the top of the stairs and scratches his head as he finds the room that he picked out the night before.

He decides he isn't tired enough to go straight to bed and finds his way to the top floor deck. He walks onto the deck, discovering

Dean and Heather arm-in-arm. They look up to see Greg and he shakes his head and says, "Throw me in a barrel of titties and I would come out sucking my thumb!" Then he looks at the obviously displeased faces of both of his crewmembers and realizes that isn't a kind thing to say in the presence of Heather. He says, "My apologies for both interrupting your romantic evening and my nasty mouth."

Heather replies, "No problem. Are you all right, Greg?"

Greg says, "Define all right. It seems that all of the damn old men are getting the pretty young ladies."

Dean says, "Give it time and you'll be an old man." He chuckles.

"This isn't the best idea. My barging in on y'all was rude. I am going to bed."

Heather says, "Just one thing there, old buddy. Have you been drinking?"

"Fuck no, I have been freebasing cocaine. Can't you see my singed hair?"

Dean looks as though he is going to line Greg's young smart ass out and just then Heather says, "Drinking, eh?"

Greg says, "Yeah, sorry, not to be rude, but I am going to bed."

Dean remarks, "I think it would be more rude to stay."

Greg makes his way through the double French doors and onto the winding staircase to the level below and goes left down the hallway to his room. He passes Ted's room and hears female laughter coming from inside. He is mad enough to bite nails in two. He slams his door open to hear the laughter pause. He yells, "Wore out? Those girls are just too tired to party with me!" Then he goes inside and passes out on his bed, alone, inebriated, and confused.

The next morning Dean and Heather are again early risers. They love the upper-level deck and sit out under the blood red moon, enjoying each other's company. Dean says, "I have a treat for today."

"Oh yeah? What do you have planned?"

He responds, "I have to wait for Jake before I know for sure." Heather, with eyebrows at full staff, says, "Jake? What does he have to do with the surprise?" Just then the commander comes walking out on the deck. He greets them, "Good morning. I hope that I am not intruding."

Dean replies, "Not at all, Commander, especially if you have good news about our surprise for today."

Jake says, "Oh yeah. Be ready at 9 am Alpha Kantabury I time and Murdock said that he would be ready and take you guys."

Heather is really curious now. "Take us where?"

"You didn't tell her, huh?"

Dean smirks. "Nope, I thought it would be a nice surprise if we could and a big disappointment if we couldn't." He then looks over at Heather. "The commander has agreed to let us go onto the base and explore, or scout the area. We need to get a good look at their runways and see what kinds of stores there are and how much housing exists on there."

Heather has a big smile on her face. "Just us?"

Dean says, "With the exception of Murdock and possibly some of his people."

"Fantastic, that sounds great. We get to go exploring!" Heather exclaims.

Dean is wearing his ole trusty, thick blue PJs and Heather has on her plush, pink robe. They are all huddled up around the fire, awaiting the appearance of the sunrise. And day two begins on Goldilocks. They watch what proves to be a even more gorgeous sunrise than the day before. It is still very chilly and they are enjoying the outdoor fireplace. Ted comes out, with Gwen and Detty close behind, and Jake actually busts out with a laugh. The other two can't contain theirs after Jake turned loose, and they all three have a short burst of laughter at this sight. Ted and the two girls, all with big smiles, kind of shake their heads and Ted says, "What?" He chuckles. "What is so darn funny, you three?"

Jake replies, "Where is your wingman, studly?"

"Greg drank a little much last night and got a little belligerent."

Jake asks, "Is he okay?"

"I didn't tuck his rude ass in last night, but I heard him come in slamming doors and cussing. It is my belief that he is okay, just a little hung over this morning probably."

"I see," says Jake.

Gwen asked if they would like some breakfast and gets a yes from most all of the crew. The two girls disappear into the home and the crew sit and talk about plans for the day. Soon breakfast was served, with no sign of Greg, and they got on with their day.

The group has Greg sitting with them in their stations when 8:45 am shows on the clock. Jake's voice comes over the comm, "Ted, have you started the PMs yet?"

"No, sir. We will begin on them around 9:30 am. We certainly haven't forgotten, sir."

"Great. Is there anything that is required of Dean or Heather?"

Ted comes back on, "Not that I can think of, sir."

Jake replies, "Dean, Heather, you can leave to meet up with Murdock now."

Dean says, "Awesome, Commander! We will be on our way in a few minutes." He then directs his attention to Ted. "I will need you to drop the shields while we exit the grounds."

"Where are you guys going?"

"Downtown! Onto the base to see what is there. To get a map if even possible." Greg sits very quietly and moves his head very little.

Ted says, "Well, no one asked us if we wanted to go."

Dean says, "Someone has to man the fort. I can tell when the shields are off by the repeaters' light arrays. We will somehow get your attention when we arrive back. Try to keep an eye out for us. Maybe we can beep the horn if Malpeada has horns."

They leave the ship and walk over to the front door of the embassy and enter. Murdock is waiting inside. They all greet and he begins walking to the staircase to the left. They pass it and beneath it, they find a door. Murdock enters and they follow. They go down a short flight of steps and through a second door to find a parking garage. They walk up to a vehicle that resembles an extra cab pickup truck. They climb inside and exit the grounds. They travel down a freshly paved road and begin to pass houses. The houses are a bland gray color and are finished with a stucco pattern. Dean says, "Funny, it is like we are back home."

Murdock speaks and the interpreting device begins to speak, "You have homes like these on your world?"

Heather says, "Homes, embassies, roads, and vehicles. They look a little different, but the shape and style are very similar."

Murdock replies, "Interesting."

They continue to pass road after road, with houses as far as you can see. Dean remarks, "There sure are a lot of them. How many people could this base accommodate?"

Murdock says, "Enough troops to defend against the wild ones on Stilligate. This base will likely hold twelve million men. This will include the barracks."

"Twelve million, huh? That will hold about half of our first Armada."

Murdock about runs off the road and responds, "How many will come with each Armada?"

Dean answers, "The commander mentioned around twenty million per Armada."

"Wow! Where are all these people going to stay? The base will be filled with the first load," Murdock states.

"They will have supply ships that will provide temporary shelter."

They turn left and arrive at a runway. It is a very long runway that has two others that meet up together at the center. They drive out onto the runway and Murdock starts to speed up. They must be going 100mph in a matter of a few minutes. Ten minutes pass and he starts to slow. They come to a stop and he speaks, "This is the end of runway A. B is the same length in that direction. There are twelve runways assembled end-to-end in this fashion."

Dean replies, "This will work well. Do you have any actual specifications for length and weight rating?"

"Yes, in the archives. I will request them for you when we get back to the embassy."

They leave here and travel a short distance to a storefront. They walk up and go through glass doors into a store. There are beverages, food, clothes, camping supplies, guns, ammunition, and all types of typical department store items. They walk through the store and a lady comes out to greet them. She is a stocker/cashier. They just say hi and make their way through the store and back outside to the truck. It is sitting in an empty parking lot, with the exception of two or three vehicles. It appears almost abandoned. They climb into the truck and Dean says, "I was kind of surprised to see someone manning the store."

Murdock asks, "Why? We still have troops that are maintaining the base. It is a small crew, but there are about five hundred people here."

Dean asks, "Should we feel safe to go here alone?"

"Has anyone issued you two passes?"

Heather replies, "No."

"As long as you have a pass, you are safe on this base. When we get back, I will see that everyone gets these and a card that will allow you to purchase items if you like."

Heather gets a big smile on her face.

Dean says, "A free credit card. Heather is going *shopping*!" Murdock just looks ahead.

They arrive back at the embassy and the lights go red on the repeaters. Dean previously explained to Murdock how they work. He pulls in and Dean and Heather thank him for taking them on a tour of the base. They say their goodbyes and go back to their respective areas.

Chapter 25

Mass Exodus

      The two weeks on Earth seem to pass rather quickly and the fifteenth of October arrives. Commander Charles sits with a few of the board members, Brenda, Woody, General Silvers, the US President, and the Canadian Prime Minister, in a control room in his facility in Las Vegas. The satellite systems have a tracking device that shows every single one of the five thousand ships as they prepare to leave. The radio has a ton of people talking on several frequencies. It is 11:45 pm and the first fleet's departure is at hand. As the clock counts down, the US President is a little concerned as this is the biggest fleet ever deployed on air, land, sea, or space, especially in space.

      He says, "Commander, a short one hundred years ago, we dismantled the space shuttle program, little did we know that it would not only start over again on this same frame but it would turn into the WRC's FTL transport ship. How will these pilots keep a formation that keeps each ship from colliding with each other?"

      The commander feels confident about how all of this will work since he was the manager over Dean Stinson and his highly skilled crew when they decided how to travel in groups. He responds with authority, "Sir, each ship has sensors that will steer them away from the other ships. They can't be within three miles of one another at any one time. In the vastness of space, they will not follow and lead. They will be wing tip to wing tip for the entire journey, and each pilot will synchronize their ship to the lead ship. They will actually resemble a flock of geese as they travel to their destination, twenty-five hundred ships per side, with the lead bird in the middle."

      The president says, "I read something about how they would get in the flock formation. Is there enough room within our solar system to maintain this gap and span? It sounds like they will be taking up a seventy-five hundred km plus wide area. Why should they not travel nose to tail? It seems they would be more organized and less likely to collide with anything this way."

The commander comes back and says, "Sir, you must realize that the sensors on these ships can detect an object the size of a bird one thousand miles in front of them. They have shields that combine together that can deflect an asteroid that is fifty miles across. In nose-to-tail formation, if one ship fails in front of the other, there is no reaction time and their shields will be interlocked as if they are under a blanket together. One ship toward the lead could destroy half to three-quarters of the Armada if it were to fail or lose propulsion."

"That is brilliant. I am happy to have you as the one making these decisions."

Charles responds, "I only led these men and agreed with their assessment of the methods."

The radio voices begin to quieten when a number begins on every television, radio, and Internet newsfeed as it is 11:59 pm and the world watches their manmade salvation leave their solar system. Ten...nine...eight...seven...six...five...four...three...two...one. And the sky above the darkened Earth lights up with the bright light from the heavens. There are people on rooftops and lying in truck beds, with their spouses, looking up to the sky to see these manmade stars that are streaking across the sky. The light from each of the five thousand FTL engines light the sky with lime green streaks in spectacular glory from Alaska to Brazil.

The group within the control room is in contact with the lead ship. It is an American replicated and piloted dignitary craft. He comes on the radio and says, "Arc 0.0, Jeff Briscoe to Earth control." The man sitting at the back of the room responds, "Earth control; go ahead Arc 0.0." The voice on the radio says, "We are all a little uneven for startup, but we expect this to plane out once we hit FTL speed. We have all ships indicating green lights on my panel and want confirmation. Also, request release from Earth control," as the voice begins to become static filled. The controller responds, "All green indicators from Earth, and permission granted to take control

210

of your fleet, Captain." The voice comes back on once again, "Understood. Arc 0.0 to all of the fleet and Earth control. We are now out of range of the Earth's communications and I now am assuming control of the Armada. Gentlemen and ladies, we are on our own. Arc 0.0 over and out." There are other voices that the group begins to hear, "Arc zero one reporting." The voices fade to a low static-riddled sound and they silence the communications channels.

It is now 3:00 am and a successful launch has been witnessed for the first of thousands of voyages to their new land. Using telescopes, people all over the world watch the lights from the engines, and many are just gazing upon the night sky. Most continue to watch until the sky fades back to black. Many will be on one of those transports within the following two years. Many have no idea the sun is scheduled to fail prior to the last ship's departure.

In Vegas, the big night is over. The commander, Brenda, Woody, and the US President all go to Commander Charles' office. They sit around a small meeting table. Woody says, "Where are all of our planners?"

Charles responds, "They were all invited, they may be on one of those ships," as he chuckles. "Mr. President, I have noticed that there hasn't been any official press release on the date of the anticipated failure of the sun or the intent of housing our evacuees in holding camps when Earth becomes frozen. I have formally released this tentative plan to the administration, with the intent that your group will decide the direction for the Public Relations and the ramifications of this PR announcement."

The president says, "It has already been leaked. I believe the Koreans have released the information. They are probably just trying to cause havoc because we aren't playing their style of hardball. At least they aren't like the out of oil and broke Islamic nations. These people have a desert to live in and are at the rest of the world's mercy for their ride to the new world. Egypt and Turkey were kind enough to allow a limited number that are not radicals to hitch a ride, but due to their uncivilized methods and attacks on countries of our world, no one would grant them passage for previous crimes that many of their

211

religion doesn't seem to condemn." The president pauses and says, "Sorry, I just can't support any religion that would encourage hatred and prejudice toward others. I also fear that if Turkey has released this information to one of the other Islamic nations, they would broadcast it as well.

"On the topic of the announcement, it isn't planned at this time, but it has already been on the Internet. The CIA has sent me links to conspiracy theorists that have obtained the information. They actually have a factual assessment, but we don't have to confirm the information and we have over a year to break this news. We must get a few safe voyages behind us before we officially release the information. *Do not* let anything stop your planners from creating these temporary shelters and creating a condition to allow us to be able to continue replication of these crafts across the world!"

Charles responds, "That was almost a speech, Mr. President. I am compelled to clap." He chuckles. He continues, "Mr. President, I have released my planners with authority to do what is necessary to create these shelters. I would be very surprised if construction hasn't already started across the United States." They are all tired from the long day. Charles dismisses the group and they all go home for a good night's sleep.

On Goldilocks, the time passes rather quickly as well. The crew goes about their day-to-day activities. They wake on the morning of the sixteenth and man their stations on the ship to go through typical work. Heather receives a transmission from Earth. It is a voice transmission from Commander-in-Chief Charles Phillips. Jake is sitting at his console in his quarters when Heather comes over the intercom. "Incoming voice transmission from Commander Charles Phillips to the Parche I." Jake's voice then comes over the comms and says, "Go ahead and play it."

Commander Charles' voice sounds thick and he stumbles his words slightly as he speaks. He says, "Parche I, you have company coming your way. The first fleet of five thousand ships launched from the orbit of the Earth at midnight last night. It was a successful launch, and you should be prepared to greet your guest in six months from today's date. I, and most of the world, have been up all night to witness the event that should become quite common over the next two years. We are all celebrating the flawless launch that has been such a long time coming. Commander Charles Phillips out."

There is silence on the bridge. Dean says, "Well, I guess this really has begun. This is indeed the proudest moment of my life."

Ted speaks up, "None of this would be possible without your hard work and brilliance."

Dean smiles, and replies, "I know!"

Ted comes back and responds, "And so humble to boot!" The room goes quiet again as they get back to their work.

Back on Earth, the big news of the first successful voyage is all over the news sources. Headlines read "WRC Sends Twenty Million Into The Unknown". Other headlines read "WRC Lights Up The Night Sky From The North To South Pole". They have talk show hosts that are interviewing people who worked in the replication facilities.

The White House has their speaker reporting with two thumbs up. In an interview at the White House, they ask Speaker Jonathan Smith about Commander Phillips. The reporter says, "This man is being revered as a superhero and no one can get any time to speak with him. Why is that, Mr. Speaker?"

He responds, "Avoiding the public eye was part of his agreement with the nations of the world. He wanted anonymity and his contract dictates that he is not responsible for any PR and is in control of the coalition but doesn't have any obligation to speak on behalf of it publicly. I believe he has made a wise choice, as this keeps his focus where it needs to be and that is on the movements of the people and the monumental challenge of building these ships that everyone must agree is at a phenomenal pace."

He calls on another reporter and she says, "Mr. Speaker, we have all seen the schedule for the movement to the new world and no one who is going disagrees that it is a tremendous task. However, there are people that will still be stuck here on Earth during the middle of next year when some sources are saying the sun will fail for its first phase. Can you confirm this as factual?"

The Speaker looks visibly shaken by this inquiry and he is privy to the fact that the sun's estimated "Red Giant" phase is predicted to begin on July 15, 2118, but he has been told not to mention it. They didn't cover if they asked specific questions concerning it and to avoid it, he must lie. He grits his teeth and begins, "There have been predictions on the end of the world since the beginning of mankind. I believe there are some predictions going on at this time. No one can say with one hundred percent certainty precisely when this event will occur. I feel confident in telling you, regardless of what happens, preparations are being made to accommodate anyone who is here and those who have a seat reserved on a transport to keep them safe. Production of the ships will continue until the last person is evacuated from our doomed planet."

Another reporter asks, "What preparations are being made, Mr. Speaker?"

He replies once more, "There are grand shelters that will hold millions upon millions of people comfortably. The manufacturing facilities that produce the spacecrafts are all being fitted with environmental controls that will keep these plants in operation through any weather imaginable. Large Alaskan road clearing machinery is being brought in to ensure a passage can be made to accommodate the replicator's raw materials and the road for the people to travel can be cleared. Massive electricity producing generators are being sized and fueled in the event that power is lost for both the manufacturing plants and the camps."

The word "camps" set off a flurry of reporters yelling out questions like, "Camps, what kind of camps? Is it a conspiracy to get the elite out and leave the rest of us to die in concentration camps?" He quickly realizes that the word "camps" could not have been a poorer choice of words and he just wants to get away from the lynching that appears is about to take place. He then walks across the platform, two special agents come to escort him and to ensure his security team meets up and surrounds him, he walks away, with a red

214

face, saying, "That is all for now. They are not camps. They are closer to large apartment complexes."

It is now Friday morning, and Brenda and Charles are preparing for their morning meeting with the planners. They sit in the commander's office watching the press meeting. When it is over, Charles says, "Camps? He actually used the word *camp*? Where did this guy come from? Camp is a bad word for use with a group of reporters. They have FEMA camps, concentration camps, and to refer to a holding facility that will ensure the survival of our people prior to being able to evacuate them is preposterous to call it camps!

"7:25 am, it is about meeting time." Him and Brenda take the familiar walk to the elevator and travel down a floor to the meeting room that has the large conference table. Joe Bennett, Virgil Russell, Woody, General Silvers, and the others wait as he and Brenda enter the room. He takes his seat at the end of the table and starts the meeting. "Where were you guys on Wednesday night?" He is looking at the planners.

Joe speaks up first. "I was in bed sleeping. Once they are in orbit, they are someone else's problem."

Charles inquires, "Problem, huh? I guess you slept well?"

Joe replies, "Always, sir."

"No matter. I just thought there would have been more interaction in the control room from you two," Charles states.

He wants an update on the efforts to accommodate the people that are left behind and to ensure the continued production of ships after January 1, 2118, as this is the first possible date that the sun could begin to burn out. He begins, "Joe, did you get in touch with the man concerning transportation?"

"I did and I have begun setting up the purchase of an all wheel drive bus that will be used at each of the American sites. I also took the liberty, since it seems that I am responsible for transportation for this endeavor, to set up equipment that can clean the ice and snow from the roads to ensure safe passage. I sent out a memo to all involved."

Charles responds, "Good thinking, as we haven't discussed this aspect. What about other areas of the world? Have you informed others of your actions and recommended they do something similar?"

Joe replies, "Yes, hell, Korea thought I was setting up theirs as well. I explained that each division is responsible for their own actions and we don't have time or resources to go around and accommodate all of the other areas. I think they got the picture."

"Virgil, have you started work on the shelters, or *camps* as our White House speaker put it?"

Virgil chuckles in a very low rumble and says, "Yes, sir. I have assembled teams at every site. They are going to work on heaters and thermostats that will produce enough heat to keep everyone at a hundred degrees, if necessary, at -60 degrees Fahrenheit outside."

Charles responds, "Should we be trying to accommodate for -459 degrees Fahrenheit?"

"No, sir. The sun isn't going to fall from the sky. It will simply be much colder. We will experience an ice age here on Earth that never recovers. It may be at absolute zero at some point, however, this will not be until the sun is completely burned out and there is no atmosphere and no orbit around the sun. By that time, if anything is living on Earth, it is because a supernatural force has intervened."

"I understand." Charles continues, as he already had prior knowledge from Randy, "I had no idea that you had this kind of knowledge of the path that our world will take during this time."

Virgil says, "I called Randy, as you suggested. He filled me in on all of this stuff."

"Okay, do you know how cold it will become?"

"It depends on where you are, but Randy said the North and South Poles would still be the coldest, but they shall only get to sixty degrees below within the first year. The Earth has a certain amount of heat within its core. The entire ordeal will take a considerable amount of time."

216

"I have never asked Randy how long total following the "Red Giant" phase before it becomes inhabitable."

Joe responds, "I did. The answer surprised me as a Christian. Randy is a true scientist and has little knowledge of the Bible. His answer was approximately seven years for anything without a shelter." The room became silent.

After a short period of time, Charles speaks up, "Well, it appears everyone has their business in order. Let's hope for the sake of the other nations that they do as well. We all need to be prepared to leave and enter into orbit next week so that we can meet our departure date of October 29. We need to be boarded and prepared to leave Area 51 on Friday, October 23. Everyone needs their counterparts that will be assuming their roles here, on Earth, versed on what must occur before we leave. Meeting adjourned."

Brenda calls her mom and asks if she is all packed up and ready to go. She explains they are going to board the ship on Monday to prepare for departure on Friday. All of the other members of the commander's cabinet share the details to their families. They all begin to pack and prepare for the big day.

Monday morning arrives and Brenda meets the commander, her mom, dad, and sister, Sheena. Sheena also has dark hair and she is a year younger than Brenda at thirty-one years of age. The guard comes out to greet the group and escort them to their new home. Sheena asks, "Will we be living here until Friday when we depart?"

The commander says, "Not unless you want to, young lady. The ship will be on a GPU–Ground Power Unit–and an umbilical that will give the craft full amenities."

"Brenda explained the inside of it is like a cruise ship. If it is like that, I may not want to leave."

"In the next six months, I fear that you will be tired of your cruise ship. If I were you, I would get checked in, find your cabin, get all of your items ready for the trip, and then go out and enjoy your last week on Earth."

"Sounds like a plan, big chief. You care to join me?"

"You know…I just might." He hands her a business card. "Give me a call if you get out and want some company."

"Don't be surprised if I call."

"Don't be surprised if I meet up with you."

Brenda's dad, Jim Smith, just looks on as if he isn't too impressed with his daughter's forwardness. He questions, "Commander, why are we doing all of this four days before our departure?"

"Brenda gets picking choice of the cabins. There are others coming through the week, but your family and mine are the first to get checked in. I was serious about you staying if you like, but I fear you'll regret it after six months in this tin can."

Jim responds, "I agree."

Wednesday night comes and Commander Phillips is at his office watching midnight approach, alone, with cameras that are affixed in the control room. He is anticipating the launch as it is scheduled once again for midnight. His phone begins to ring. He answers, "Hello." It is Sheena on the other end. She explains she is down at the Foxtail Nightclub and would like some company. Charles tells her he is preparing to watch this week's launch.

He asks, "How would you like to come here and we can watch it from the roof?" She is a little surprised as it sounds somewhat romantic but agrees. She arrives after about a half hour. They greet and he asks, "Are you ready? It is now 11:30 pm. We can get up there and get settled before the show." They get into the elevator and arrive at the top of this large skyscraper. The wind is fairly strong and there is a chill in the air on this October night. There is a garden area with AstroTurf, padded lawn chairs, and a small portable heater. The two make their way to this area and the commander fires up the heater. They both sit in a love seat made just for two. They talk some more but get quiet when they know it is close to the time for the launch. They both look up at the crystal clear night sky and once again, the streaks from the ships cross the horizon. They have had

218

another successful launch. The two spend most of the rest of the night up there talking about the trip and getting very well acquainted.

It is near 4 am when Sheena says, "I have had a wonderful time. You will be on our ship for the voyage?"

Charles cheerfully responds, "Yes, absolutely, and I would very much enjoy doing this again with you." They make their way down the stairs and into his office and she leaves.

The next morning Brenda and Charles meet to start their day and she goes to fix coffee and comes walking back out with a red and white scarf. She carries it into Charles' office. "Sheena's?"

"Yes, as a matter of fact, she watched the launch with me last night."

Brenda makes a humphing sound. "I see."

It is Friday morning and they all meet at the ship near the large runway. There is a fairly large crowd boarding. Brenda, Sheena, and her mom, Janet, all board the ship and find their way to their luxurious quarters. It doesn't take very long and they feel the spacecraft move. The captain comes on the intercom and says, "Ladies and gentlemen, this is your captain speaking. I am Captain Dalton Coleman. Each passenger must find their way to the launch seats. If you could direct your attention to the television sets in your rooms, there is an instructional video on where each is located and how to use them. It is just like a commercial airliner seat. There are many attendants throughout the ship stationed in the hallways outside of your cabins. If you have any question about what seat is the launch seat or how to fasten your lap belt, please call on your attendant to assist you. It is a cool forty-seven degrees in Southern Nevada this morning and a slight breeze from the West. We are first in line to depart and I expect we will be underway shortly.

"Ladies and gentlemen, enjoy our launch. I will be back in touch when we are in orbit over Earth and it is safe for you to move about the spacecraft." They all glance at the television and there is a video showing where those seats are located and how to use the belt. The video plays continuously.

219

In very short time they are on the runway and into the air. It is a very smooth liftoff and soon they are seeing blue flashes outside of the ship through the television monitor. There is a feeling of uneasiness among the group as they pass through the atmosphere into outer space. Soon they are in orbit and everyone is free to move around.

Chapter 26

Breaking New Ground

On Goldilocks, the group is becoming somewhat bored of the little area they are staying in. They have all hung out with security, learned how the cameras work, heard stories of the battles they have fought, and spent time with the gardener, maids, and the handyman. They all find it pretty dull. Heather goes to Jake in his quarters. "I want to go shopping."

The commander says, "Huh, shopping? Where? What do you want to buy and with what money?"

"With the charge card Murdock gave us. He said if we need anything to use the card. We haven't been back to the base to try it, but as far as I know, it has as much money on it as I want to spend."

"A woman with a limitless charge card. I don't know about that. I imagine the WRC will have to pay for what we buy while we are here."

"Are my earnings from my paycheck going to be any good in stores?"

"Good point I suppose. Let me get with Murdock again and I will see if he or one of his men can take you and Dean shopping."

"Sir, don't you think it is safe for us to go alone? Dean and I will both take a gun."

"Okay, but Murdock still needs to lend us a vehicle and teach you how to drive it. I will also ask if he feels like it is safe. If not, then you shall have a chaperone."

A short time passes and Jake calls Murdock. He inquires as to rather he is available to meet with him. The two agree. Murdock wants to see the spacecraft, so it isn't very long and he is standing by the side of the ship where the entrance ramp drops. Greg says, "I see Murdock standing near the ship on camera one." He goes over the comm, "Commander…"

Jake responds, "I invited him, let him in. I am on my way to meet him." The big metal door clicks and Murdock hears the sound of servo motors lowering the ramp. Once it is down, he walks up the ramp to see the bridge, with everyone working at their stations. He sees the holographic imagery at the front of the room and everyone on their computer monitors. He says, "I never expected to see all of this inside of here. It reminds me of our monitoring area at headquarters. We don't have any real life video like that, though." Dean looks up and sees the image of Chillikreet that he had been studying. Just then, the commander walks through the door.

"Good morning, Murdock!" Jake says with a smile.

"Good morning, sir."

"Let's walk around the bridge here and I will show you our ship." They take a walk around the bridge. Murdock looks at the big chair in the middle and says, "Yours?"

Jake replies, "Of course." Jake points everything out and what everything does while they are walking around. They look up at the display at the front of the room and Murdock asks, "Chillikreet?"

Dean speaks up, "Yes. I am looking at the TOPO maps that were made while we were in orbit above the planet."

Murdock says, "Interesting."

Jake asks, "Do y'all have any type of holographic devices?"

"Life-like pictures like that? No, we have nothing that appears as a real representation in a picture." They leave the bridge and walk down the corridor to the break area. Jake walks up to the food replicator and says, "Coffee, black." He sticks his coffee cup under a nozzle and coffee flows into his cup. He then says, "Chocolate cake donut covered with chocolate." A box resembling a microwave begins to move a nozzle inside back and forth, creating a donut. After a few minutes, the display reads "READY". He opens the door and asks Murdock, "Would you like one? They really are tasty."

He declines and responds, "So this box and this spigot creates your food?"

"That is right. It is what we call a food replicator. It takes material and prints three-dimensional items, depending upon your request. We have a large storage area that is used to feed this machine. You would be surprised how little raw material is used to create food with this device, though. We expect this system to keep us fed until the first of the transports arrive in April."

Murdock says, "We could help to eliminate world hunger with this technology."

Jakes replies, "Well, the supplies that feed the unit still must be acquired, but it is much cheaper than raising animals and growing food."

"Animals and growing produce are the only ways that we have for food. No replicators here." They tour the gym with the racquetball court that changes to a basketball, handball, and volleyball court, then go into Jake's office. Murdock seems quite impressed.

Jake says, "I invited you over to discuss our situation and condition. How safe do you feel we are right now?"

Murdock replies, "With the shield of death over us? I feel that you are nearly untouchable."

"Okay, suppose we would like to travel around the base. Are your fellow Malpeada military personnel as acceptable of us as your group is?"

"Absolutely, sir! They know that you have taken over and many of them are very interested in meeting you and learning about you. The people that are currently here choose to be here and were told why the base was abandoned. The only ones you need to fear are the people of Chillikreet and Berlinkat. These people would probably murder you on sight."

Jake continues, "Do you believe that any of these people could be on base?"

"No area is ever fully secure unless you have some shield of death like you have placed over this compound, but I don't believe any of the king's soldiers could get on base without being detected."

"I have a restless crew who want to come and go as they please. Do you think this is acceptable?"

"Acceptable, yes, but unnecessary. There are five of you. I have thirty-five guards at this compound. We should accompany anyone that moves about outside of the embassy grounds."

"It just seems like a bother."

"No bother, sir. This is our job. To make it easier, I will have someone dedicated and prepared to go any time day or night to accompany you. All you need to do is to let Gwen or Detty know if you require them."

"This will be ideal. What if we desire to leave the base and explore the area south of here?"

Murdock says, "I would like to go in your ship since it is protected to explore, but if we need to go without it, then I would like for our group to take an entourage of at least five of my men. If possible, I would like to have a day's notice that you want to leave the base."

"Understood and thank you." He escorts him back up to the bridge. They shake hands and down the ramp he goes.

Greg closes the outer hatch. Jake sits at his station and says, "Dean, are you and Heather wanting to go onto the base?"

Dean responds, "Yes, sir. Murdock gave us each a charge card and it has been burning a hole in her pocket ever since." Ted and Greg both have a little chuckle from this.

Heather says, "He gave each of us one."

They all look at Heather and ask in unison, "Huh?"

Heather says, "Seriously." She opens a drawer under her console and pulls out passes and charge cards with everyone's name and picture on them. She passes them out.

Jake says, "I wonder who ultimately pays."

Ted says, "I have over half a million dollars in a doomed bank on a doomed planet. They can have that if I can get some Stirpeto souvenirs." He laughs. Then he asks, "Seriously, Commander, what is to become of our currency or monetary worth that was earned and saved in earth's currency?"

"I have no idea. I assume the banks and their records will be coming and set up here. I speculate we will have the same as we had when this happened. I have not seen that memo, though." Jake continues, "Anytime that any of you are done with your work and want to go onto the base, then feel free. I would just like to know when you leave so I can kind of keep track on you." This message is very well received by everyone.

Heather inquires, "So, if I am done now, I can go, Commander?"

"That is right."

"Heather, can you give me about fifteen minutes to finish this scan?" asks Dean.

Heather says, "Certainly." Then in a high-pitched, muffled voice she says, "I'm going shopping! I'm going shopping!"

Jake says, "Just locate Detty or Gwen and let them know your wishes and coordinate the dropping of the shields with another crew member."

Dean is not content with the little shopping trips onto the base. He wants to go south and explore what is there and where all of these people are going to stay. How populated is it exactly? Are there bad guys behind every tree, or is it very sparsely populated? He asks, "Commander, do you have a plan for finding a safe location for setting up the influx of earthlings that will be happening in a few months?"

"Not exactly. We need more resources to clear land and secure a place. We will have a lot of men and machines when they arrive,

225

but the base will not hold all of the people that are coming on the first Armada."

Dean says, "We need to go exploring."

"Agreed, Dean, but how do we proceed safely? I have spoken with Murdock concerning trips away from the base, and he is intent on sending a troop of people for protection for us."

"They know this land and they know how to keep us safe. They seem very sincere in their objective and loyal to us. Can you grant me and Ted permission to head south with the Malpeadan military within the next couple of days?"

"No, Dean, but Ted and I shall go."

"Why you two?"

Jake says, "If the worst were to happen, you could fill my position and keep everything on track for our incoming ships, and Greg could take Ted's place if necessary."

"Perhaps we could take the ship," Dean replies.

"I will consider this, but it is difficult to imagine disengaging the shield array that is in place and uprooting everyone after such a long journey. I don't want to travel to the southern border, I just want to go about fifty miles south. This will give us some idea of how the first month of the evacuees will be situated. There may be more bases here that they haven't mentioned. There could be areas that could be cleared that are forests. I guess the bottom line is, we don't know how heavily populated or what kind of situation we have to our immediate south, other than the TOPO maps and they lack a lot to be desired."

Jake goes back to his quarters and drafts an email to Commander Phillips.

Dear Charles,

We have now settled into the embassy that Malpeada has so graciously released to us. This is a very nice dwelling. I would not be surprised if you would like to take this facility and make it home base for your staff. They have military personnel here to assist us with everything from guarding the perimeter to accompanying us onto the base. They have issued everyone passes and charge cards so that we may move freely about the base and obtain goods. Things are actually going very differently than I had imagined when I made first contact. They are very gracious people. I need to do some exploring for recommendations for where we shall place all of the incoming people. I know I must travel south, but that is where the hostile natives reside. I am struggling to decide if I play it safe and take the ship or travel with the guards that are at the compound. I will follow up with another communication when we decide. I received your voice message concerning the first Armada and expect that you are getting very close to departing yourself, given it is near the time that you planned to leave.

We have found adequate runways for the transports to land. I will be sending coordinates as well as specifications when I can. The base here will hold twelve million people, so we can comfortably accommodate the first Armada with some in shelters, obviously, but as a temporary means. I feel sure there are enough hangars and open areas for us to set up housing for a few days, then ship them out to the next area where they will be housed using the supply and military ships.

Brenda and I have always had a thing for one another, but I would not ask her to jeopardize her relationship with Dale. She probably wouldn't have anyway, but now that she is a free woman, we are going to try to see where things lead. Keep my beautiful Brenda safe, sir! I look forward to hearing back from you.

Sincerely,

Jake Conley Commander WRC Parche I

He presses ctrl and enter on his keyboard and his email is on its way.

Jake then takes a walk up to the bridge to find Ted sitting at his station. "Where is Greg?"

"He went to his room to go to bed. He isn't feeling well."

"No doubt," Jake answers. "I am headed over to discuss a trip south with Murdock. Would you like to attend this expedition?"

"Absolutely, are we going exploring or to seek and destroy?"

"Ted, we have worked together for quite some time and I want you to understand that I don't mean to be ruthless, as it seems that I keep explaining, with taking these people's land away, but this is survival of the fittest at this point. I hate to put this in such strong words, but I want you to understand that if I have to exterminate fifty million Berlinkat radicals in order to save twenty million earthlings, then I will do it. Our objective is clear. I would like to negotiate with them and I am not a war monger, but some have already made their intentions clear by firing on our vessel. If it is *necessary* to rid this land of these people, then I will do it. We will begin as honorable and as diplomatic as is possible, but in the end, I will have a safe haven for the Commander-in-Chief to come to."

"I completely understand, Commander, and know that I will be by your side regardless of the lengths that must be taken. Dean sounded a little democratic when we discussed forcing Malpeada's hand. I do not feel that way. If you hadn't negotiated in the way that you did, we would not have this opportunity and we quite possibly would be at war with them. I have many loved ones that are depending on us, sir."

"We will leave in the morning at 0900 if Murdock is prepared for that. Have you gotten your PMIs done for today?"

Ted chuckles, and says, "With a pretty sick Greg, we did. He was in bad shape before I released him, but we completed our duties, sir."

"Very well, if I don't see you later today, then I will see you on the deck at 0800."

Ted responds, "Aye aye, Commander."

Jake then goes down the walkway and sets the trip up with Murdock. There were no issues with them leaving at this time in the AM and he was content to send a convoy to accompany them.

A while later, Ted sees Murdock's truck at the gate, with Dean at the wheel and what looks to be Jerdek riding along, so he lowers the shields and they enter the compound. They park and it isn't long before he sees Dean and Heather approach the entrance. He lowers the door. They enter with Heather carrying several packages. Ted says, "What did you buy me?"

She responds, "I actually did get you something."

Ted replies, "That's a shocker!"

She hands him a scarf.

They continue on and head to Dean's quarters. Heather has several new Malpeada blouses and other gifts for the crew.

Dean says, "Now! I have been waiting for two days to get you alone!" They decide to stay the night in Dean's quarters on the ship.

The next morning, the usual meeting place finds Ted and Gwen sitting out under a cloudy sky, looking like it may rain. They sit near the fire as it is especially chilly this morning. Ted has Gwen held tightly and she meets eyes with Ted. "We should go in," she says as a streak of lightning lights up the black morning sky to reveal storm clouds rolling across the top of the embassy.

"Why? The shields will protect us from the lightning and wind."

"I still don't care anything for getting wet," Gwen replies.

"The shields will block the rain as well." The flame that is from the fire only flickers as the temperature within the protected area changes due to the front that is blowing through. The commander steps through the door and rain can now be seen from the light above the compound. The lightning picks up and a loud crash of thunder is heard. It sounds like a cannon was fired off of the deck. Gwen is obviously a little uneasy in Ted's arms.

Jake has a seat and says, "Do not fear the weather. Our shields will protect us from anything that it has to throw at us." Just then a bright flash lights up the entire shielded area, causing a blue crackle and what looks like lightning all the way around the area the shields

229

are protecting. They feel a dousing of rain. It quickly goes away. Gwen jumps up and runs inside.

Ted chuckles, and says, "She thought they failed, perhaps. That is the first direct hit from lightning that I have seen on the shields. They are only at twenty-five percent." They hear the spacecraft power up. It is a distinctive high-pitch whistling turbo sound until the low quiet roar of the engines becomes a slightly more energetic louder roar.

Jake says, "Dean is up. I guess he decided we needed a little more power for Goldilocks' Mother Nature."

A few moments pass and Gwen comes back out in her uniform and asks, "Would you like breakfast?" They both agree that it would be nice.

Jake asks her, "Please go to the ship and ask Heather..." Crash, boom, the lightening hits the shields again but no rain gets through. "...to prepare an omelet 'Jake', bacon, and sausage and biscuits, please."

Ted asks, "Will you be okay to walk over there alone?" Crash, bang, bam, the storm rages on. The weather is really getting busy all around them and they can hardly get their words out without the thunder and lightning interrupting them. She stands there trembling, obviously scared. Ted says, "I want toast, eggs over medium, and two orders of bacon."

She responds with a trembling voice, "I may learn to make this in our kitchen." She actually sounds sincere.

Ted says, "Pretty lady, do you think I would have you walk over there alone?" He gets up to accompany her and they disappear.

Murdock then comes walking out onto the veranda. He sits. "Commander, is it still your wish to go on our trek today?"

"Do you have flooding in these areas?" The tablet repeats each man's words in their respective language.

Murdock replies, "With deep water? We rarely have this occur. It is possible, but I find it unlikely."

"Let's give the storm a little while to settle down." As the clap of thunder is heard again and the lightning lights up the shields again, Murdock almost jumps off the deck and replies, "I need shields. Could you share this technology?"

"Someday, I'm sure."

"When you are ready, or after the storm passes, we shall go. The shields of death are amazing. I can't believe this strong fall storm and we don't have a drop of rain upon us."

"Believe it. Murdock, I know how your government feels about murder and we do not want to do anything to put our alliance in jeopardy with Malpeada. When we travel south, what if we encounter the king's military or the savages? Will it be clear that we may have to take a human life?"

"If there was some problem with engaging the king, we would have made this clear when you blew up two of his castles and killed hundreds. We have not seen any hostility from the Gargalik Tribe. I encourage you to try diplomatic means with them. Chief Greybird has proven to be a reasonable man, and I would not consider him a savage. They could be a good ally as well, but you must work with him to establish what must be done to coexist."

Jake responds, "If they attack, we have a protocol that is referred to as 'rules of engagement'. It provides rules in case we are fired upon."

Murdock says, "We are not unreasonable people. We clearly understand that and with my men, there will be no reason for you to take arms as we shall protect you. You must also understand that not everyone south of here has allegiance to the king or the Gargalik tribe. They are innocents that will likely be willing to join your group."

"That makes sense. We will take this into consideration as we work on our relations. We have a method for communication that allows messages to be written on the night sky. Perhaps we should communicate in this manner soon."

"You can write on the sky?" Murdock looks shocked.

231

"Yes, we have used it back on Earth for emergency communications, and it may be a good propaganda tool here."

Gwen and Ted walk back out on the deck, with breakfast. Ted says, "I took the liberty of bringing you some, Murdock."

Murdock says, "I will try, but your food has a great deal of sodium. I don't care that much for the taste of raw sodium." They sit and eat, watching the storm above them rage on. Gwen seems much more comfortable and she is eating as well.

Greg comes walking out. He says, "Good morning." They all greet him. "That is a first for replicated alcohol and maybe not the last, but the last for a while! I apologize, Gwen. I realize that I was out of line the other night. Where is Detty?" asks Greg. Thunder pops and the dim morning sky is lit brightly.

Gwen says, "Some of our people can't handle ale as well. It isn't anything that we haven't seen before. Detty is sleeping in. I believe that Ted made her very tired last night." The group laughs as the storm rages and cracks. She looks confused as she didn't say this for a joke.

Ted looks at her and says, "I will explain later," giving her a wink. Ted had learned a new card game and played it with them until very late the night before.

They finish breakfast, with the storm making a lively morning that seems to never end. They each go to their stations and patiently await the break in the storm so they can go exploring.

Chapter 27

Next Stop Goldilocks

It is Wednesday morning and the day the third Armada leaves orbit and takes the commander and his staff to Goldilocks. Brenda wakes up in her cruise ship styled quarters and realizes she has a premium suite. She goes out her door to her mother and father's room. She knocks on the door, her mom answers with a novel in her hand, her thumb between pages. Brenda says, "Good morning, Mom. Would you like to have coffee?"

"Sure, dear, but could we go out on the viewing deck?" Brenda thinks *you mean the holographically generated viewing deck*. The ladies are still in their housecoats with little WRC logos on them. They take the short walk down a carpeted hallway past a glass front room, and both smell bacon cooking, freshly brewed coffee, the sweet smell of chocolate lattes, and espresso. Brenda says, "We must be near a coffee shop."

Mom replies, "Just down that way," as they enter an area that has large round metal rails and a view of the dark ocean beyond it. They both walk up to the rail and gaze out over what appears to be the ocean and a night sky filled with stars. Mom asks, "Brenda, will there be a sunrise?"

"The replication is used for smoke and mirrors, surely it will have a beautiful sunrise." They both have a seat in lay-down lawn chairs that are just beyond an awning. The awning is used to block the bright replicated sun they will get to view later this morning.

Brenda says, "Well, Mom, is it all that you expected?"

"I expected a room full of seats like a commercial airliner. I never expected this would be a cruise ship theme. If you and your boss are going to kill us in this bucket of bolts, I guess we will enjoy it until it happens." Just then they see a streak of light across the darkened replicated sky. They both enjoy watching the sun rise.

"Mom, you aren't afraid, are you?"

Brenda's mom looks into her big blue eyes and says, "Are you not, even a little?"

"The only real fear I have is for the people that are left behind and the people that are already on the planet. I have a real fear for them. I don't know what our Savior Jesus Christ will think of us all abandoning Earth. I have a fear that I will miss him. We must be living in the final days, Mom."

"Never question our Lord above. He knows and supports our choices or He would not have given us this ability or a place to go." The sun has now lit the big beautiful ocean scene that is created for the passengers. Brenda and her mom are both very impressed by the details and the beauty of the scene they see before them. They are both very relaxed.

Back in the room, Brenda's father sits in front of the seventy-inch television set, watching his local Vegas morning newscast, and he hears them speaking of their fleet that is to leave at midnight. He has a big green cup that says Remington on the side, in white writing. He is having his usual morning coffee and daily dose of the news. He watches for a while and decides to find out what else is on and when he changes the channel, a banner pops up on the screen that says PREPARE NOW FOR YOUR NEW LIFE ON GOLDILOCKS. Below, it has a second smaller caption that says Learn how to build shelter, replicate food, and gather supplies for survival, channel 00. It piques his curiosity and he changes the channel to 00. A show begins with building a cabin using pre-replicated logs. It shows a supply ship that has a replicator creating log cabin style logs that are nearly twenty feet long. It goes on to show how to clear and level an area for the dwelling and explains how the military will be there to assist with transportation of the materials and will supply all items necessary for the dwelling. He decides that this is a pretty important TV show and decides to watch it the rest of the day. Brenda and Mom gets back and he sits in the easy chair, reclined, wearing his thick PJs, white socks, and old house shoes laying on the floor. He is drinking coffee and is engulfed into the plan that they have put together for shelter on the new planet. Brenda goes over and gives him a peck on the cheek and says, "I have to go report in."

Dad says, "Not even a day off during our cruise?"

"Dad, this isn't like going to the office. I have to check and see if Commander Charles needs anything, and check my email, etc." They all say their goodbyes and Brenda takes off to see if everything is set on go for midnight.

She arrives at Commander Phillips' room/office and she just thought that she had the honeymoon suite. She walks in the front door to find a fireplace, fine furniture, real wood paneling, a study with a library full of books, and a marble tiled dining area where she spots the commander sitting, enjoying his breakfast in his blue WRC robe. She says, "Good morning, sir. What a nice place you have here!" Sheena comes walking out from the kitchen area and Brenda gazes upon her with fire in her eyes. Not to be distracted, she says, "Oh, well, good morning."

Sheena says, 'Hey, good morning, sis. It isn't how it looks. I just came over to visit with the commander this morning before he has to go to work."

Brenda says, "Not my affair," with the pun intended. She directs her attention to Commander Phillips. "What is in store today, sir?"

He responds, "Check on your correspondence and make sure nothing is hot, then enjoy your last day in orbit over planet Earth."

"So this is it? No holdups?"

"Nope, all set to leave at midnight on our little six-month cruise." She wishes them both well and heads back to her quarters. She gets on her workstation and checks the commander's appointments and looks over a few emails from the day-to-day operations from Vegas, but nothing is pressing. She goes in the bathroom to find her bathing suit to go work on her tan from the replicated UV light from the holographic sun. She lays face down in her personal viewing area. Her tight white bikini almost shines on

235

her golden tanned curves that glisten from the lotion she has deeply massaged into her beautiful youthful skin. She is relaxed and very content when she hears, "Damn, girl!" She looks back to see her dad out for a stroll. She says, "Dad?" He shakes his head and chuckles. She can hear him say, "Thank God for mothers," as he continues on his stroll.

Nightfall soon comes and with it midnight arrives before anyone really realizes, or they are distracted and adjusting to this false wonderland that has been created for them. Brenda is in the front of the ship on the bridge with Commander Phillips, Pilot Dalton Coleman, and the other crew members. Brenda asks, "We begin our acceleration to FTL speed in ten minutes?" The time is now 11:50 pm.

The commander says, "That is correct."

"We don't need to be strapped into a seat somewhere? Seats upright and luggage stowed?"

Charles chuckles, and says, "Not at all. The anti-G system on this vessel will keep you from even being able to tell that we have taken off."

Brenda replies, "Why did we feel like we were riding a bottle rocket when we took off from Area 51 then? Does it not work on the surface?"

"We could have used it, but it takes a lot of power with the forces of gravity at work. Out in space, when the serious acceleration begins is when it is necessary, and it is much more efficient," answers Charles. She then asks, using the ship's nickname in lieu of Arc 0.3, "Where in the Armada is the WRC Phillips–our ship– going to be?"

"Lead ship. You sure are asking a bunch of questions for someone who has sat in on so many of these meetings that determined these things." He chuckles.

"I must admit when our staff has spoke of several of these things, I didn't exactly understand and I didn't listen that closely."

He says, "I see." Soon they hear a countdown from the communication's station. The other ships in the fleet are projected on the hologram image at the front of the room. The ships begin to move, and they can also see stars that look like they are also moving. The pilot begins to speak to Earth command and before you know it, they have released control of the group to Commander Phillips and their voices are static filled and begin to fade. Dalton looks back at Commander Phillips and speaks, "All systems are normal. All ships are now synchronized in the flock formation. We will be at full FTL 20 in about twenty-two Earth hours."

Charles says, "Fantastic. You have control, Coleman." Charles and Brenda exit the bridge. They walk back to their respective cabins and the trip to Goldilocks is well underway.

Back on the surface of Earth, a new day comes and General Jeremy Enlow has assumed responsibility for Commander Phillips' operations on Earth. He even occupies his office. He took the role with the understanding that he will not leave until December of 2118. Commander Phillips is still in charge, but for WRC's Earth presence, Enlow now has control. He is very comfortable in the role and has clear instructions and understands the direction that Commander Phillips has for the operations on Earth. He anticipates a repeat of the events that have occurred for the foreseeable future. He sits at his office and his telephone rings. It is Korean President Kim Sun Pang. He pleads his case with the top official. He gets no satisfaction, and they both hang up the phones in anger.

General Enlow has decided to travel to check on the status of the shelters that are being constructed. He has a personal jet waiting at McCarran International Airport. He arrives and meets members of his staff, his secretary, Lisa Hill, and Joe Carrington. They are both former CIA agents and dress in typical special agent attire. Joe is sitting inside the terminal, having a burger at Ruby's Dinette, across the table from him sits Lisa. Lisa is a light colored brunette, with green eyes. She is about five foot three, with a small body frame. She often found herself used by the CIA as a distraction in certain cases when necessary. She is qualified for a lot more than just being a "distraction". Joe has curly, dark hair. He is about five-

237

eleven, with a fairly slender build, and has a peculiar perspective. He sits with the beautiful brunette and they appear to be an unusual couple. Soon the pilot arrives, as well as the general. The pilot is well over six feet tall, brown hair, dark eyes, with a very physical physique. The general is a large man who is physically very fit and wearing a blue Armani suit. He has dark, short hair and is in his late thirties.

They all leave the airport and head to the jet and are soon in the air. They are headed for the largest of all of the facilities located in California. They get in the air and travel for a short time and land at LAX. It was a comfortable landing. They enter the terminal to a team of protesters. They are holding signs that say: WHY ARE THERE CHOSEN ONES? and WE ARE LEFT OUT IN THE COLD, WE DON'T GET TO LEAVE EARTH UNTIL IT IS TOO LATE.

The group is surprised to see this as they try their best to avoid them, but the protestors begin to shout obscenities at them and question why some are lucky and some are not. They manage to get past this group and into their black SUV without any altercations, and speed away from the terminal.

It is now about 5 pm and everyone is tired. They go and check into their hotel just outside of Los Angeles. They meet in the lobby a little later and order a pizza so they can stay in for the night. They agree to meet in the lobby the next morning at 6 am.

The next morning comes to find Joe sitting in the hotel's breakfast dining area. The smell of fresh coffee and bacon fills the air. He sits alone at a small booth, with a plate of food, a banana, cup of cherry yogurt, and a cup of coffee. He is waiting on the others to arrive. The hotel has a very nice reception area, with the food bar on one side of the entrance where the attendant sits. A second sitting area is on the far side of the entrance. Large windows fill this area and very few people are in this area because it is a little after 5 am. He sits with a thought of the protesters from the day previous, thinking what a bunch of frigging ungrateful losers. They should be banned from the trip altogether. A friendly, elderly gray haired lady sits at an adjacent table and he scowls at her and looks away.

He soon finishes his breakfast and decides to go out front to have a smoke and check for more protesters before the others come down. He stands out front of the hotel, looking out at the interstate in the distance, smoking his cigarette, and dreading the traffic to the facility. It isn't long and a shuttle pulls up and asks, "Mr. Smith?"

He rebuffs, "Not me, Captain." The driver gives him an odd look and says, "Good morning," as he passes. Joe has no reply for the lowly bus driver. Soon, several people come out to catch the shuttle to the airport. The same elderly lady walks past and says, "I hope you have a nice day." He just stands and looks at her as if she had offended him. Soon, through the smoke glass windows, he sees Lisa walk into the breakfast lounge.

He goes back in and slips into a seat without her seeing. She gets a bagel and some cream cheese, along with a glass of orange juice. She begins to go and find a seat. By this time, the area has several people eating breakfast when she spots "Mr. Joyful" and considers acting as if she didn't see him, but decides to go and sit with him. She sits down and asks, "When did you get here?"

"I have been down here waiting on you all since five."

She says, in a very kind voice, "We weren't supposed to meet until six, though."

"I didn't think you two would sleep all day, though." She knows he is a grumpy, unhappy fellow and decides to eat her bagel and keep to herself. Soon General Enlow arrives. He grabs some coffee to go and says, "If you guys are ready."

They walk out of the hotel and get into the black SUV, with Joe driving, and travel a few miles on backstreets until they come to a construction site. It looks almost like an ocean of activity, with a large twelve-foot chain link fence that stretches as far as you can see. There are concrete trucks hauling concrete from one of several ready-mix facilities within the fence as they drive down a road along the fence. They travel for about half an hour and finally reach a sign that reads ENTRANCE. Below the sign, it reads No Admittance Without Official Business Needs. Another large sign reads WRC FUTURE HOME OF TEMPORARY LODGING FOR EVACUEES.

They pull to the guard shack and a guard comes out, with a gun on his side, and walks to the door of the SUV. General Enlow pulls out his ID and presents it to the guard and says, "We are here to see the superintendent, Dan Green." The guard motions for them to pull around to the side of the shack. A short time passes and a young, twenty-something-year-old construction worker, complete with hardhat, walks up to the driver's side of the SUV and greets Joe.

Joe says, "I have brought General Enlow to view the site." The young, blond haired man says, "I am Dan Green. I am running the show here."

Joe says sarcastically, "Okay, I am impressed."

Dan asks, "How do you all want to do this? I can climb in the SUV and we can drive around the site, or we can jump into a yard truck. Most of the yard dogs aren't very clean or comfortable."

Joe says, "Get in," with a scowl.

He walks around to the far door of the vehicle and climbs in the back beside General Enlow and behind Lisa. He says, "Darn, y'all even got pretty girls up there at headquarters, huh? Pardon me, ma'am, but you even smell good." He then directs them around the site. The next three hours are spent nonstop driving around this enormous construction site. He shows them six ready-mix plants, they pass at least fifty concrete trucks, and a multitude of cranes and steel beams are everywhere.

They finally get back to the guard shack and get ready to drop the superintendent off and General Enlow asks, "Will we finish this by January 1, 2118?"

Dan says, "Yes, sir. It is ten times the job that I have ever led, but I was in charge of the new football stadium last year, downtown, and this is a very simple building. It is just large and has enough heat to warm up the world. We will be done, sir."

The general asks, "Is there anything that you need?"

"No, sir, just good weather to keep us from getting behind, but we have a month to burn, so we should comfortably make your deadline."

General Enlow asks, "How many facilities have you constructed, Mr. Green?"

"Sir, I have done nearly forty buildings for CC Constructors and General Contractors."

"One more thing. Do you see anything that is not typical or could be unsafe with this facility?"

"I see no issue, except they usually have an awful lot of earthquake protection through a California building. I don't see so much on this one. If the big one hits, I'm not sure what the outcome will be."

The general says, "Well, let's hope that isn't part of the plan over the next couple of years."

Dan says, "Hope not, sir." The general hands him a card with his contact information on it, then Lisa hands him one with her contact information as well. He walks away and they leave. He looks at the back of Lisa's card and it says in a handwritten note: Marriott Hotel on Figueroa St, room 523. I leave in the morning and would like some company tonight.

They leave the site and decide to drive by the replication factory. They drive further toward the desert and find another massive building. They are rolling a space frame out of the large doors and through the back. They drive slowly and see more protesters with signs. They line the large chain link fence that protects the front of the facility. Joe speaks up and says, "The protesters could get ugly before this is all said and done."

General Enlow replies, "I wonder what these goofy fucks are protesting. Maybe we are polluting their environment that will soon be gone." They all chuckle and drive back to the hotel.

They all have a good night's sleep. Leaving the hotel, they pull around to the front and up to the drive that enters the road. They

241

hear the general in the back seat say, "Isn't that ole Superintendent Dan?" Lisa just smiles. The general and Joe both think what a hoochie. They return to Vegas and Lisa contacts all of the American replicators and airports that are hosting the next round of flights. It is Wednesday, the twentieth of October and another fleet is due to leave tonight.

She completes her calls and goes into Jeremy's office. "Sir, all stations are reporting good statuses for next week's flights." They all get into somewhat of a repetition stage of setting up the transports each week this way and become confident in their day to day needs of their newly gained positions. They travel around occasionally and visit the different shelters being built. There are obviously delays due to weather and rescheduling requirements, but they are quite competent decision makers and work each issue out for an Armada of five thousand ships each week, as requested by Commander Charles Phillips.

On WRC Phillips, the voyage is going remarkably well. Commander Phillips continues to track the progress on Earth and hears some off topic news about Lisa. He thinks to himself, *you are just now figuring out that pretty young girl gets around*? Some don't know how to enjoy life. He says out loud, "Hell, I had her before everyone else." Brenda is the one that no one can have, but little Miss Sheena is beginning to be a real factor. Just then his door buzzes. He says, "Enter." It is Dalton Coleman. He is a tall man with graying hair. He is wearing a blue WRC jumpsuit. They both are old friends from back in the academy days.

"What's up, Dalton? Are you doing okay? How is this thing to fly?"

"Sir, I am doing well, but I haven't seen the roster for the return flights. Will I be scheduled for the trip back?"

Charles says, "Only if you want to."

"I have my entire family on this vessel. I would very much like to stay and help them get started. What land will I be given? Is any of this determined?"

Charles looks a little surprised. "Are you interested in land, Dalton? You have, ever since I have known you, been a military man and committed to that lifestyle. I had some thoughts about you being a big part of the new base."

Dalton says, "No, sir. I am ready to turn in my flight suit. I have enjoyed my long career and have always dreamt of moving off to some secluded part of the world for retirement. I honestly thought I would buy a replicator and head to Alaska to try my hand at trapping."

Charles says, "Please excuse my shock. I really didn't see you as this type of a person. Do you currently own land on Earth?"

"I bought ten acres last year, but it isn't paid for. I financed it for the next five years."

"When things get settled and we begin again, there will be many changes, but I am heading up everything. Many people on Earth that own land didn't come. We can find some that you could claim. The way it will work is when we land and settle, we will have each country, providence, state, and county tallied up for total area of mass. We will then ask the population to put in a claim on what they had on Earth. If this claim can be substantiated and validated through deeds and public records, then they will be assured the same amount of land. If someone wants land, they have to put in a request for a maximum of one hundred acres. It will be divided up among the requests once the assured land is issued. The government will be no exception. They will continue to own an adequate parcel of land for parks and wildlife. There will also be an allowance for the inhabitants. All of this is being compiled right now on this ship. I hope to know how much is available before the claims begin coming in.

"The banking system will be a little trickier to sort out. People will not have their typical jobs and for them to pay a debt that was incurred on Earth would be difficult. The debt for all of these people will essentially be wiped clean. I wish we could adopt a system like what is currently in place on Malpeada. They don't have any bankers and it is illegal there to earn money based on the use of money alone.

243

Lawyers are paid for by the government through taxes. Taxes are at a minimum."

Dalton says, "This sounds fantastic. I have a deed for the land that I own with a lien. If I could receive equal land, or one hundred acres that are free and clear, then it would allow me to live life to the fullest. In answer to your question concerning flying the ship, sir, it is amazing how your design engineers have concocted a program that replicates every airplane flight control that has ever been built in modern time and implemented them here. I personally like the Lear Jet settings and have selected Lear Jet controls. I suppose this was to be able to accommodate the various multitudes of pilots that will be necessary over the next few years."

"That is exactly right. We have such a multitude of pilots that are necessary to get these transports to Goldilocks, it was necessary to capitalize on the computer generated simulations for every modern airplane that is in existence. All captains will have heavy commercial or military airplane experience, but for the copilots and others that will take the helm while en route, we needed to facilitate a control that was familiar to them.

"Have you watched the informative videos on the television sets in the rooms?"

Dalton replies, "No, I have watched the morning news and I saw some banners about infomercials or something."

"Look closer. We have compiled information from the planet and have put 'how to' and methods that will be used to sustain each load of twenty million that are coming. We even have hands-on labs that allow you to build a cabin down in the lower area of this ship. I feel sure that we will lose a few due to their ability, but if you follow this information, it will be much easier to put together housing for you and your family if this is the direction you want to take. We have sent enough food replicators and specialty device replicators to accommodate everyone with daily meals and drinks. It also goes into details of a method for building shelter and acquiring the raw materials from the supply ships. It is important that everyone views

244

this information or they will not have any idea of what they are doing once we arrive."

"Sir, I know you have accommodations for me waiting, but as I said, I will really want land, and to help my family get established. Weapons? I brought my gun safe. It is full with all of my guns, but I will not have ammunition to last for the next ten years."

"Watch the videos. That is all covered. We will take care of our people once we are there. I fear there are dangers from the current inhabitants, though. We will be taking what is theirs."

"That is regrettable, but we must save ourselves, sir."

"We have tried diplomacy and will continue this attempt, but things aren't looking too peaceful on Goldilocks for our old friend, Jake Conley."

"Understood, sir. Well, I should get back and check on the bridge. Thank you for the information."

Chapter 28

Go South Young Man

On Goldilocks, it stormed the rest of the day they planned to go south. The next opportunity they have to go south was upon them. Ted and Jake are both up and in full combat dress. They have WRC Camo on, gun belt complete with ammo, machine gun with a sling over their shoulder, and they are carrying a high-tech helmet packed with extra electronics for remote sighting for their guns and remote vision. They have a supply of small drones and units called peak-at-you—PAY. The PAYs are balls that can be thrown. The camera is always aligned with the horizon and can be seen remotely through a viewer in their helmets. They are standing on the bridge at about 6 am and Dean and Greg look on. Dean says, "Sir, it isn't too late to let me go. It has been a long time since you have been out on a maneuver."

Jake clearly insulted replies, "Don't worry about me, ole man. I can handle anything this place has to throw at me."

"Old man, huh? I didn't mean that as an insult, sir."

Ted and Jake walk off the bridge and down the ramp without any additional words.

The garage door opens and they see Murdock in gear that is meant for tactical use. He has on some camouflage, a gun belt, and carrying a typical helmet. The two men walk into the garage and Jake notices one of the many vehicles are gone and no one else is accompanying them. Jake, Ted, and Murdock all climb into the big four wheel drive pickup. Murdock starts it up and they pull up and over to the parking lot exit. They see the lights for the shields turn red and they leave the compound. They drive a short distance and Jake says, "Two things" as the interpretation device repeats his words. "First, we are headed north, and second, I thought we had plans of having several troops accompany us."

Murdock answers, "We are headed north to the vehicle depot. The others are there now going over the equipment and getting ready for our journey."

It is a cloudy morning on Alpha Kantabury I. All the streets are wet as they pull through in the large pickup. Soon they arrive at a large hangar that has tracked vehicles, jeeps, and space-age looking tanks. They are all somewhat similar to the ones back on Earth but still unique in their own way in comparison. They pull up to the front in the large white truck and the men get out. They walk up to an all-terrain vehicle that is like an SUV. It would remind you of a Humvee. It has guns on mounts on the top and is camouflaged. They all climb in and another soldier walks up. He appears to be the troop leader, as he was directing the others. He comes over to Murdock and says, "You gentlemen ready?" Murdock responds, "Yes." He fires up this army vehicle and the man gets inside and motions to the others with a wave of his arm to follow.

They pull out and Murdock says, "Goltarik, let me introduce my earthling friends. This is Ted and Jake from the planet Earth." The man looks their way and says through the interpretation device, "Glad to meet you, gentlemen."

He then directs his attention to Murdock and says, "Zelicwi finally going to let us wipe out the vermin south of here?"

Murdock says, "President Haulk is going to give all of Stilligate to the earthlings."

Goltarik responds as he looks at Jake, "How do King Sedimo and Prime Minister Jimelclay feel about this decision?"

"Jimelclay was okay to head back to Malpeada, but the king is who we are preparing to defend against. He fired surface-to-air missiles at their spacecraft."

Goltarik asks, "So you guys are expecting a confrontation?"

"Not expecting, but prepared if there is one." They pull up to a large guard shack that is the entrance to the base. The guards have the barriers down as they approach and two soldiers, one on each side of the road, salutes the convoy with a closed fist to their forehead as it rolls through the gate, on its way south.

Jake speaks up, "I have comprehensive maps of the entire landmass, but I have no clue as it pertains to occupation. Do either of you guys have anything that shows where King Sedimo lays claim or Chief Greybird's land is located?"

Goltarik answers, "Nothing official, but I can give you pretty good coordinates of what they occupy. I go down there a lot."

Murdock responds, "He wants to go about fifty miles. Are there decent roads that far out?"

Goltarik says, "We can make it."

Murdock remarks, "That wasn't the question. Is there fear that we could have issues with travel since the rains and the terrain?"

"There will be issues regardless of the rain. The southern area is not developed. The king's men have all-terrain vehicles and horses to get around. The Gargalik tribe is usually on foot or horseback. The roads down there are ones that tanks and half tracks have cut. We can bring the tank out front and we can go anywhere you like, sir." It gets quiet. The only sound is the screeching and metallic pings heard from the tank and military vehicles that follow.

Goltarik asks, "What is it that we are looking for?"

Jake speaks up, "A place for three billion earth people."

Goltarik says, "Holy shit! Are you serious, man? This place is going to be more crowded than Longenthros! Are these people going to be here soon? Oh wow, this is frankly unbelievable, sir."

"They are on their way. Our first transports of twenty million souls will be here in April. Then we will have twenty million delivered each week for a year. We will then start greeting forty million a week."

Murdock speaks up upon hearing this, "No one explained this to me. You realize that there are large reptiles in this land to deal with, King Sedimo, the Gargalik's tribesmen, and a very uncivilized countryside to try to deal with?"

248

Jake had seen the dinosaurs as they passed through on the Parche, but replies, "Large reptiles? No one said a word about any huge animals. Regardless of the challenges, we have an entire world full of inhabitants that are surely going to die because our sun is failing. The world will be dead within two of our earth years. This will equate to about three of Alpha Kantabury's years. We simply do not have a choice. When we first entered orbit, we were resolved to overthrowing Malpeada if necessary. We declared Eminent Domain on Longenthros."

Murdock said, "Eminent Domain was declared to whom?"

Jake says, "To President Grainta Haulk!"

Murdock replies, "Wow! And you are still alive? You have a "set", don't you, my friend? I bet that was a very uncomfortable conversation."

"You see us in Stilligate, don't you?" Then both of the soldiers chuckle.

They arrive at an area where the nice concrete road ends. It is a red clay path. They are all jogged around in their seats. They see Murdock reach down and pull up a lever they assume must be for greater traction. They have traveled about fifteen miles before hitting this area. Soon they come upon a man, who in appearance looks like an Indian, riding on what looks like a horse with a camel's head to the WRC members. It is an unappealing animal. They slow as they get near and Ted and Jake both place their hands on their side arms. They pass without incident, however, they see the man and the camel cut off in a gallop onto a trail that goes to the left.

Murdock says, "That could be trouble."

Jake responds, "Is that a horse?"

Murdock chuckles. "Of course that is a horse. What does it look like to you?"

Jake says, "The interpreter is not always an exact depiction of your language. That thing looked like an Indian on a camel. What would make you believe that is trouble?"

Goltarik responds, "An Indian on a horse. I am unsure of what this camel is that you speak of. That is a member of the Gargalik tribe and they will be in contact with others to alert them that we are in the area with you two." Just then a broadhead arrow grazes across the window of the Hummer. It was clear that it was meant for Jake.

The convoy comes to a halt and another arrow narrowly misses Murdock and they all roll their windows up. Goltarik climbs up and stands on the seat to man one of the guns on the top of the vehicle. Automatic gunfire is heard from the half-track behind them. It is a battle in the middle of this trail, with a clearing on both sides that is near the size of a football field, then dense forest on either side beyond the clearing, and what appear to be natural berms in no particular arrangement. They have been ambushed. They then see muzzle flashes coming from the woods. They hear the automatic rifle that Goltarik is manning fire short bursts into the woods.

Murdock exclaims, "Those sons a bitches have guns and they are shooting at us! This vehicle will protect us from their small arms and arrows. They are in direct violation of the treaty!" Then a deafening sound of the tank's big gun is heard and more muzzle flashes come from the dense tree line. They hear a voice on the radio, "I am turning loose of the eliminator, please everyone, stay down."

Immediately following this, Goltarik hops down on the seat beside Ted. A sound like an engine starting without a muffler is heard. They look back and there are what appear to be three machine guns on a rotating turret, spinning and shooting as it turns. There is a massive amount of firepower coming from the half-track that is clearing everything in a two-hundred-yard radius. Trees are falling over, revealing several Indians high-stepping as they retreat and hundreds laying dead all around the tree line. This assault continues for what seems like an hour but is in fact about ten minutes. There are fallen trees all around the edge of the clearing and a continuous plume of smoke darkens the already overcast sky as the sound stops.

Murdock says, "I really didn't want to kill anyone today. They shouldn't have waged this attack. Malpeada's leaders may eliminate these savages for you. This convoy is not at war with these people and we have kept peaceful relations with them. I don't care who is riding with our convoy, it doesn't excuse them for attacking our group! This could be war!"

Suddenly a huge animal with smooth, light brown skin runs up to the convoy. It looks around at the mess and walks slowly past the group. Goltarik looks up at Murdock. "Eliminate the threat?"

Murdock answers, "Not without a reason." The enormous animal walks through the clearing, bends over, and picks up one of the fallen savages with its long carnivore teeth. A deafening sound of the tank's muzzle is heard. A huge gush of blood spews out of the backside as the animal drops the corpse and begins running toward the convoy. Another shot is heard from the tank as the animal plummets forward to the ground with such force the men in the convoy can feel the impact through the ground. A small shower of blood peppers the Humvee.

Jake says, "What the fuck is that?"

Murdock calmly says, "That, my friend, is a large reptile. We call them Torntauks."

"That is a freaking dinosaur!" exclaims Jake. "We had these on our world back before civilization."

"They are a force to be reckoned with. It is nice to have a tank, but it could have been scared away by several other means. We didn't have to kill it. If we had left it, then it surely would have scavenged these fallen men."

Ted says, "We may need a little of this Torntauk repellent!"

The convoy begins its trek again. They leave the dead and wounded for the tribe to retrieve. They continue on for about ten miles and come to another clearing. It is plains land and goes on for miles. They see a group of teepees off in the distance and the convoy stops once again. Jake says, "This is what I need to note here. Areas like this could be used for a place to build shelters for the people that are coming."

Murdock asks, "Have you seen enough?"

"Not really, but I don't want to see you all wage war with everyone down south on our behalf. Would it be possible to have Goltarik spend some time with Heather to assist in identifying the populated areas, as well as structures that exist down here?"

Murdock says, "It would be possible for me to spend a little time with Heather!" He snickers.

Ted interrupts, "Sorry, guys, ole Dean just about has that little earthling wrapped up. You never know, though, some females from Earth are really attracted to the whole mercenary soldier type. We call them "bad boys" back home."

"I can't imagine more "bad boy" than us two. In answer to your question, though. Yes, he can spend as much time identifying the area as you all need."

They have plenty of room to turn this convoy of four around. They begin the drive back to the base. They drive down this mushy road, with densely covered foliage on each side, for a fair amount of time until they come to the dead Tyrannosaurus Rex, or Torntauk, lying in the clearing. They see no sign of fallen savages or of anyone. The Torntauk had been cut up and nothing remained except a big pile of guts and a very large, bloody skin.

Jake asks, "They cut up the dinosaur?"

Goltarik answers, "That is a big meal for the tribe."

"I guess the food replicators of our world have me somewhat in a different mindset than of these people."

Goltarik says, "Had we not been on official business, I would have gotten the tenderloin out of him myself. We hunt these animals. The tenderloin will feed my family a meal a week for nearly a year."

Ted says, "Wow, we are actually discussing eating dinosaur meat. Is it good…tasty?"

Murdock speaks up. "Ask Gwen to cook up some. We have some at the embassy."

Goltarik says, "Ask her to do this while I am there providing the information for your map."

Ted agrees, "Sounds like a plan!"

They continue on until they reach the concrete road. They soon reach the base and go to the depot. Murdock, Ted, and Jake all get in the big pickup truck and make their way back to the embassy.

The next morning, the usual meeting on the deck with the group has everyone in attendance to see the sunrise. Jake and Ted tell their story of the battle with the Indians and what their horses look like and the dinosaur they encountered when Ted says, "Gwen, do you think you could cook up some Torntauk for dinner tonight?"

"Certainly, we have plenty of Torntauk tenderloin. It is absolutely delicious to us."

Goltarik soon arrives and meets with the group. He is there bright and early and works with Heather and Dean to detail the map for the people that live in the different areas. They continue their fact gathering and the daily routines. They would like to have as much research and information to the evacuees as is possible prior to their arrival.

At the end of the day, they make their way over to see when Gwen would be serving dinner and an aroma of deer tenderloin and gravy filled the air when they entered the door. Goltarik says, "That is the tenderloin that I have been missing!" They all go down to the bar and have a fine meal, and they find that it tastes very much like venison tenderloin, only much larger, and it is pretty tasty. It is in appearance very similar to chicken fried steak, only a little thinner due to it being pounded on with a tenderizer. They all ate until their stomachs hurt. They thank Gwen for the delicious meal and call it a day.

Several weeks pass with the day to day routines being fairly consistent. They decide that with the information from the study of the structures and the layout of the tribe's men, as well as the king's land, that they have provided all of the pertinent information to Commander Phillips. His team is releasing it to the military leaders of the countries in order to plan a strategy against the inevitable invasion.

Chapter 29

Grand Union Station

On Earth, the fleet carrying the Korean group is set to leave. As with all other flights, it is midnight and General Enlow is atop the large office building in downtown Vegas, having a glass of wine with Lisa. They are wrapped up in blankets, with the heat on high when the stroke of midnight arrives. They watch the streak across the sky and go to the general's office. He sits at his desk and she sits in a chair in front of it. They discuss the timeline of the failure of the sun. She inquires, "Have you prepared a place for us?"

The general says, "I have beefed up the heat in this office building and I have a Super Duty in the parking garage, with large tires. We will be comfortable here. I have put in a large enough generator to keep everything running for the duration." The two end up staying the night in his office.

Early the next morning, he receives a communication from Commander Phillips asking for an update on the heating and shelters that are being built. He returns the following email:

Dear Commander Phillips,

Today we sent the eighth Armada that contained the Koreans. They continued to protest right up to the very last flight. I would be cautious of their arrival as they feel that the WRC is not being fair to them.

We have had great progress here in America for the shelters. The ones in Oklahoma, Arkansas, Texas, and Louisiana have been completed. We continue to see protesters at each site, as we have since the beginning. We have tried to accommodate them with information concerning the reason for our "CAMPS"<sarcastically> and how they should feel privileged to have a country that cares enough about them to have a contingency plan so that they do not all freeze to death before they can leave Earth.

I have been in touch with General Patterson concerning the shelters for the ones left behind. They are all complete in the US and await the influx of people when it all begins. My staff and I are all set with at least a six-month supply of fuel and a method of leaving the building in Las Vegas when the time comes.

I pray that all is well with you and your flight, sir. We have not had any catastrophic failures here in the US and it has been business as usual, except for the every week argument with the Koreans. We have had a few construction accidents, but we have been able to handle it all here.

General Jeremy Enlow

WRC Earth Acting Commander-in-Chief

On the WRC Phillips–Arc 0.3–the group is enjoying their voyage. They are sipping margaritas on the observation deck, swimming in the pool, and having themselves a six-month vacation. The time seems to pass very quickly. The military advisors on the WRC Lynch in the fourth Armada have received the information concerning the inhabitants' positions. They are formulating a plan for attack and defense.

The one thing that gives them difficulties is how to defend against the dinosaurs that were detailed during Jake's visit south. They have meetings concerning different ways to eliminate the threat, but they don't want to kill off a natural resource that could be quite valuable. During one of the meetings, President Lynch says to the group of planners, "Didn't one of the emails from Goldilocks say that Malpeada had a type of repellent?" He explains they need to determine what the repellent is. And also, if there was in fact a war waged between the savages and Malpeada.

President Lynch's administrative assistant, Barbara Kennedy, is asked to draft an email to Jake and President Grainta Haulk to find out how to develop this method of repellent.

She drafts the following email:

Dear Brenda Smith,

I have been tasked with finding out more details concerning the repellent used to control the dinosaurs on Stilligate. Is it possible for you to contact Jake and the President of Malpeada to determine what this repellent is and if it will be possible to equip our people with this? We have devised a plan for the inhabitants of Stilligate, but this seems to be a difficult undertaking for our advisors, as they don't want to kill them all. I think they all find it a novelty they want to preserve.

Sincerely,

Barbara Kennedy

Administrative Assistant to President Robert Lynch

Brenda receives the email and forwards it to Jake. Jake had already asked Murdock about how to repel them and responds to both Barbara and Brenda. Brenda and Jake had become quite regular at correspondence, as they write emails just about each afternoon to keep up with their experiences. He explains in his correspondence that the native people use a low-frequency sound as a repellent. It disturbs their balance and they will move away from an area that has this loud, low-frequency tone.

The day of the first ships to arrive and orbit Goldilocks seemingly comes without warning. Jake sits somewhat nervously at his controls on his ship. Dean, Heather, Greg, and Ted are all manning their stations and patiently awaiting radio contact with the lead ship. It is around noon on April 15, 2117, when the radio has the sound of Jeff Briscoe's voice. "Arc 0.0 to Parche I. We indicate we are in range for you to receive radio transmissions."

Commander Jake takes the communications and says, "Jeff Briscoe! It is very nice to hear your voice. We read you loud and clear. Please bring your fleet into a low Earth, uh, low Goldilocks' orbit. Protocol dictates that your transport ships are at 100 km higher altitude than your supply, dignitary, and military ships."

Briscoe comes back and says, "This will take a little time with the number of ships that we have here, sir."

"Understood, Captain. We plan for the first arrival of a dignitary ship to be yours, followed by all of the other ships in order from WRC Arc 0.0 through Arc 1000.0." The numbering scheme for each fleet is the ship number–Arc X, then the fleet number–.X.

"We have coordinates for all of your ships to sit down using a vertical descent. Once you are all safely on the planet, we will begin to land the transport ships one at a time. We can handle about twelve transports on the ground at any one time. We shall get the first group of vertical descents down and set up for a receiving area," states Jake.

Twenty-four hours pass as the group gets into formation above the planet. Once again, Jeff Briscoe's voice comes over the Parche I's communication's link. "Arc 0.0 to Parche I, we are all in formation and requesting coordinates and permission for Arc 0.0 to enter the planet's atmosphere."

Jake returns his request, "Permission granted. You should have received coordinates for the location that you will need to enter the atmosphere and to set the ship down at. If contacted by any control tower, including Stirpeto's tower, please use identification Arc 0.0. We have apprised the locals and they will recognize their respective call number as our incoming ships."

Jeff Briscoe's voice comes back on the line, "Arc 0.0 beginning descent, over."

Jeff and his crew then begin their flight into the ionosphere of Goldilocks. They have the same holographic image that is projected at the front of their bridge as the Parche 1. All of the passengers are strapped into their seats, and it is quite a bumpy ride. They see blue sparks dance all down the sides of the craft. It shakes and shimmies as it passes through the ionosphere. After time passes, they emerge to a big beautiful planet. They see oceans, lakes, rivers, mountains, and plains.

They pilot the craft to the coordinates provided. A voice comes over their communications system, "Stirpeto Tower to unidentified vessel. Please identify your craft." The newly constructed ships incorporated the interpretation application into their system. Jeff says, "Wow, they speak English."

His navigator, Shelly Cole, replies to the tower, "Stirpeto Tower, this is Arc 0.0 requesting permission to land at coordinates 62 deg 33'51.24" N and 105 deg 23'33.94 E." The voice from the tower comes back on and says, "You have clearance to land at these coordinates. Your craft does indeed have vertical descent capability?"

Shelly says, "Affirmative, tower." They then arrive at an enormous parking facility and slowly and methodically land the ship.

The fleet then begins an organized landing pattern for each craft. They are five minutes apart from one another and all begin to descend on the planet one at a time. At this rate, it will take three days to get all of the support staff on the ground. They will only send the smaller ships at this time and accommodate them in an area that doesn't interfere with the runways that are necessary for the larger transports.

Murdock meets Arc 0.0 and provides transportation for Jeff Briscoe, Shelly Cole, and the other two within his crew to the embassy. He parks the large truck in the garage and enters the embassy. They walk into the foyer and Gwen and Detty are there to greet them. Murdock says, "I will escort Jeff to meet with Jake and the others. You can assign these three quarters if they like."

Murdock takes Jeff out of the front of the large mansion and across the circle drive to the parking lot at the side of the embassy. They walk up to the entrance ramp of the Parche I that is already down and walk up the ramp. Jake, Dean, Ted, and Heather all stand awaiting his arrival and to go through a debriefing concerning his flight and the status of his ships. They all go into Jake's quarters where it is more relaxed and have a seat in his living area. Jake says, "How was the trip? Did you have anyone that had issues?"

Jeff says, "I know that we had a few, but per protocol, any that was out of hand was put in confinement and sedated. I don't believe there were more than one or two throughout our entire fleet."

Jake continues, "Did you run into any debris?"

"Absolutely! There was twice that we encountered meteors. I was very happy to have the flock formation, as I am unsure if a single ship's propulsion and protection would have had enough strength to keep damage from occurring. The flight through this ionosphere was the most worrisome. We traveled a long way. It was possible that we could have had some undetected damage with the shields or the ceramic tiles."

Dean says, "No tiles. These crafts are printed to have a continuous ceramic coating. If it were cracked, the sensors would have indicated it."

Jake says, "We are now capable of transporting the inhabitants of Earth over twenty light years away. We have made the first voyage with the safety and efficiency of a modern airline. This day should be a holiday here on Stilligate."

The ships continue to come in one after the other. The only ones invited to the mansion were the dignitary ships with WRC officials and the operation's crew of each ship, but few of them actually go to the embassy as many don't know Jake. Three days straight, the military and supply ships continue to land. They finally get three complete enormous parking lots full of these ships and are ready for the transport ships to begin entry into the planet's atmosphere.

Jake is in contact with the crew of the transport and explains there are twelve runways to choose from, but the traffic controller will direct him to the appropriate one. He also explains that once the craft is on the ground, it will be important to unload and get back into orbit because others are waiting to set down as well. The traffic controllers will have their hands full and the entire base will fill up within a couple of days from the evacuees. Each person has instructions on where to go and what to do once they exit the spacecraft. They are to meet up and wait for a shuttle that will take them to base housing. There will be about ten people per house until they can prepare a location for them to begin to build their own

259

shelters. This will be in a matter of days, not weeks or months because they have another Armada due in one week of their landing.

Jake and Heather speak to the incoming pilot of Arc 1000.0, his name is Allen Jeffers. Allen comes over the radio and says, "Arc 1000.0 requesting permission to begin my descent into the planet's ionosphere."

Jake gets on the radio. "Jake Conley, Commander of the Parche I. Permission is granted to begin your descent." It is quiet, the crew of the Arc 1000.0 have the hologram set to monitor the sides of the ship and blue lightning bolts dance across the outside of the shields as they make their way through this dangerous part of their journey. The huge craft begins shaking violently as the hologram shows the blue lightning bolts penetrating the outer area of the shields when radio silence is broken and the pilot comes over the comms and says, "The shields are being penetrated! I repeat we have…!" A large pop, crackle, and then static comes over the bridge of the radio in the Parche I.

Jake begins to yell, "Abort! Abort! Pull back up out of the descent!!" He stops yelling, waits, and listens.

Again, he yells into the microphone, "Arc 1000.0, please respond if you are receiving this transmission. Please Lord! Please respond."

Silence…nothing but static on their channel. A second voice comes on the radio, "Sir, this is Commander Simpson of the WRC Arc 1001.0. I regret to inform you that we have lost Arc 1000.0. There was a large fireball, then the craft could be seen falling to the surface." There is then a very somber and sobering transmission.

Jake replies, "You are absolutely certain Arc 1001.0? Could it not be that the flashes from reentry made it appear that way?"

The reply comes in a stern but shaken voice, "No…no, sir, there is not any doubt. The Arc 1000.0, with five thousand souls aboard, has perished. The question now is what do the rest of these ships do? We can stay in orbit indefinitely."

Jake responds, with an obvious heavy heart, "I have Dean Stinson standing by to investigate this failure. We have all of the data logs from the vessel that were collected within Arc 1000.0. We shall determine what has happened with this ship and advise."

Jake says, "Dean…"

Dean interrupts and says, "Sir, I am already logged into the recorded data from the craft Arc 1000.0 and I am now reviewing the logs."

Jake then contacts the Military Vessel Arc 10.0 that is already on the ground. He speaks on the radio to them. "Military Vessel Arc 10.0, please respond to the last known coordinates of Arc 1000.0, search the area for survivors, and confirm debris from the ship on the ground if possible."

A voice comes over the air, "Arc 10.0 Commander Gifford reporting, requesting permission to depart."

A voice from the tower comes over the radio, "Arc 10.0, you have clearance to depart from location PL1 when you are ready." Soon the hologram at the front of the Parche I shows the military vessel rising up from the base and flying above the embassy at a very high rate of speed.

Ted comes on the radio and says, "Captain Ted Snider, Pilot of the WRC Parch I, to Military Vessel Arc 10.0. Per protocol during reentry, you had your shields up and this wasn't a concern, however, during a flight south of here, our vessel was fired upon by anti-aircraft installations that resided within castles. I respectfully recommend activating your shields at eighty percent to protect your ship against this threat."

Commander Gifford replies, "Shields set, Captain. Thank you for the heads up on this potential threat."

Heather then sets the Parche I's hologram image to intercept the image that is being projected on the Arc 10.0. Ted, Greg, and Jake all watch as the ship accelerates to near Mach 10. The ground is passing beneath it and it simply looks like a quilt of varying colors. They near the same area where the Parche I was shot at and they see a

261

plume from some type of projectile being launched. But the craft is there and gone before the projectile can get in the air. The navigator did direct the hologram to the rear of the ship to see the gunfire, then back again as they all look on, with the exception of Dean who is studying the logs of the destroyed ship.

Dean speaks, "Sir." Jake immediately directs his attention to Dean. He continues, "I have reviewed the strength of the shields for the Arc 1000.0 and found that the larger ship has ten percent less capacity than the smaller ships, simply due to their enormous size. The strength was based on the most stress calculated that would ever be placed on the space frame. I am also convinced that human error was involved due to the setting of the shields was not at maximum. They were set at one hundred percent, with the engine's throttle at eighty percent. This, in conjunction with weaker shields, caused the spaceship's demise."

Commander Conley replies, "So all that is required is to ensure the other ships' throttles be set at one hundred percent through the ionosphere in order to supply the shields the power they need to protect it?"

Dean says, "This is not all we need to do. I recommend that we divert power from the rear shielding through plasma conduits to the front shields to help with their strength. I also see that the path the ships have taken has been at the Equator of Goldilocks. The force seen by all of the ten ships I reviewed experienced greater forces on their shields than the Parche I did. We took a far southerly path. My full recommendation to safeguard any other transports against this is to re-route the rear shielding to help the front shields. Throttle *must* be at one hundred percent per original protocol, and the ships should enter at the same southern location as the Parche I during its final flight to Stirpeto."

Jake says, "We have five thousand family members, loved ones, and Earth residents that have placed their trust in us. They are now perished, burned, charred, and strewn across this world. I ask you, *are you certain that this will safeguard against this potential?*"

262

Dean says, "Absolutely. I would go pilot one of the vessels to test it if it were possible. I would allow my mother to ride down on these transports pending these modifications."

The hologram now shows twisted, bent, and burned metal strewn across a plains area. There are small fires, but the ground is wet from a rain shower that occurred the night before. The Arc 10.0 slowly passes across the wreckage, looking for any sign of life. There is nothing over the size of a car hood and none of it is recognizable. The commander of the Arc 10.0 comes over the radio, "Arc 10.0 to Parche I."

Heather answers the call, "Parche I here, Arc 10.0, please go ahead with your transmission."

He continues, "We are not finding any signs of life whatsoever here at the crash site. We have flown a grid pattern over most of the wreckage and have only seen charred remains of the Arc 1000.0."

Jake speaks up, "Please, let's have a moment of silence for the passengers and crew of this American ship. The radio and everyone in the room is silent for a moment...a few quietly pray. Jake then says, "Arc 10.0, please return to base and prepare to process our incoming evacuees."

Commander Gifford replies, "We have a correction for this error this quickly, sir?"

"What throttle position was your craft set at during reentry?" Jake inquires.

"One hundred percent throttle and one hundred percent shields, sir, per protocol."

Jake replies, "This is to you and to all other Arc Transports that hear this broadcast. The logs show that the Arc 1000.0's shields were set at one hundred percent, with a throttle position of eighty percent. We strongly feel that human error is much to blame for the failed entry, however, we want to take additional precautions that are now being updated in your ship's directory. Please confirm prior to reentry that the rear shields are redirected to reinforce the forward shielding. The angle of descent has been changed by a couple of

263

degrees, and the coordinates for reentry has moved south by quite a large distance. Please review and confirm this data and follow the new protocol, as air traffic control will have a check-off list that everyone must confirm to ensure a safe reentry."

Arc 1001.0's pilot comes over the radio, "Arc 1001.0 to Parche I, we are requesting permission for reentry."

"Parche I to Arc 1001.0, your reentry request is granted. Please proceed with the check-off list with air traffic control, then contact us again as you begin your descent," stated Commander Jake. The radio becomes quiet as Heather shuts down the channel.

"I want to know when they begin their descent."

Heather says, "Of course, Commander. I will put them on the hologram sir."

The pilot of the Arc 1001.0 comes over the radio, "Parche I, we are now beginning our descent into the planet's ionosphere."

Jake replies, "Feel free to enter at the coordinates provided."

Heather places their hologram image from the Arc 1001.0 on the Parche I's projector for all to see. Dean is studying the data as the enormous ship enters this area. The blue lightning dances all around the outside of the shields. The sides of the enormous ship shake slightly. They stay in this area for a very anxious five minutes. A view of the ice-capped mountains at the south of Stilligate are seen on their projectors. The entire bridge rejoices and cheers for the fact that the ship made it through unscathed.

Jake then comes over the comm, "Parche I to Arc 1001.0, good job, Captain. We look forward to seeing you and all of your 5,000 passengers at Stirpeto's base."

A new schedule is necessary for the transports in order to get everyone onto the base and temporarily housed. The schedule is one ship per every ten minutes across the six runways in order to get all of the fleet on the ground before the next Armada arrives. This proves to be quite an undertaking, but in orderly fashion, the ships begin to arrive one right after another. The military members are there with shuttles to take them to temporary housing to await their final destination.

The next place depends upon the country of their origin. The WRC sent out a proposal to all of the world leaders that divides out the continent so that each one has at least the same landmass as they had on Earth. The military crafts serve as shuttles to take the evacuees to each respective area. They are all issued weapons and Torntauks, or dinosaur, repellent and, of course, each military vessel has shields and a superior complement of weapons to the Parche I. They will be able to take care of themselves against the inhabitants. None of the world leaders has agreed to the division of land, so they take a tentative map provided by Commander Phillips and use it for the locations that the people are going to and hope the final decision isn't too drastically different than the proposal.

Chapter 30

Well Oiled Machine

The parking lots and the airstrip are eventually emptied and the second Armada arrives and is dispersed. This is just in time to do it all over again. The first ship to set down from the third Armada on the PL1 site is the WRC Phillips. They have their own transportation at this time and a map of how to get to the embassy. With Woody driving a WRC Super Duty, Charles Phillips rides up front, with Brenda in the back seat. They pull up to the entrance and Jake hears Ted say, "Now that is a sight for sore eyes."

Heather, Dean, and Jake all look up at the hologram and it is the WRC truck. With the security tightened through guards that arrived from Earth, the shields for the ship have been down for a couple of days. They pull in and park near the front of the ship. They all walk up the ramp and Charles says, "Permission to board, Commander."

Jake says, "By all means, Commander Phillips. Welcome, very welcome! I am so very happy to see you, sir! I am very happy to see this young lady right here as well." He shakes Charles' and Woody's hand and gives Brenda a long needed hug.

Commander Phillips says, "Your team has been doing such a splendid job that I got the feeling I wasn't truly needed."

"I am turning gray with all of these difficult decisions."

"I have my planners with me and we shall be setting up in a pretty nice command headquarters on base. I would be happy to see you all choose what you would like to do for some downtime. We can take it from here."

"Sir, the Parche I is ours? Is it acceptable to take it to our designated land and begin to set up shelters and find a claim for ourselves and our families?"

Phillips seems to dwell on it for a few minutes then says, "Yes, the ship is yours for as long as you need or want it. We will not be sending her back out unless we decide to go exploring again, but one of the discarded dignitary ships would probably be more comfortable for that due to its lavish interior."

Charles and Jake then make their way to Jake's quarters. They walk in and Jake goes to his personal replicator and says, "Water and Crown, on the rocks. Anything for you, sir?"

Charles says, "You know, I haven't had a good drink in a while. Give me the same." They both take their clear glass and sit down to discuss their situation. Charles says, "I read your report. We lost a transport, did we?"

Jake lowers his head, and says, "Yes, sir. There was nothing I could do. We changed protocol immediately following the incident. Dean reviewed all of the logs and he determined that it was largely due to human error."

Charles says, "We are doing the unthinkable. If this is the only ship that is lost, you realize that we will be lucky."

"Yes, sir, but it seems that you have put together a system that has been as reliable and efficient as a modern day commercial airline."

"Jake, even commercial airlines have issues sometimes. I kind of expected to see a couple of million homeless people upon landing. Where did you put everyone?"

"We used your map and staged them at the base. The military, supply, and dignitary ships served as shuttles to bring them to their respective areas. They will build base camps and use the ships for protection from the inhabitants."

"Can their shields extend around an entire camp?"

Jake replies, "I am unsure. I believe that Dean had developed instructions on using several ships and combining shields. I can't say they are safe, but they have weapons and enough people that they can defend themselves against an attack."

"I see. The world leaders wouldn't agree on the distribution of land. I honestly think they are laying all of that on the WRC. If so,

267

then they will get what we give them and the proposed map will be the law. They will have more than they had on Earth." The two men finish their conversation and Jake is relieved of duty for his role at the embassy.

He has a meeting with his crew. He explains that the duties of receiving the evacuees will now be handled by Commander Phillips' staff. He asks for their desires. He explains that his intent is to take the Parche I to use as shelter somewhere between a lake and the ocean and claim land.

Ted asks, "The WRC has given you this vessel?"

"Well, if they need the vessel, then I feel sure they will call on me. But I prefer to think of it as *ours*. We can still use it for as long as we need to in order to establish our place here on Goldilocks."

Ted says, "What about Alicia and our families?"

"They are welcome as well. I don't plan to leave today. I want you all to get your families together, and if there are enough, perhaps we could request the use of Commander Phillips' dignitary ship."

Dean inquires, "What about King Sedimo and the tribe in this area? Is there not a war that was waged with them? Will there not be a serious potential of attacks and battles that could be waged against our people?"

Jake says, "After the king saw the influx of the never-ending and continuous flow of transports and military vessels flying over their land and heard of the slaughter that occurred with that tribe, they surrendered without a shot fired. The WRC staff is working out a deal for where they will relocate them and the Indians will work out a deal soon, I feel sure. Neither of these groups stands a chance against our technology."

Ted says, "That was when we lowered the shields, Commander?"

"Yes, but we have all been so challenged with trying to accommodate incoming ships that I haven't had an opportunity to discuss it."

268

They all take the next week to gather family members, including Brenda and her family, and a dignitary ship and head south and find suitable land that they all agree on. They find a fresh water lake that is likely a thousand acres or more of water. They claim thousands of acres of shoreline between them and begin to change their roles from exploration astronauts to wilderness families. Jake performs a marriage in the great hall of the dignitary ship for Heather and Dean. They all pretty much retire on this piece of property, building fine shelters, raising animals, and growing fresh vegetables.

A year has passed on Earth. Everyone there feels the certainty of impending doom. Very few businesses are in operation. The big cities are pretty much ghost towns. The stream of ships continues every Wednesday night at midnight when the first transports begin to return to Earth. They immediately begin landing these ships on alternate sites to give them a full Preventative Maintenance check. Resources are beginning to run low for people that can perform this type of work and the pilots are forced to review many of these issues themselves. Many ships have to be taken out of service because there is no one to repair them.

Months pass and it is now August of 2118, and Commander Jeremy Enlow is feeling very good about the number of ships that they have been able to dispatch to the new world, seeing as how it is past the target date of the phase shift of the sun. On the morning of August 10, he is in his office in a meeting with his staff, trying to figure out a way to combat the lack of skilled labor when a bright flash is seen in the sky through his windows. The sun dims and immediately the temperature in Vegas drops from over one hundred degrees to fifty degrees. There is a newscast that comes on the television set outside of his office in the lobby, he heard them say, *today must be the day of reckoning*. The reporter is explaining that many doubted this day would come. It is near noon and it appears to be dusk outside due to the sun morphing into another state.

Jeremy looks over at his staff, who have all gotten up from the table, and says, "We all knew this day would come." A bright entity appears from the east. It is a very beautiful yellow sheen on the horizon. A brilliant white light passes across the landscape in an instant, he turns to look and half of his staff is gone. He sees what appear to be flashes of light rising up from the city. He realizes that the Rapture has come. It truly is the day of reckoning. He quickly scrambles to find how many pilots and staff he has left as it begins to snow. He gathers Lisa and what is left of his staff and sets out to get on a transport, as this shall be his last day to command the WRC on Earth. He finds a ship that is prepared to leave for orbit. They board the ship and he sends out a communication to all of WRC. "Today we have seen the Rapture. There are very few souls left to operate the fleet of ships that are traveling to the new world. Please gather as many as is possible and launch for the orbit of the Earth. The voyage that is to leave on Wednesday night shall be the final trip to Alpha Kantabury I."

The time comes and the ships streak across the sky one last time. General Enlow and his crew sit on the bridge of the ship, looking deeply into the hologram of the Earth as it grows white. Soon, there are people living in the shelters that were built for the ones to be left behind, but they are only about half full and not at all in some cases. The world soon becomes in a stage of an ice age with a plethora of snow that extends above the landscape at depths of ten to twenty feet deep in some areas.

All the ones left behind can do is survive in their shelters.

The End

The following is a sample from Book 2 of the Series
Imminent Domain: Left Behind. It will be released within
the next few months.

Imminent Domain

Left Behind

Neal JB Verne

Chapter 1

Charmed Life

A lady walks along a row of tomatoes in her garden. She is carrying a hoe and snipping out stalks of grass that is trying to consume the water and fertile soil she has provided for her plants. It is a peaceful morning, but there is no sunrise. There is no change in the weather as she looks out across the large garden to see trees and an enormous domed metal roof above that extends up high above the trees for miles. She lays her gloved hand across the end of the hoe handle and looks back up to her home. It is a small cabin with a porch. Her husband, Danny, sits with a mason jar of what appears to be moonshine.

She calls out to him, "You best not be getting drunk this early in the morning, you ole motherfucker, you!"

Danny, without saying a word, reaches behind him and grabs a deer rifle and points it down toward the garden.

She yells at him again, "You best not be shooting at me, you old bas…"

KaaaBOOOOM. The rifle is fired, echoing all throughout the closed-in shelter and she shrieks and drops to the ground, lying flat and lifeless.

Danny stands and holds a hand flat out above his eyes, as if to block the light from above, with the rifle in his other hand, and says, "I got 'em!"

Riddled with fear, she looks toward him on the porch, stands, and turns to look at what he is looking at. She sees a whitetail buck deer lying dead at the end of her garden.

She yells out again, "You about gave me a fucking heart attack, you old son of a bitch!"

He chuckles, and says, "Go get my damn deer and skin 'em before I grab the round in there that says *BITCH* on it!"

She finishes the row that she is on, then goes and starts dragging the deer back up to the cabin. She isn't a big strong lady and she struggles, as a blood trail is left behind. She manages to get the bloody carcass back up and into the barn. She ties the hooves of the animal to cotton rope that is threaded through pulleys on each side and anchored to a rafter on the roof. She then grabs the other end of the ropes that have a hook at the end and connects them to a rack on the back of an ATV. She pulls forward, tightening the ropes and dragging the lifeless animal vertical as blood streams from its shoulder and onto the concrete floor of the barn, turning it red.

Danny comes walking in with an ice chest and a knife. He says, "I sharpened your knife." Without speaking a word, she takes the knife and makes an incision in the animal from the groin to the neck and looks at Danny while she cuts.

Without hesitation, he says, "I will be in the cabin if you need me." He quickly leaves the barn.

She butchers the animal with speed and precision, leaving bones and entrails in a large pale beneath the hooves that hang from the ropes that she tied earlier. The large ice chest that he brought was full of fresh meat after she was done slicing up the deer. She backs the ATV up and struggles with lifting the heavy container with the entrails and disconnects the ropes. She pulls the four wheeler up to the cabin and parks it. She steps off and up to the front porch, leaving small blood tracks on the steps. She sits down on the lawn chair and relaxes, looking out over her garden.

A few moments pass and Danny comes walking out in his overalls and a pistol strapped to his side. Not a word is said as he makes his way down to the ATV. The motor cranks up and he is off to the replicator refueling area.

He travels for about five minutes when he reaches his destination. It is at an outer wall of the shelter. There is a six-inch-wide concrete barrier that protrudes deep within the ground several feet and goes all along the outer wall that keeps the ground-dwelling creatures from overwhelming the shelter. The area on the other side of the wall now has thirty feet of snow and an ice age has fallen on the earth. The location he has arrived at is a very large pit that has an opening to the ground outside. It is at least twenty feet deep and is lined with a glass like surface and half filled with snakes, moles, and other animals that have traveled through the ground, seeking shelter and food. He pulls the large bucket from the four wheeler and dumps it on the top layer of doomed animals, splattering them with blood and the other parts of the deer that are left.

He flips a lever marked "FILL" and a wall begins to traverse across the bottom of the pit like a trash compactor. The sign near the pit reads "REPLICATOR FUEL." He waits while the pit is seemingly cleaned and a green light illuminates on the control panel. He presses a button on a screen that reads "PUMP A." This pit is part of a large system that processes bio matter and turns it into fuel that is used for the food replicators used to sustain their food supply. He turns on this button and hops on his ATV. As he pulls away, he wonders how terrible life must be for these pour animals that were freezing to death and to find shelter only to be destroyed in order to sustain human life.

He takes a trail that brings him in the opposite direction of the cabin and feels as though his wife would be better off alone for a while. He travels down a trail, looking up at the lighting as he goes. He makes a trek around the outer wall of the shelter once a week to inspect for collapses, failed lighting, and to ensure nothing or no one has breached the outer walls. He rides and remembers a short time ago when he was in his own hunting grounds and how it would get dark at this time of day. The light remains consistent as he reaches the wall farthest from his home. He is about a two hour ATV ride from his cabin and stops at another pit that reads "REPLICATOR FUEL." It is the same as the other, but doesn't have quite as many animals in it. He presses the button and walks over and sits on his ATV.

He sits for a while wondering why the transports never came for him, why he had spent his life as an atheist. He has been in the shelter for about six months now. He wonders about the ones destined for Goldilocks. Were they there? Did God empty the transports? He thinks of all of his wealth that was in the banks across the world. He had amassed great riches in the world as the founder of an investment banking group, Chimera, and it was all gone, all he has now is this enormous shelter and Kelly, his little southern, swimsuit model that he was with when the end came.

He becomes angry as he recalls the three hundred million dollar checks that he wrote to the WRC in support of the relocation efforts. He hears something at the side of the pit. A small rodent looking creature sticks his head out of one of the many holes that are in the back side. Danny pulls out his pistol and shoots the rodent! The animal disappears and Danny decides that he must have missed and it ran back into the hole, but then he sees blood trickle out of the hole and down the side into the pit below. He screams, "Take that! You get some fucking pity. It was over for your sorry little life just like that." Just then, a very large snake comes straight through the same hole, mouth gaped open with the small animal toward the back of its throat as it widens this hole. It flies across the top of the pit and stretches almost the entire length of the pit, rapidly approaching Danny. He takes a firm grip on his pistol, as its tail clears the hole, it begins a descent into the blood stained concrete bottom below as Danny walks over to look at this enormous animal.

He spits over the side and says, "Not today, you foul son of a bitch, not today." He decides he will be as humane to the other animals as possible and not leave the snake there to

275

eat them. He takes a step to the control panel and flips the "FILL" lever, then says, "I hope that hurts, you bastard!" The energetic sound of a hydraulic ram and squashing flesh is heard. He jumps on the wheeler and takes off back to the cabin.

He takes a different path home. On his way he passes large open pits that are filled with boiling water. The shelter was placed in an area that has natural hot springs. This helps to keep the temperature warm by using the Earth's core heat. He comes to a "Y" In the trail and turns left. As he passes through the trail, he reaches a paved road.

He turns right on the road and in a short time he comes upon a white building with a red cross on the front of it. He slows as he passes, then takes off until the road disappears under two large metal doors that are similar to aircraft hangar doors. He turns down into a drainage ditch and back on dirt, through a small patch of woods, and into the west side of his field.

A large, black pit bull comes running up to him as he has slowed to a crawl, trying to ensure that Kelly isn't in a sniper position somewhere. He stops and the dog runs up and puts his front paws up on the gas tank of the ATV. He reaches down to pet him and says, "Charlie, she let you out to play?" The large dog rubs his head against Danny's leg as he strokes the back of his neck. He pushes him away and says, "Come on, boy, let's go see if Momma is still mad at me." He rides up to the little cabin. There is no sign of Kelly as he walks up on the front porch, and the pit bull, Charlie, runs over to a love seat and climbs up and lays down with a high-pitched moan accompanied by a yawn. He looks over at the dog and says, "She got you, too, huh?" Charlie looks like he is getting comfy there and has no interest in going in there with Kelly.

He walks in the front door of this beautifully constructed log cabin and immediately smells the aroma of freshly cooked deer tenderloin. Kelly walks out with a short pair of Daisy

Dukes that shows her long tanned legs and skips up to him, hugs, and kisses him.

Danny asks, "I guess you are over the whole deer thing?"

"I wouldn't say over it and if you do that again, and I have that .40 S&W on my side, I will shoot your ass grave yard dead."

Danny replies, "I understand. I smell something good!"

She looks at him. "Yeah, I know how much you like fresh tenderloin and I figured you would like to have that rather than something replicated. I haven't cooked for you in a few days, so I thought that I would be nice."

"Daisy Dukes, too? You must be feeling good."

COMING SOON!

www.ingramcontent.com/pod-product-compliance
Lightning Source LLC
Chambersburg PA
CBHW060545180626
46817CB00002B/739